BY A JURY OF HIS PEERS

By the same author:

Backstage at the Palace

Canadian Cataloguing in publication data

Steinberg, Henry

By a jury of his peers
ISBN 1-895854-42-3
I. Title.

PS8587.T44B92 1995   C813'.54   C95-940424-4
PS9587.T44B92 1995
PR9199.3.S73B92 1995

To receive our current catalogue and be kept on our mailing list
for announcements of new titles, send your name and address to:
Robert Davies Publishing,
P.O. Box 702, Outremont, Quebec, Canada H2V 4N6

Henry Steinberg

BY A JURY OF HIS PEERS

ROBERT DAVIES PUBLISHING
MONTREAL-TORONTO-PARIS

This book may be ordered in Canada from

General Distribution Services,
☎1-800-387-0141 / 1-800-387-0172 FAX 1-416-445-5967;

in the U.S.A., from Associated Publishers Group,
1501 County Hospital Road,
Nashville, TN 37218
dial toll-free 1-800-327-5113;

or call the publisher, toll-free throughout North America:
1-800-481-2440, FAX (514) 481-9973.

The publisher takes this opportunity to thank the
Canada Council and the *Ministère de la Culture du Québec*
for their continuing support of publishing.

Publisher's note

Appeal Court Justice Henry Steinberg
passed away suddenly in January, 1995.
This novel is his legacy.

Dedicated to the memory of the late
Henry Steinberg

1

Serge Tremblay sat on the hard bench, his cold gaze fixed upon Marie-Lyse Lortie. She gripped the cell bars, eyes burning with intensity. If she'd had the strength she would have ripped apart the bars to get in and strangle him. Anger enhanced her appearance. She took a deep breath and held it a moment. Her chest rose, then relaxed as the air was released through her lips. She could not penetrate the mask of this impossible man. How could she represent a client who refused to discuss anything that happened on the night of the murder?

"Where were you that night?" she demanded.

"They say I was at Le Wiz."

"They, they! What do you say?"

"Right now, I say nothing."

"Right now you're on trial for murder. If you won't help, how in the world can I defend you? They're not playing cops and robbers upstairs. This is the real thing, and you're facing life. The trial will begin today. Don't you understand that?"

"Yeah, I know, but I didn't do it. They won't prove what I didn't do."

"They're trying hard enough. And you, you won't defend yourself.

Dammit, you won't even tell me where you were that night. Did you go to St. Denis Street?"

Tremblay looked at her impassively, and said nothing.

"Look, even if you're ready to spend the rest of your life in some jail for a crime you didn't commit, I can't let you. Tell me something. Say something!"

"I told you I didn't do it and that's all you need to know right now."

"Are you afraid? Did someone threaten you?"

"No, I just can't talk."

Marie-Lyse released the bars and feigned calm. "All right, all right, maybe that's all I need to know right now. But what about later?"

"We got time."

"You'll get more time than you ever wanted if you don't help. Don't you realize we start choosing a jury as soon as they get their act together in the court upstairs? Say, do you want another lawyer? Someone older, more experienced?"

"No, you're doing good."

"Tell me about the night of the murder."

"It's not time."

"They placed you at the scene of the murder. They know you had a fight with Lepine. They arrested you with the gun, and you say it's not time to try to do something?! . . . Are you guilty?"

"No, I'm not."

"Then tell me what happened that night." Marie-Lyse waited for an answer that didn't come. At that moment she hated his aloofness and his apparent smugness. Did he equate silence with manliness? If he didn't want to help himself, then why couldn't he think about her, on her first murder trial?

"Who killed Lepine?"

"No comment."

"No comment? You know, because you were there, weren't you?" Again Tremblay stared impassively. "The jury members will ask the same questions I'm asking. They'll want to hear your story. Will you testify? I can't even start to think about it if you won't tell me what happened.

Look, think of *me*. What do I say to the judge when he asks if we have any witnesses for the defence?"

"Let's decide later."

"Do you realize that if you don't testify, they'll think you're hiding something, and send you back to jail forever? And if you do testify, the moment Talbot begins his cross-examination they'll find out about your criminal record. Attempted murder at the age of eighteen isn't exactly a character reference!"

"I told you I wasn't guilty of that either."

"But you pleaded guilty."

"Lawyer said I had no choice. I was young, and I took his advice. Got me twelve years. I kept my nose clean in jail and got out in four."

"This time you have a choice: tell me what happened and try to defend yourself, or plead guilty and it'll all be over in a few moments. Is that what you want? Do you want to plead guilty?"

"I don't need a lawyer to plead me guilty."

"Serge, do you think I want to lose my first murder trial and not even know what happened, because my tight-lipped client wouldn't trust his lawyer?"

"I trust you, but I can't talk right now."

The sound of footsteps echoed behind her. Marie-Lyse forced a smile. "They're coming for you now. I'll take the passenger elevator and see you upstairs . . . . There's going to be a big crowd when you enter the courtroom. Don't look surprised, and try not to look so damned tough."

The footsteps stopped. Without looking back, Marie-Lyse turned and walked briskly past the steel door.

* * *

Rick Hayes was outraged when he received a summons for jury duty. His company had just landed a big contract. If he lost two weeks now, he'd have to make it up later and miss his holiday. His anger grew when his request for exemption was refused. The sheriff had listened sympathetically when he explained that his job in the machine shop was important. She responded that others had also asked to be excused, and his reason just wasn't good enough. He still could hope to not be chosen. After all, they summon about a hundred and twenty people, and only twelve are picked.

April first arrived—the day stated in the summons—and here he was in court. He'd been waiting since 9 a.m.; they hadn't even had the decency to start on time. If he came late they'd probably jail him, or at least fine him. What kind of a game was this anyway? Who the hell did they think they were, the court clerks who delivered funny-looking papers full of stupid expressions, and threatened to jail him if he didn't show?

Rick wasn't the only irate jury candidate. Over a hundred and twenty people were jammed into the overflowing courtroom. They were all over the place — sitting on the audience benches and in the jury box, standing in the aisles, and leaning against the walls. The ventilation couldn't handle such numbers. The crowd became restless, waiting for the judge to enter.

Rick could smell the impatience and agitation of the crowd. He stood back as far as possible, pressing into a corner, and hoped he wouldn't be noticed. It'd be hard to miss him, dressed as he was. He had seen no reason to get all dressed up. If the lawyers didn't like his clothes, they could send him home—which would suit him fine.

He wondered where the judge was. Judges don't wait around in crowded unventilated rooms. They probably have fancy offices, soft chairs, and good-looking secretaries. They sure get paid enough. Last week, the papers said the judges wanted a raise. Rick couldn't remember what they were earning, but it was too much if this was how they treated the public. It was almost as bad as the damned hospitals. The doctors make you wait too, but they don't send bailiffs to force people who are minding their own business to come and do their work for them. Who the hell wanted to be a juror? Why couldn't the judges do their jobs and leave him alone? He didn't ask for their help in the machine shop.

Rick had a simple philosophy about police and the law: the less he saw of them the better. They had bothered him when he was young, but he didn't have a record or anything like that. A few times, he was picked up with a couple of joints but they'd let him go. He never got into the hard stuff because it was too expensive. He still smoked the odd joint . . . and why shouldn't he? It was his money, and cigarettes were so expensive that he might as well enjoy the real thing.

He scanned the room. Some of these people probably welcomed a chance for free entertainment, and maybe a meal or two, but he had a good job and would rather be in the shop. A woman dressed in a black robe sat at the front taking attendance and writing notes. She looked kind of cute, and would have looked better in something other than that black robe. She was speaking to a younger, even better looking woman with blue eyes and blond hair. They looked like two crows in those robes. Nice crows. Rick had seen the second one carry a few books into the room and put them where the judge would sit—if he ever arrived. She was nervous, kept opening the door and disappearing into the back hall.

Over on the right side of the courtroom he saw the empty prisoner's dock, guarded by a uniformed cop who leaned against the railing. The door at the rear opened again, and Rick strained to see into the distant corridor. This time he saw a black and red gown walk by. Well, at least the judge was in the building. Now if he'd come into the courtroom, they could get started. It was almost ten, and they were supposed to start at 9:30.

* * *

The Honourable Mr. Justice Samuel Berne paced the corridor outside his office, looking at his watch for the tenth time in two minutes. He hated to keep a panel of jurors waiting. After eight years as a judge, and four with jury trials in criminal cases, he still could not accept the inevitable delays in the jury selection process. Some people arrive at the last moment, and registration can take longer than expected. If the members of the panel arrive on time, the prisoner is delayed, and there's little he can do when the blue bus transporting prisoners to the garage is late. A prisoner who goes berserk in the basement retards the delivery of all other prisoners to the courtrooms. Then there are the inevitable labour problems. The guards always explain it's not their fault, but the fault of someone at the Parthenais Detention Centre. What was the reason for today's delay?

He had a thing about punctuality. He arrived early even for trivial appointments, and seethed when he couldn't meet schedules. At such times he felt a loss of control. He'd read that this attitude caused a predisposition to heart attacks, in the same way as repeatedly pushing the buttons in an elevator so the doors would close faster. Sam broke the elevator controls habit the next day, but the concern for punctuality remained an integral part of his personality. He learned to conceal it, but could't change it. His heart would just have to adjust, as it had to his overweight condition. He didn't think of himself as heavy—just a little too round at the waist. People sometimes said he looked leaner than the last time they'd seen him. It was an illusion he couldn't explain. He would just laugh and suggest that whenever he departed, he left a fat impression behind, an impression corrected by his subsequent reappearance.

The quip contained some truth. His self-assurance and controlled energy, buttressed by his title and stubbornness, made his presence felt even when he was silent. Since becoming a judge he used more body language. The nods, winks, shrugs, raised eyebrows and hand gestures were unrecorded by microphones, but readily understood in court.

He re-entered his office suite, masking annoyance over the delay with a smile. But his secretary Jackie, and the court usher Linda, weren't fooled. They tried to distract him.

"Monsieur le Juge," Linda said, "I'm not used to working in the Criminal Division, but there's a shortage of ushers today. I hope you'll overlook small mistakes."

"Linda, just relax. Everything will be fine."

"I'll try, but I'm nervous."

"Is it a French or English language case?"

"French."

"Good. That'll make it easier."

She usually accompanied judges in the civil and family divisions. Despite her half dozen years at the courthouse, this was her first assignment as usher in a criminal trial.

"Did you phone down to see if they're ready to start?" Sam asked, as he passed his secretary's desk. She was organizing the day's forms into piles.

"Stop making the girl hyper. You know they'll call when they're ready," Jackie said. "I remember your first time in the assizes. Ha-ha! You expected the first case to be a simple little robbery, and they gave you a murder."

"Enough, Jackie," he protested, "It was a long time ago."

"Your knees wobbled so much when you left the office that I was afraid you'd catch your gown in the elevator doors. When you came back after the first morning you looked like a ghost. Do you remember the lawyer for the defence in your first case, how she got to you? Every time you blinked, she made a motion for a mistrial, and you worried."

"Well, I was inexperienced. Even so, the accused was convicted of manslaughter, and neither the conviction nor the sentence was appealed."

"Beginner's luck. In your last trial, the accused was acquitted and the crown prosecutor was so incensed that he went on TV to complain that your charge to the jury was the worst he'd heard in twenty years."

"Yes, my wife wasn't happy either. She blamed the acquittal on my 'shadow of a doubt'." Turning to Linda he continued, "It was an interesting case, and I'm sure you'll find your first criminal case exciting as well."

"I feel better now, but I'm still a little uneasy because today's April first. How do you call it . . . the poisson d'avril?"

"April Fools' Day."

"April Fools' Day," she repeated, wrinkling her nose.

"You just reminded me," Jackie interrupted, "Rocket called yesterday with greetings from The Maintenance. He wanted you to know the government's fiscal year ended March 31."

"Happy New Year to the government and its accountants," Berne replied.

* * *

The department that provided and maintained buildings, furniture, and equipment was called *The Maintenance* by court personnel. Propelled by its own peculiar logic, its sole motivation was to remain within the budgetary constraints imposed by the Treasury Board. Building repairs were undertaken or deferred according to the annual maintenance schedule and budget. Innovation was rare, but funds were always available to repeat last year's activities. The budget divided building repairs, furniture replacement, and equipment acquisition into watertight compartments. Money allocated for elevator maintenance couldn't be diverted to purchase computers; funds set aside for new furniture couldn't be used to replace carpets. The budget had to be respected on a line-by-line basis.

Hubert Racine presided over *The Maintenance* in the Montreal Courthouse. He had started as a court clerk, where his pleasant disposition, willingness and efficiency had earned him the nickname *Rocket.* Despite approval and accolades from judges, attorneys, and litigants, his career had stagnated, and he had requested a transfer to building maintenance.

The enthusiasm which characterized his previous activities had caused him to exceed the budget occasionally, which hindered his advancement in the public service. Rocket learned the hard way that needs could only be accommodated within budgetary constraints. While others undertook daring initiatives such as replacing a broken typewriter or plastering and painting a cracked wall, Rocket responded to each request with a unique blend of solicitous concern and a flurry of paperwork. Over the years, his coworkers erred and disappeared into nothingness, and eventually Hubert emerged as the undisputed leader of *The Maintenance.*

During his tenure, many requests were sacrificed to the Budget Deities. Each year he received a letter of commendation from his superiors, and a modest salary increase. The energy and willingness of his early years as a court clerk disappeared forever, but he retained his nickname. Rocket Racine matured into an obsequious procrastinator.

"Rocket has more news," Jackie volunteered. "At the last moment he noticed money in the budget which hadn't been spent. I don't know if they're lazy or can't count. Anyway, they bought new chairs for some of the courtrooms, including the one where you're sitting today. You'll have the privilege of breaking in a new chair."

"I'm honoured. Please thank Rocket and his defenders of the government properties," Sam said, pulling the red-trimmed black gown over his shoulders. "It's almost ten. Let's see what's happening."

Linda picked up several books and opened the door. Justice Berne followed, clutching the notes of his speech to the jury candidates. The elevator descended the twelve floors slowly, stopping to disgorge some judges and ushers and to collect others. Shop-talk and banalities were exchanged.

"Where are you sitting?"

"That damned case still going?"

"Did you hear about the new appointments?"

"See you for lunch?"

"I hear parking rates in the garage are going up."

"'Bye. See you in the club for drinks."

They left the elevator on the third floor, and walked down the long hall, Linda always a step or two ahead on his right side.

"Linda, when we're crossing the main lobby to get to the courtroom, move quickly and have your key to the private corridor ready. Then I'll wait in the office behind the courtroom. Check that the court clerk has completed the attendance list, and find out if the prisoner has arrived. There'll be a guard near the prisoner's dock; you can ask him about our guest of honour. If he hasn't arrived, tell the guard to see me."

Linda nodded and unlocked the door. She turned and disappeared into the courtroom.

*   *   *

Halfway down the corridor a uniformed constable was grinning. Sam signalled him to come to the office. The constable moved with an ease and assurance that marked him as a courthouse regular.

"You're Constable . . . ?"

"Parent, Denis Parent, Monsieur le Juge. I've been assigned to the jurors in your case, together with Wilfred Harvey and Gisele Boisclair. Gisele's a hostess, but Fred and I are full constables with the right to carry guns." He patted the revolver protruding from the holster hanging from his belt and continued, "Do you have any special instructions?"

"Not right now. Have you been working with juries long, Constable?"

"Twenty years, Monsieur le Juge. I'm the most experienced jury constable in the Palais de justice. It's strange we haven't met before."

"Well, I've been sitting in the Criminal Division for a few years, but like all new judges my first trials were in the smaller towns around Montreal."

"I see . . . .Would you like a cup of coffee, Monsieur le Juge? We have a machine in the jury room and the coffee's ready."

"Not right now, thanks."

*   *   *

From the corner of his eye Sam saw Linda emerge from the courtroom. She walked over, speaking excitedly. "The courtroom, it is overflowing. I've never seen such a crowded room. The clerk has taken the attendance, but the prisoner hasn't been sent up. The guard said the bus was delayed, but the prisoners will be brought up shortly. The guard will see you in a few moments."

"Good. I'd like to present Constable Denis Parent, the senior jury constable in the Palais de justice." Linda made a mock curtsy and Parent smiled. "You'll have to check with Constable Parent often during the trial to assure that all jury members are present, and to find out about their problems. You can only get this information from the constables, because you and I aren't allowed to speak to the jurors outside the courtroom."

Parent left and walked down the corridor. His name struck a familiar chord, but Sam Berne couldn't remember why. It'd come back. He glanced at his watch. Five to ten, and he could feel the irritation of the jury candidates radiating through the wall of the adjacent court-room. A guard entered the office.

"Monsieur le Juge, I'm Constable Ovide Demers. The prisoner has arrived from detention and is in the cell behind the court, wearing handcuffs and chains. Have you any instructions before we bring him to the dock?"

"Do you have any special information about him that I should know?"

"He may be dangerous. We treat all prisoners with caution."

"I'm sure you do. But what's special about this man?"

"Nothing, Monsieur le Juge, but he's charged with murder."

"I see. Take off the handcuffs before he enters court. I don't want jury candidates to form the impression he's guilty before we start."

"And the chains?"

"Keep them on. With over a hundred people in court I don't want to take chances. Clamp the chains to the floor hook, so that if the prisoner wants to escape, he'll have to take the building with him."

"I understand," the guard replied. "We'll be ready in five minutes."

Berne turned towards Linda. "Watch through the doorway crack and tell me when the prisoner's in place." She scurried out like an eager youngster. Actually she was a youthful twenty-nine, married and the mother of a five-year-old.

Sam still felt a tinge of nervousness in his stomach each time he spoke to a panel of jurors. Seeking distraction, he went to the washroom and checked his image in the mirror. His hair was still black—most of it—but the bald spot was expanding. He was proud of his appearance and watched for the telltale signs of age—to deny their existence to himself.

"They're ready now," Linda announced, poking her head back into the office, eyes shining in anticipation.

"Let's go . . . .Speak loudly and clearly when you open the session. Remember there's a large crowd and possibly some reporters."

She tilted her head slightly, so that her blond hair fell to one side, "Yes, I'll be careful . . . and loud." Linda pressed the buzzer, opened the door and entered the courtroom.

21

As the crowd rose noisily, Sam Berne briskly mounted the two stairs to the platform and remained standing in front of the judge's desk.

"The Superior Court, Criminal Division, presided over by The Honourable Mr. Justice Samuel Berne, is now open."

* * *

He surveyed the room, nodding to the prisoner, the attorneys, and the clerk, who bowed slightly. He attempted to sit down, but the chair was about eight inches higher than usual. He was frozen in a strange posture, neither sitting nor standing, knees protruding above the desk.

"Please be seated," Linda continued.

Rocket had done it again! New chairs had been placed in some courtrooms but no one had bothered to check their height. Berne was uncomfortably balanced in the air, on a four-legged object that was neither a chair nor a barstool, poised like a baseball catcher coming out of his crouch to whip the ball to the second baseman. He hoped the audience wouldn't notice his peculiar pose and discomfort. There was no time to do anything about it. The wall clock said five past ten and the jury candidates were waiting.

"Ladies and gentlemen, welcome to the April session of the Superior Court of Montreal. I appreciate that many of you wonder why you've been summoned. You have undoubtedly asked yourselves, 'Why me? Why was I chosen?' A computer selected your names at random from the electoral lists, to be candidates for the jury. Twelve people from among you will form the jury in a trial which will commence today."

Sam felt like an utter fool. It was hard enough to speak to over a hundred people in a hot crowded room under normal circumstances. Perched in mid-air on that new chair, the task was impossible. Soon his nervousness was replaced by an urge to send Rocket to the moon with a swift kick in the butt.

Rick Hayes leaned back and stared. The judge seemed bigger than he'd expected—fatter anyway. He couldn't figure out why the judge's knees stuck out above the desk.

The judge continued, "Serge Tremblay, seated to your left, is charged with the murder of Frank Lepine. His lawyer, Maître Marie-Lyse Lortie, is seated at the table in front of him. The attorney for the prosecution, or the attorney for the Crown, is Maître Vincent Talbot, seated to your right.

"In a few moments we shall adjourn. Please leave the courtroom and remain in the adjacent corridor while I receive those people who request an exemption, or who are related in any way to the accused, Serge Tremblay, the victim, Frank Lepine, Maître Talbot or Maître Lortie, or who have any personal knowledge, connection or relationship with the facts of this case . . . ."

Berne was now speaking mechanically, all thoughts focused on himself, his predicament, and Rocket. This chair is impossible, he thought. I feel like a parrot on a swinging bar. Where do they find these chairs? And why did they have to put one in the courtroom the day I'm receiving a panel of jurors? On an ordinary day, I could adjourn for a few moments and have the chair fixed or replaced. But you just cannot stall a hundred or more jury candidates. Something must be done about this chair.

" . . . Once again, I thank you. Please remember, following the adjournment I shall receive those persons who request an exemption on general grounds, followed by those who are related to the accused, the victim, or a lawyer, as well as anyone having some connection with, or personal knowledge of, the facts of this case. After the exemptions have been decided, we'll proceed with the selection of the jury. The court is adjourned. Thank you."

* * *

As the candidates left the room, Berne departed through the rear door. "Did you see my new chair?" he asked Linda.

"Non, Monsieur le Juge. I sit on the chair below your raised desk. I can see the whole courtroom, but not you. Was there a problem?"

"Yes, and I don't think it was a poisson d'avril. That new chair

Rocket bought is about a foot higher than chairs should be. Get someone to fix it, please. Call *The Maintenance* . . . .Call that constable who's been around for twenty years; he may know about chairs. Ask him and the other constable to lower the chair." He paused for a breath, and continued, "The court clerk may know something about chairs; get her as well and come back to see me when it's all organized."

Sam entered the office behind the courtroom, lifted the receiver and dialed.

"Judge's chambers," Jackie answered.

"It's me."

"I know. The number of the downstairs office is on my telephone screen."

"Then why do you answer as if a stranger were calling? . . . Forget what I just said. I'm just upset. Your friend Rocket bought a chair that's too high and wasn't adjusted. I just adjourned to allow the experts here to fix it . . . .The office door's partly open, and I see they've managed to move the chair into the hall and wrestle it to the ground. They're twisting and pushing it . . . .A policeman just gave it a kick, but it didn't help. Can you call Rocket to come down and help?"

"Today? Non! It's Wednesday, his regular day off. If I call, they'll write a memo which won't be typed till Friday, and we won't hear from him till next week. It'd be best to wait till tomorrow. I'll call him early in the morning."

"Yes . . . no . . . yes. *Oh, I seem to have forgotten something else. Why is the constable's name, Denis Parent, so familiar to me?*"

"You're really having a bad day. He was the constable during Judge Boyer's first jury trial."

"Oh yes, I remember now, thanks. I'll have to live with the chair problem for a day. Did anyone call?"

"No, only you. It's quiet so far."

"Okay, see you later. There won't be time to come back upstairs until after the jury's chosen."

"Bonjour."

"May I enter?" Linda asked as he replaced the receiver.

"Of course. What's the problem?"

24

"You announced in court that you'd soon proceed with the jury selection. Is it going to take long? Will the lawyers question the candidates?"

"You've been watching American TV again. This isn't *L.A. Law*. The accused has the right to an impartial jury, not a made-to-measure jury that's partial to the defence. As I said in court, the candidates are chosen at random from the election lists. We assume they're impartial and only allow questions if the trial has received a lot of publicity, or if a lawyer gives a good reason to challenge a candidate for cause. There'll be few such challenges in our case, or none. Go and see if they fixed the chair."

"Immediately," she replied and left. A minute later she looked into the office, grinned, and shook her head impishly from side to side.

"Get the chair back in the courtroom. I'll survive somehow till lunch. Our fifteen minutes have passed."

Berne waited a moment, then walked into the courtroom. Only the accused, the attorneys and the court personnel were present. He resumed his place. "Constable Parent, please summon the individuals who request exemption. Call them one at a time." Parent nodded and walked to the public corridor.

*   *   *

The first half dozen requests were routine. Two of the candidates were self-employed and couldn't spend the time in court without suffering considerable financial loss. Judges usually exempted insurance agents, self-employed repairmen and truck drivers, and convenience store owners on the grounds of financial hardship. They did the same for mothers with very young children, and people with serious medical conditions.

Judge Berne listened half-heartedly, distracted by the absurd chair. Then he reached down and turned the knob at the end of a lever beneath the seat. Nothing happened. The candidate in the witness box worked as a cashier at the front desk of a major hotel. She had been told by her boss to request an exemption.

25

"I'm sorry. I fail to see that you or the hotel would suffer if you were absent for two weeks. Exemption refused. Please call the next candidate."

A squat woman in her fifties, of Asian origin, explained that she worked in a local hospital, and asked for an exemption because she wouldn't be paid for the days she was absent. The personnel department had informed her that the union contract only provided for payment for day workers summoned for jury duty, and not for night personnel. Sam thought there must be an error. The best jurors were employees of public institutions, school boards, universities, and large companies— precisely because they didn't have to fear financial loss or hardship. He made a note to check it out personally.

His right hand grasped the knob under the chair once again, and pressed downward. Suddenly, the seat plummeted two feet in a free fall. Like a comic book character, Sam peered over the desk at the surprised faces of the lawyers.

They didn't know whether to laugh or be alarmed. Before they could decide he began to rise from the crouch . . . and the seat of the chair followed snugly. He moved his body up and down several times, seeking a comfortable position before releasing the knob.

Well! The day's first major problem had been solved. During the next adjournment he would adjust the chair just right, and teach the guards how to do it as well.

He looked at the woman standing in the witness box and ruled, "Exemption refused." She shuffled out slowly. "Next."

Constable Parent entered the room, followed by a young man.

"Come forward and stand in the witness box, please," Berne called.

The candidate walked to the front of the court, and the clerk asked, "What is your number?"

"Seven dash one twenty-two."

The list of jury candidates showed his name as Robert Blain, a student. "Mr. Blain," Berne enquired, "Why do you request exemption?"

"I'm a student and I have to write exams this month."

"I understand. When is your last exam?"

26

"May fifth."

"Fine. I shall exempt you for the present term, and order that you return on May seventh, when a jury will be chosen for another trial. Does that suit you?"

"Well, Your Honour," he replied, "I've been thinking and really, I'd rather stay and serve now."

"Good. The request for exemption is withdrawn. Mr. Blain, you are most welcome to remain."

Parent waved his hand from left to right, signalling that there were no more requests for exemption.

"Are there any people in the corridor who are related to the people involved or have personal knowledge of the facts of the case?"

"Non, Monsieur le Juge."

* * *

The judge's voice announced, "We will now proceed with the selection. I request the clerk to read the charge to the accused."

Serge Tremblay was seated in the prisoner's dock, wearing a dark leather jacket and jeans. He had short dark hair, and the pale complexion of someone who has been indoors too long.

The judge continued, "Mr. Tremblay, please rise."

Marie-Lyse Lortie stepped back towards her client and whispered something.

"Serge Tremblay, the attorney general has charged that on or about October seventh, 1991, at Montreal, in the Province of Quebec, you did unlawfully cause the death of Frank Lepine, thereby committing a second degree murder. How do you plead, guilty or not guilty?"

Tremblay was in a trance.

"How do you plead, guilty or not guilty?" the clerk repeated.

Marie-Lyse grabbed his right hand. He stared at her blankly for a few seconds before answering in a low monotone, "Not guilty."

"For trial on this charge, you have placed yourself upon God and your country, whom the jury will represent. The candidates who have been summoned to form a jury will be called into the courtroom one at a time. You may challenge twelve of the candidates without cause, and as many as you wish for cause. Be seated." The clerk shuffled the cards, pulled one out and read, "Number seventy-eight, Henri Lanctot."

Denis Parent had stationed himself at the door. Now he stepped out into the corridor and repeated in a resounding voice, "Number seventy-eight, Henri Lanctot." Within seconds the door reopened; Lanctot entered and advanced timidly to the witness box. "Please remain standing while the attorneys review their notes."

Both attorneys looked down and flipped through the booklet of forms completed by the prospective jurors, to read the meager information provided about candidate number seventy-eight. Sam looked first at Lortie, who smiled and responded, "Content, My Lord," and then at Talbot. "Satisfied."

"Please swear the juror."

The clerk intoned, "Place your right hand on the Bible. You swear to consider carefully all the facts which will be adduced in evidence in this case; you swear to render a verdict based solely on the evidence; you also swear to keep in strict confidence, during and after the trial, all discussions and deliberations in which you will participate."

"I do."

"Juror number one, please be seated in chair number one in the jury section."

Constables Harvey and Boisclair had been standing quietly beside the jury box, while their senior colleague dominated the scene. Now they sprang into action. Harvey relieved the bewildered juror of his jacket, while Boisclair guided him to the chair closest to the judge.

Meanwhile the clerk reached into the wooden box, selected another card, and called, "Number five, Natalie Elie."

Parent's voice echoed from the hall, "Number five, Natalie Elie." The candidate entered, strode resolutely toward the witness box, and stood there rigidly. According to the form in the book, she was fifty-six years old, divorced, and listed her occupation as Head Nurse, Notre Dame Hospital.

"Peremptory challenge," announced Lortie.

"Ms. Elie, you have been challenged and will not form part of the jury in this case. I thank you for coming to court today, and remind you that you must return on April thirteenth, same time, same courtroom, when a jury will be chosen for another trial. You are free to leave, and thank you once again."

Natalie Elie turned and left as stridently as she had entered.

Rick Hayes waited in the corridor, watching the candidates enter the courtroom. Each time a rejected candidate emerged, the people in the hall rushed to inquire what had happened. Hayes tried to keep a running count so he would know when twelve jurors had been chosen. Others appeared to be doing the same, but it wasn't easy. The process had accelerated, and apparently some of the challenged candidates had remained in the courtroom to watch the proceedings. He sure as hell wouldn't stay one second longer than necessary.

A rejected candidate came out and announced that eight jurors had been chosen. A collective sigh rose from the crowd. Thereafter whenever a name was called, the person called groaned loudly, and the remaining crowd roared in relief. Only three places remained . . . two . . . and finally one.

* * *

"Forty-nine, Rick Hayes," bellowed Parent.

"According to my notes," Judge Berne announced, "the Crown and the defence have used up their allotment of peremptory challenges." Talbot looked down for a moment and replied, "Yes, My Lord." Lortie smiled helplessly, acquiescing. They were obliged to accept the next person to walk through the door as the twelfth juror.

Eleven jurors were seated in the jury box at the front of the courtroom. They stared at the back, waiting for the next candidate. When the door opened, Rick Hayes entered, wearing cowboy boots, tight jeans, a leather jacket, sunglasses, and a leather cap. He chewed gum as he walked to the stand. Berne was unable to suppress a grin and a raising of the eyebrows as he glanced at Lortie.

She looked back at him and breezily announced in a loud voice, "Content, My Lord."

Vincent Talbot scowled, then grinned gamely, "I too am satisfied, Monsieur le Juge."

A flabbergasted Rick Hayes exclaimed in a whisper loud enough to be heard by everyone in the room, "Aw, shit!"

Berne clenched the arms of his chair. Lortie and Tremblay turned their heads to conceal their laughter. Hayes spurned Constable Harvey's offer to take his jacket as Constable Boisclair guided him by the elbow to the vacant seat in the jury box. The jury selection was complete.

2

"**P**lease swear in the jury constables."

Parent had already positioned himself in the witness box, anticipating the judge's order. He placed his right hand on the Bible, while the other constables put their hands on a Bible resting on the far corner of the jury box. They swore to guard the jury faithfully and to protect them from contact with strangers during their deliberations.

"I make the following orders," Judge Berne intoned. "The jurors will be permitted to separate during the trial, and until their deliberations begin. This will enable you to go home in the evenings during the trial. I order the sheriff to reimburse the jurors the cost of their daily parking or other transportation to the courthouse for the duration of the trial . . . .Please ask the remaining candidates in the corridor to enter."

The smiling candidates who had not been chosen, obviously relieved, shuffled back from the hall into the courtroom.

"Ladies and gentlemen, as you can see, we have completed the jury selection. The twelve men and women facing you will be the judges who will decide the guilt or innocence of the accused in this case. We appreciate your attendance today, and regret any inconvenience. You are released until April thirteenth, when your panel must return to this room, at 9:30. At that time a jury will be chosen from your panel to try another case.

"Members of the jury, this trial will resume at 2:15 this afternoon. Arrangements have been made for you to eat lunch in the building, together with your guards. You will be given access to telephones so that you can call your employers, family and friends. If you have any problems, please inform the guards and we'll do our best to assist you. The court is adjourned until 2:15."

"All rise," Linda called.

"Your Lordship," Marie-Lyse called, "Before we adjourn, would you please order that the accused be given hot meals at lunch for the duration of the trial? Otherwise he'll have to eat cold sandwiches."

"So ordered. Please enter this in the court record and I'll sign the forms later."

"Thank you."

A flicker of acknowledgement passed over Serge Tremblay's face. Then he felt the guard's hand on his shoulder guiding him towards the door to the cells.

* * *

It was 12:30. With the jury now chosen, the case could begin. Judge Berne was pleased with the morning's progress. He lingered in the hall waiting for Parent.

"Constable, please have a talk with juror number twelve and see if you can get him to remove his cap and sunglasses, and to stop chewing gum."

"No problem, Monsieur le Juge," Parent replied with assurance. "Oh, what is your policy on jurors having their meals outside the courthouse?"

"I have no policy about meals. Those decisions are made as the trial progresses. I do, however, have a policy prohibiting guards from encouraging jurors to ask permission to eat their meals outside the building."

"I would never do such a thing," Parent exclaimed with feigned innocence.

"I'm sure you wouldn't, but perhaps you can say something to your less experienced colleagues."

"Oui, Monsieur le Juge," he replied, his credibility now fully restored.

It was known among the judges that Parent frequently encouraged jurors to make a variety of demands which, if uncontrolled, could transform a jury trial into a gastronomic adventure at government expense. After the constable left, Berne turned to Linda. "Let's go upstairs. Jackie will be waiting to hear about your morning in the criminal courts. You did very well."

She preened, pirouetted, and walked to the elevators.

*   *   *

Denis Parent gathered the jurors in the jury room.

"I'm Denis Parent, senior Jury Constable in this courthouse. I've been around since the building was opened, a lot longer than most of the judges. If you have any problems, bring them to Denis. I'm the guy who arranges the meals, sorts out the parking, reserves the hotel rooms, calls the doctor, and deals with the judge for you. Let's face it, I take care of a lot of things around here."

Rick wondered who the hell the clown in the tight uniform thought he was. These guys are always the same. Give a guy a uniform and a gun, and he thinks he runs the world. Take away the gun and he's just a leering old guy who wouldn't last a day in the machine shop.

"Hey, Parent!" Rick called.

"Constable Parent," he corrected.

"Look, Parent, don't pull that rank crap on me. You heard the judge. We're the ones who decide if the poor bastard on trial is guilty or not. You're supposed to help us, and I need help. Are you gonna help or do I have to ask the judge?"

"What do you want, kid?"

"I'm not your kid or anyone else's. You wanna help me?"

"Okay, but only if you take off your cap, and stop chewing gum in the courtroom. It burns the judge where he sits. What's bothering you?"

"My vacation. I'm supposed to get two weeks off before we start this big job in the shop. The boss said if I got chosen, no holiday. I don't care if I sit around this place for a few days, but I want to do it on the boss's time and not mine."

"Is that all?" asked Parent.

"Uh-huh."

"Look, I told you I know my way around. Tell your boss the judge ordered you to stay here, and if there's any trouble with your vacation, you'll ask the judge to get involved. The law says they can't fire or punish you for being on a jury. Screwing up your holiday is a punishment, and they can be fined for it. I haven't been around for twenty years for nothing."

"Sounds good. Thanks . . . .When do we eat around here?"

"Right now." Parent raised his voice. "Ladies and gentlemen, we're going to a special dining room in the courthouse. You heard the judge say that you're going to decide if the guy on trial is guilty. Well, you're sort of like judges, so you get to eat in a private dining room like the judges do. Leave your jackets and things in the jury room. We lock the door when we leave . . . and follow me, 'cause we don't use the public corridors, like tourists. I've got a special escape route through the marriage office; leads right out . . . .Let's go. Constable Harvey, please bring up the rear."

"But," a voice protested, "I need a phone. I have a business to run!"

"When we get upstairs you can use the phone, but you'll have to wait your turn," Harvey replied.

"Wait for a phone?" the voice asked incredulously. "Not me. Tomorrow, I'll bring a cellular phone. Got to stay in touch."

True to his word, Parent led his charges through an office crammed with desks and clerks, to an elevator in the main lobby. They rose two floors, and walked single file to the reserved dining room. Rick had left his cap in the jury room. As they entered the dining room, he spit his gum into a garbage container.

* * *

When Sam and Linda got back to the private office upstairs, Jackie greeted them. "I've been reading about your case in the morning paper."

"Are they still writing about that acquittal of last week? I thought it was all finished. The TV interviews by the crown prosecutor, and the digs from my wife, friends and devoted secretary, almost convinced me the decision was made by me and not by a jury."

"Calm down. The world's not interested in your innocent murderer. *Le Journal* reported that the trial in the Tremblay case begins today, and that you'd be the judge."

"I didn't know you read *Le Journal*. Tabloids are for sports and crime fans, and you're neither."

"I read the tabloids when they write about you."

"Then why didn't you tell me when I came in this morning?"

"Because I didn't know. Nantel dropped by with a photocopied clipping from *Le Journal*. He asked me to tell you, 'Hot stuff! Monsieur le Juge, hot stuff!'" She cupped her right hand, raised it towards her mouth and blew hard on her finger nails. "Hot stuff!"

Linda looked on, bewildered. "Jackie, is it true that the case was mentioned in *Le Journal*?"

"Oui."

"Why did Monsieur Nantel—"

"Allow me to explain," Berne offered. "Your colleague Nantel is an avid newspaper reader who follows the careers of the judges in the Criminal Division. Each morning he clips out the newspaper crime reports which concern us, and brings a copy to the judge mentioned. He usually adds a comment of one or two words. Calls it his *jurisprudence.*"

"Really?"

"Oh yes. Apparently he wheedled three filing cabinets from Rocket to store his collection of old clippings. Keeps the new ones in the fire hose cabinets. That's why Rocket pasted signs around the building saying the cabinets shouldn't be used for storing newspapers, cups and other personal objects."

"I'll ask him to show me the scrapbooks," Linda said. "Monsieur le Juge, I think I like working in the Criminal Division."

"Don't be so impulsive," Jackie cautioned. "Wait till the jury starts deliberating and you end up spending a weekend with him in the courthouse." She nodded towards the judge, as if Linda couldn't figure out who the him was.

"Do juries really sit and deliberate on the weekends?" Linda asked incredulously.

"Yes, but I try to arrange matters so it won't be necessary. Oh, Jackie, I managed to figure out how that new chair works, so you won't have to bother Rocket . . . .It's almost one o'clock; I'm going down for a sandwich."

"Bon appetit. Linda and I will go to a restaurant to discuss the case privately. Oh—you had a call from your wife. She's going out and will call later. Also, Maître Asselin phoned. He'll be in his office for a while. I said you'd probably return his call when you come up from court."

"Get him, please. He's probably calling about the annual court-house visit by the Hudson High School students and their teachers. If they come in the next day or so, my case should interest them. Bon appetit. I'll see you both at two."

*   *   *

Jackie and Linda were in good spirits when they returned to the office from lunch and sat down by the window. They had managed to find an extra table and two chairs which were set up cafe style behind the working area. At Christmas, Sam had bought them a teapot and half a dozen china cups. The two women, seated at the table drinking tea, sharing gossip about the trial, added an air of civility to the otherwise institutional atmosphere. Linda was still exhilarated by the morning's experience, and her enthusiasm was contagious. "Tell me about Constable Parent and Judge Boyer. Jackie knows the story, but said you can tell it better. Please?" she asked as Samuel Berne entered.

"I'm not accustomed to compliments from Jackie—not even indirect ones." Jackie glared at him; her tongue darted out in mock defiance. Sam shrugged as if he didn't understand what she meant, then replied to Linda, "I'll tell you later. Put on your gown, and let's go down to the courtroom."

Minutes later, they crossed the wide lobby and walked along the corridor separating the judges' offices from the courtrooms. As usual, Linda walked on his right, one step ahead.

Sam walked into the private washroom, looked in the mirror and ran a hand through his thinning hair. He bent forward to see the bald spot that seemed to have grown larger since morning. The tap was leaking. He felt the drops of cold water with his index finger, then tried unsuccessfully to shut it off. Perhaps when there was time, he'd ask Jackie to call *The Maintenance*; otherwise it would drip forever. Linda knocked on the outer door. "Ready, Monsieur le Juge."

"Good. Don't ask the people in the room to sit until the last juror, number twelve, has taken his place."

"But I can't see him from my chair. Your desk blocks my view."

"I'll signal you."

When the jurors filed into the hall, one was missing. Parent walked forward and volunteered, "Monsieur le Juge, it'll just be a moment. Number twelve is phoning his boss." He continued with a self-satisfied grin, "I convinced him to remove his cap and to not chew gum. As for the sunglasses, I'm working on the problem. I, Constable Denis Parent, will prevail."

"I've no doubt . . . .There he is now."

Linda pressed the buzzer, opened the door, and announced, "Please rise." As the jurors entered, she looked up at Judge Berne. He nodded, and she called, "The hearing will now resume. Please be seated."

* * *

Berne looked around the room, acknowledging the attorneys, the clerk and the accused. This was his first opportunity to study the jurors. Six women and six men, a good omen. Two of the women seemed quite young. He hadn't bothered to check their ages, but they were probably in their early twenties. Number four, Betty Major, caught his attention. She was shapely, with long auburn hair. As their eyes locked, she flashed a warm inviting smile. Sam wondered if they'd met before. An exceptional memory enabled him to recall entire paragraphs of judgements, legal texts, and contracts, even numbers on a balance sheet, but invariably he forgot names and faces. A warm flush rose through his body as he waited for number four to turn her head, but she stared straight at him. He looked at number five, Lucy Morin, and number six, Phil Pasquin. Twelve, Rick Hayes, peered ahead stiffly, eyes concealed by sunglasses. At least the cap and gum were gone.

Although most of the jurors wore their Sunday clothes, Berne knew from experience that that would change as soon as they got into the trial and felt at home. Number six, at the end of the first row, was particularly well dressed, wearing a double-breasted suit in the latest Italian style. That must be the fellow who complained about the phones. The list of jurors read simply, 'number six, Phil Pasquin, business executive'. The luck of the draw had placed him immediately in front of number twelve. Like magazines on a book store rack: *Gentlemen's Quarterly* and *Popular Mechanics*.

Parent sat on a wooden chair beside number twelve, on the floor a foot lower down. As Berne spoke, Parent drifted off to sleep, eyes tightly closed. He'd probably heard opening remarks a thousand times before. Berne was disconcerted but carried on.

"Ladies and gentlemen, you have been chosen with great care by both the attorney for the Crown and the attorney for the defence, to try this case and decide whether Serge Tremblay is guilty or not guilty of the murder of Frank Lepine. That is the only task that you have in this case, but it is a vital one. To discharge your responsibilities properly, you must act calmly, dispassionately, without preconception or prejudice.

"Our system of justice is adversarial. This means that the Crown must establish the facts of the case, and the accused is entitled to be present and have his lawyer question each witness to determine if he or she is telling the truth. The Crown has the burden of proof, the obligation to convince you beyond a reasonable doubt that the accused is guilty of the crime charged.

"The accused does not have to prove anything, and cannot be compelled to testify. He is presumed innocent throughout this trial, until the Crown has made you morally certain of his guilt. That is the most important principle of law which you must apply throughout this trial, and during your deliberations."

Berne focused on the accused, wondering if he was guilty. All he knew with certainty was that Serge Tremblay was tall, slim and composed, cool as a spectator at someone else's trial.

*   *   *

Serge rubbed his wrists where the handcuffs had been removed. The judge had asked if anyone in the courtroom was related to him. He had no relatives—as though he'd just spontaneously appeared, in the motherless cold flat on Champlain Street. He had always had to take care of himself. Independence and self-sufficiency can come too early in the east end. He could remember being small, but had few childhood memories.

His father, Marcel, had worked as a seasonal employee assembling aluminum lawn chairs and tables at the factory on Frontenac Street near the river. From January to July he went off at seven in the morning, and left Serge alone. After the shift at the plant, he'd spend a few hours at the tavern.

Each July, Marcel Tremblay was laid off. He found odd jobs making deliveries in the east end for a pharmacy or other store, but these jobs were always temporary. Invariably there was a shortage in the money collected. He would explain that it wasn't his fault if a customer had shortchanged him or wasn't able to pay the account. But the odour of beer on his breath would betray him, and he would be fired. Then he would drift into a neighbourhood tavern and spend entire days drinking, until the urge to work seized him once again and the cycle would begin all over.

There was a regular flow of money, paycheques from the factory in winter, and unemployment insurance cheques in the summer. The cash earned from the delivery jobs supplemented the government cheques. This routine continued from year to year. Serge had learned how to live in the small flat and avoid his father. He knew instinctively when to clear out of the living room and leave his father alone with the TV set and a sixpack of beer. Experience taught him to retreat into the bedroom. He didn't recognize his father's friends—only the sound of their voices. It was safer that way.

Sometimes the men played cards, but usually they just watched the hockey games, shouting till late at night. Sometimes they broke furniture, but that could always be replaced with 'new' things from the Salvation Army.

Girls didn't exist in Serge's world. He was about as conscious of their presence as of the lamp-posts on the streets. Serge didn't even know that he had a mother until he was seven or eight, and found out where babies come from by listening to the big kids.

Women visited his father, and sometimes moved into the flat, but the relationships never lasted long. These women faded from his memory as quickly as the new ones appeared. Claire, Thérèse, Jeanne d'Arc, Sylvie, Marie, . . . yes, there were many Maries. Invariably the Maries had double names: Marie-Jo, Marie-Thérèse, Marie-Marthe, Marie-Jeanne, Marie-Ange, and 'the little Marie': la 'tite-Marie. One was even known as Marie-Marie! They stayed only a few hours or days, and he ignored them.

Nature had provided for Serge in her own way. In the winter when his father was at work, the flat was a safe haven, and in the summer and fall the streets were more accommodating. On cold or rainy days Serge went to school. At other times he'd hang around with other kids. No one seemed to care what they did, except the owners of the stores where they stole at will. Serge liked Oscar, the biscuit store, best. They always kept a box of broken biscuits near the door for the neighbourhood kids, a crude but effective form of protection.

Until he was twelve he had managed to escape police attention, but then he was caught stealing a pair of jeans. The police threw him into the back of their car and drove to the station. Charges weren't laid because the police had more important things to do. A few hours later he returned to the streets. He continued to steal whatever he wanted, but he had learned his lesson, and was shrewd enough to not get caught again.

He had always been stronger than he looked, and it was this strength that helped him survive in the east end. He knew many of the street kids, but they weren't his friends, just guys he hung out with till he decided to do something else.

To insulate himself from the people around him, he acted the same way as when his father returned from the tavern. His face lost expression; his unseeing eyes stared straight ahead, and only his ears absorbed the surrounding sounds as he closed and bolted an invisible door to the world. He didn't mind if people were disconcerted by his cold unfeeling gaze.

*   *   *

The judge's voice continued, "Throughout this trial you must listen and observe everything in the courtroom. Don't only listen, but watch each witness. You will have to decide who is telling the truth, and who is not. The way a witness stands, looks, and acts may be revealing.

"The court clerk will read the charge, to which the accused has already pleaded not guilty. Then, Maître Vincent Talbot will make the opening statement for the Crown."

I don't believe what's happening, Rick thought. What am I doing in here with all these people? It's a bad joke, as if I had fallen into the TV set and wound up in the middle of *Night Court*. Look at the judge; he moves well, but he's too heavy. Must spend his life making speeches and eating. I wonder if he knows what it's like in the real world. Bet he's never seen a machine shop in his life. I'd be surprised if he could tell a die from a jig, or a punch press from a lathe. These guys are all talk. This bloody building's all talk. There goes the lawyer, talk, talk, talk.

"I am Vincent Talbot, attorney for the Crown, and I will talk to you briefly about the facts of this case. Serge Tremblay, the accused, lives on Visitation Street in Montreal. The Crown will show that on the night of October 7th, 1991, he went out to visit the bars on St. Denis Street. Around midnight, a fight occurred between Tremblay and Frank Lepine, in the bar known as Le Wiz. The police were called, no one was hurt, and no arrests were made.

"At 3:15, after the bars closed and their customers poured into the street, Frank Lepine was shot and killed. Because of the crowds and traffic on the street, the killer was able to get away.

"Two weeks later, the police were informed by a resident of the house where the accused was living, and he was arrested. She and her partner will testify, and tell you how Tremblay came home the night of the murder, white as a ghost, and then terrorized them for two weeks.

"Police witnesses will identify the gun used to commit the crime, and establish that it was in Tremblay's possession at the time of his arrest. The evidence will be sufficient for you to conclude beyond a reasonable doubt that Serge Tremblay fired the shot that killed Frank Lepine, and that he intended to do so. Thank you."

"Will you call your first witness?"

Talbot called Juan Luis Torres, who entered with a flourish and bowed. An expectant mood permeated the room as he began speaking before reaching the witness box.

*   *   *

"Good day, everybody. I am Juan Luis Torres, eyewitness to the crime. I tell you exactly what I saw: exactly, because I was there, at Le Wiz."

"Mr. Torres," the judge interrupted, "please wait until you have taken the oath, and the clerk writes down your name and address. Then,

42

Maître Talbot will ask you questions, and you should reply while looking towards the jury. Do you understand?"

"Yes, Your Excellency. Juan Luis Torres wants to tell the whole story, but he will wait for the clerk."

"Thank you. I am a judge, not an excellency."

The clerk administered the oath, then asked his name.

"I have already said my name, Juan Luis Torres, witness to the crime. My address must be a secret. These wild young people might visit Juan Luis Torres at his home."

Berne leaned forward, "I authorize the witness to write his address on a piece of paper and give it to the clerk. The address will remain in a sealed envelope and will not be revealed."

"Thank you, Mister Judge," said the witness, "Now I tell you what happened?"

The judge nodded.

3

"**J**uan Luis Torres is a citizen of this country for ten years. He is forty-two years old, and understands the world. On the seven day of October he goes to see the crowds on St. Denis Street. It is late at night, but that does not bother Juan Luis. In his country, where he was born, the people go out late for eating and shows. Juan Luis visits Le Wiz. That is a funny name, *Le Wiz*. In this country they give a bar the name of a cheese! There are many people in the bar and they all have good time drinking beer, and talking, and singing. Juan Luis is alone that night, so he sits at the bar and watches television for a while. There is a hockey game, and Juan Luis is still learning all about hockey like a good citizen.

"Suddenly, there is noise in the bar, and Juan Luis sees people fighting. They do punches like this." The witness began gesturing vigorously and striking at the air with a flurry of jabs, upper cuts, and kicks. "Juan Luis thought, someone must call the police. The guy from the front door comes and tries to break up the fight, but he is not big enough and he is only one. Juan Luis would help, but he is too old for this fight. Well, the police come in and push the guys away, one from the other."

"Were any of the people in this courtroom involved in the fight?" asked Talbot.

The witness stared intently at the jurors. Then his eyes wandered around the room, from one person to the other, until they settled on Marie-Lyse Lortie. "The lady in the black dress at the table, yes, she was in the bar, standing beside the woman they fight about." He inclined his head towards her and asked, "Were you at Le Wiz on October seven? Did you not see the fight?"

Lortie was visibly embarrassed. She stood and addressed the court. "My Lord, I tell the court on my oath of office that I was not at Le Wiz on October seventh. In fact, it is some years since I have gone to bars late at night."

"I understand," Judge Berne said, "You don't have to make a statement under oath. Perhaps the witness was just a little confused and overwhelmed by the court atmosphere." She sat down and Judge Berne continued, "Mr. Torres, is there anyone else in the court that you recognize from the bar?"

"Yes, I just noticed the man on the side, near the policeman." He pointed at Tremblay. "He was there."

Talbot interrupted, "For purposes of the record, the witness is pointing to Serge Tremblay, the accused."

"Juan Luis has seen that man in the bar," he continued. "I did not see him before in this courtroom, but he was in the bar. Juan Luis does not make mistakes with the faces of people."

There was a slight titter among the jurors, and two of them covered their mouths with their hands. Rick peered ahead impassively.

The witness, seemingly unaware of the incongruity of his last statement, continued, "The police pushed them away, and forced some of those young guys out of the bar."

"Did you see what they were fighting about?" Talbot asked.

"Juan Luis knows why they were fighting. It is always the same with those young guys. They fight abou' money and girls. Tonight . . . no . . . that night, they fight abou' the girl with the frien' who look like the lady in the black robe there." He caught his breath and smiled at Marie-Lyse Lortie, "That guy over there, near the police, wanted to dance with the girl, and she—I don't know if she wanted to dance. Her frien' that look like the lady in court said something to this other guy. Well, this guy went over and push the guy over there, and soon everyone in the bar was fighting. I was not fighting, because I am not young like the others."

"I'll show you a picture. Do you recognize the person in the picture?"

"Yes, that's the other guy who was fighting with the guy over there. What do you call him?"

"For the court record, the accused has recognized the photograph of the victim, Frank Lepine," Talbot noted. "What, if anything, happened between Frank Lepine and the accused?"

"That fellow near the police, that's the *accuse?*" asked the witness.

"Yes," replied Talbot.

"Not much. Police came before they finished the fight. They punched each other, and then they were holding each other. The cops, they made them go apart, and that guy, the accuse, lef' the bar. But he came back later."

"Was anybody hurt in the fight?"

"Yes," replied the witness. "One man, he was bleeding from his globe."

"You mean his head?" asked Talbot.

"Yes," replied the witness, "The globe on his head."

"I'm sorry, I don't understand. Did you say the globe on his head?"

"Yes, the globe."

"What globe?"

"The globe. You know, the globe from his ear."

"That is called the *lobe,*" Berne suggested.

"That is what I say. He was bleeding from his globe."

"Who was the man who was bleeding?" Talbot asked.

"It was a little guy."

"Which little guy?"

"It was the little skinny guy. There was a fight between a little fat guy and a little skinny guy in the corner of the bar, under the TV, and the little fat guy musta hurt the little skinny guy."

"Were the little fat guy and the little skinny guy involved in any way with Frank Lepine or the accused Serge Tremblay?"

"I don't know."

"Do you remember the time of the fight?"

"It was after midnight. Juan Luis went to the toilet at midnight. There is a clock and a phone near the toilet. Not in the toilet room but on the wall. A little while after I came out, the fight started."

"Did you see any guns or other weapons during the fight?" asked Talbot.

"Yes, at the end of the fight."

"What did you see? Who had guns?"

"The cops who came into the bar. They had guns, but they didn't use them. The cops only pushed everybody away from each other."

"And then?"

"The two girls lef', and musta gone home. I did not see them again that night."

"Did you see the accused again that night?"

"Of course. I told you Juan Luis saw the crime. At a quarter to three, you know, they serve the drinks two for one. They shout Last Call; the customers pay for one drink and get two. So everyone order two more beer. They drink the beers fast, because in fifteen minutes at three o'clock all the bars close up.

"Just before they shout Last call, I see this guy Tremblay—*the accuse* you call him—is back in the bar. He sit in the corner and jus' look at Lepine. I know he's mad but nothing happen. He jus' looks and looks. Then the bar closes up, and we all go in the street. There are thousand people there, in front of Le Wiz. More people go in the streets closing time than in the day. Many cars shine their lights, honk. The police are standing every corner."

"I asked if you saw Tremblay."

"Oh yes, Tremblay is leaning on a car by the sidewalk staring at the man in the picture—Frank Lepine?"

"Yes."

"He didn't look like a Frank. Well, I see Frank go up to Tremblay, and push him. People jump back to make a circle, and Frank push

Tremblay again. They shove each other a minute, and the accu—Tremblay run away.

"Suddenly there is a loud noise. Juan Luis turn aroun', and see Frank lying on the groun', holding his heart. I shout—everybody shouting. The police come over and push everybody away. They call the ambulance and take poor Frank to hospital. Next day, there's a picture in the newspaper. They say he's dead."

"Did you know the victim, Frank Lepine, before that night?" asked Talbot.

"Yes, I saw him in bars sometime."

"Thank you. No further questions."

"The court will adjourn for fifteen minutes." It was a quarter after three, and the witness had spoken for an hour without a pause. Berne knew that Lortie would welcome a few moments to prepare her cross-examination, and juries have difficulty concentrating for more than an hour without a break. He watched the jurors rise from their places.

*　*　*

Hayes led the jurors back from the courtroom. Parent accompanied him, speaking. "Our trial goes well, does it not?"

"Yeah, they finally got going. This fellow Juan Luis is a character! So excited to have an audience that he can't stop talking. Did you see the look on Lortie's face when he said she was in the bar? I thought I'd bust out laughing."

"Me too."

"Look, Parent, I'm going to rush ahead so I can be the first to the can. See you soon."

Rick smiled as he closed the door behind him. He could easily imagine the scene at Le Wiz on the night of the crime. Those bars are all the same, except maybe the gay ones. Once or twice a week he went down to St. Denis to have a good time, the best place to meet people, even if fights happen now and then.

A knock on the door reminded him that others were waiting for the toilet. The jurors were seated around the long rectangular table drinking coffee. Their animated conversation was interspersed with laughter. Everyone spoke at once about the testimony of Juan Luis Torres, and recreated the scene on the night of the crime. One juror bowed deeply in imitation of Torres, and repeated, "Good day everybody, I am Roger Lebrun, juror number three, and witness to the trial." The other jurors howled.

* * *

Berne heard the laughter as he walked down the hall to stretch his legs and restore circulation. "Well, Constable," he said to Parent, "our jurors are getting their money's worth. They seem to have come alive."

"It's always like this," he replied. "First they're mad about being chosen; then they laugh. Soon they'll become bored . . . and then serious. I've seen juries for twenty years. Each one thinks it is special, but in some ways they're all the same."

"Some things never change."

"Monsieur le Juge, do you think tomorrow is the time for them to have a lunch outside the courthouse? There's a restaurant, Le Vieux Port, where the prices are most reasonable, no more than eating in the building, and the jurors are always happy to eat out."

"Have you mentioned this to the jury?" Sam asked, staring into his eyes.

"Non, I would not do such a thing, especially after you spoke to me. But if you decide they can dine out, I must call the restaurant early in the morning so they can prepare."

"Is there a separate room for the jury in that restaurant?"

"No, but they set a large table in the back and move the other tables a proper distance. We've been going there for years. The food is good and the prices are cheap."

"I know. I ate on their terrace last summer. Don't say a word to the jurors about restaurants or eating out of the building unless I authorize you. Do you understand?"

"Oui, Monsieur le Juge."

Berne turned towards the courtroom. "Linda, are the lawyers ready?"

"Maître Lortie requested five more minutes."

"Okay. Watch the courtroom and tell me when she is ready."

* * *

The jurors anxiously awaited the cross-examination as Marie- Lyse Lortie rose.

"Mr. Torres, have you known the accused, Serge Tremblay, a long time?"

"I seen the guy before, at the bars, but I didn't know his name. He is not my frien', and we never speak together. But I reconize him today. He is the man who had the fight in the bar Le Wiz. I, Juan Luis Torres, was witness of the fight."

"Do you like to watch fights?" Lortie asked.

"With people?"

"Of course, What other fights are there?"

"The bullfights. Juan Luis Torres is true to his name. In my country, there are bullfights which I watched all the time, before I came in Canada. Now I watch hockey on television. They fight a little, the hockey players, but not so much."

"Mr. Torres, I believe Maître Lortie was asking about fights between people only," Judge Berne interjected. Things were drifting away from the subject.

"Yes, I like to watch the people fights on television. Sometimes I watch wrestling, but they are not honest. I would not pay to see them. The bulls are honest; they fight for their lives; the toreador fights for his life." He gestured and extended his arm to taunt an imaginary bull in some distant arena. Then he suddenly returned to the courtroom. "Excuse me, Juan Luis wanders his mind. What was the question?"

"Do you like to watch people fight in bars?" Lortie repeated.

"No, it disturbs the television. Those guys fight too much; they fight for girls, money, and I told you—no, I told the other lawyer."

"Did you see the victim, Frank Lepine, involved in fights before?"

Torres replied, "With guns? Never."

"Do you go out to the bars every night?"

"No! I am not as young as when I was young, and I don't go out so much now."

Lortie questioned Juan Luis Torres for the rest of the afternoon. He repeated each detail over and over, never failing to delight and entertain. Despite the thoroughness of the cross- examination, little new information was provided. The clock on the wall indicated 4:30 when Marie-Lyse announced her cross-examination was completed. Berne made his final remarks of the day.

"Ladies and gentlemen, I thank you for your attention throughout the day. Before we adjourn I wish to remind you to not discuss this case with anyone, including the members of your family, and friends who will be curious and may question and try to engage you in conversation about the case. Please do not jump to conclusions about the guilt or innocence of the accused. A body of evidence is best understood in its entirety. Keep an open mind until you have heard all the evidence, the attorneys' summations, and my charge. Good afternoon, and I shall see you tomorrow morning at 9:30. The court is adjourned."

*   *   *

From the corner of his eye Berne saw Hayes manoeuver himself beside the young woman juror who sat diagonally in front of him, Lucy Morin. Hayes' interest may have been simply that of a fellow juror, but Berne guessed otherwise. It wouldn't be the first time romance blossomed among jurors during a trial. He nodded to the jurors in the hall, and followed Linda up to his office.

"Tell me about Judge Boyer and Constable Parent," she implored.

"Sure. You may remember that Judge Boyer was appointed a few months after me. As a result we had adjoining offices and became good friends. Well, we both asked for a term in the Criminal Division at the same time. He didn't get sent to the outlying courthouses, and his first criminal jury trial was in Montreal. The coordinators assigned Denis Parent, their most experienced jury constable, to the case.

"On the first day of the trial, right after the jury was chosen, Parent asked the judge, 'Did you notice juror number five? Did you see her? What a beautiful woman!' Judge Boyer was a little nervous, concentrating on the trial, so he hadn't paid her particular attention. He watched the next time the jury entered. She was attractive: blond hair like you, about thirty-five years old, slighty overweight.

"Well, from then on whenever Parent had to speak to the judge, he began by commenting on the beauty of juror number five. After the trial ended, Judge Boyer didn't see Parent for a long time. Two years later they finally met again, and Parent asked if he remembered the trial with that beautiful juror number five. When the judge said he did, Parent told him it had been love at first sight, and they had been going out together ever since the trial. They'd finally decided to get married and wanted Judge Boyer to conduct the marriage ceremony."

"Did he do it?" Linda asked.

"No. Unfortunately," Berne replied, "we only do divorces."

"Too bad. It would have been so romantic . . . .Does Judge Boyer still sit in criminal cases?"

"Yes. As a matter of fact, he's sitting with a jury in the courtroom down the hall. Unusual situation: a young accused charged with a triple murder is out on bail."

"In the street?"

"Uh-huh."

"And in the courthouse?"

"That's right. He enters the courtroom before the jury and sits in the prisoner's dock. During the adjournments he's free to walk around the halls, or even go across the street for a sandwich."

"Really?"

"Yes, most unusual. I guess Judge Boyer thought he wasn't danger-ous and would show up for trial."

Jackie pretended to be absorbed in her typing and didn't look up when they entered.

"What are you so busy with?" Sam asked. "I haven't asked you to type anything in a week."

"I'm not busy, I'm working for the administration. They send me these files, and I have to type funny green forms in each of them. How's the trial?"

"Ask Linda; she's the expert. Did you call *The Maintenance* about that leaking tap downstairs?"

"Yes, but as usual they weren't listening. I can always tell. When they say *yes* more than once in a conversation, it means *maybe*. When they continue to repeat *Yes, yes, yes,* it means they aren't listening at all. I think you should call them. They may listen to a judge."

"That's what you think! I'll call Rocket tomorrow. I can't cope with construction and maintenance problems after a day in court."

*   *   *

Betty Major walked through the lobby of the Four Seasons Hotel and down the stairs.

A voice called enthusiastically, "Here comes the judge!"

"C'mon, it's only me—Betty—and I'm a juror, not a judge. Really I'm a barber who calls herself a hair stylist so the customers will pay more," she protested as she entered the barbershop.

"Maybe in court you're a juror," persisted Tony, "but here in Tony's Salon, you're a judge. If you're not a lawyer or a criminal and you go to court, you must be a judge. I think you're more of a judge than the judge. The real judge can't decide if that fellow is guilty, so you have to do it for him. If you don't want to be a judge, put on the white smock and cut hair."

"Tony, you're sweet."

"How long are you going to be a judge in court?"

"I'm not sure. They say two weeks, maybe less. Is that all right? Can you manage without me?"

"Betty, it's never easy to manage without you, but I try. When your customers call, and I tell them you're off for jury duty, they don't want to see me instead. Every one of them wants to come in and hear firsthand what it's like to be on a jury."

"Tony, you're really sweet. Can I help you this afternoon? We finished a bit early."

"No, you cannot be a judge and a barber at the same time. It's against the rules of the barbers' union to be a judge, and it's against the rules of the judges to be a barber. Tell me, Betty," he asked solicitously, "Do they feed you well there?"

"Do I look underfed?"

"No. You look—" he kissed the fingertips of his right hand loudly. "Where's Emile today?"

"He had to leave early. His wife dragged him to a meeting in school. They're having trouble with their younger son."

"Then you're alone?"

"It's no problem. I'm very lucky: business is bad. But don't worry, with all the appointments we booked for the week after next on your chair, you won't have time to eat. And I, Tony, will retire."

"Tony, be serious. How are you managing?"

"I'll tell you my secret. In this business two heads are better than one, so I think I'll start to work on two chairs at once, like the dentists."

"Be serious."

"My regulars have kept me busy enough. Are you sure you'll be back in two weeks?"

"Sure. I don't think these things take long."

"Have you found us any new customers in the courthouse?"

"Not yet, though I'm working on it. I found an old one. Remember Pasquin? The man with the fancy Italian suits, who comes in and reads *Playboy* magazine backwards? He's on the jury. I don't think he recognized me yet."

"How can he miss a beauty like you?"

"He's too busy thinking about himself. My father used to say people like him fall in love whenever they look in a mirror."

"Are you going to find out why he reads *Playboy* magazine backwards?" Tony asked.

"Good idea. I think it's because there are more pictures of naked women in the back of the magazine. He likes the pictures more than editorials and letters."

"Betty, I see you're a good judge of men. They chose the right person to be on the jury."

"Thank you."

"Betty, can I ask you something about the trial?"

"I don't know; the judge said not to discuss the case." She wagged her finger from side to side, and then lifted it to her mouth.

"I'll ask you the question, and if you don't want to answer, don't."

"No. My question is: Do they give better haircuts in the jail than at Tony's Salon?"

"Tony, you're impossible!"

"Answer the question."

"No, of course not."

"Then how come they have so many more customers than I do?"

"Tony, it must be the food! . . . Look, Mr. Kay is coming down the stairs. Does he have an appointment with you today?"

"Yes, and he's right on time."

"Are you sure you don't want me to stay and help?"

"No, go home and relax, Judge. I'll need you in two weeks."

"Ciao, have a good rest of the day."

* * *

The events of the previous afternoon were featured prominently in the morning papers. The journalists had enjoyed the testimony of Torres and were determined to describe every detail to their readers. Special attention was given to his comments about bullfighting, wrestling and hockey. However, the report was generally accurate. *The Gazette* followed its usual practice of not mentioning the judge's name. Lower down on the same page, a brief paragraph stated that the Crown had appealed the acquittal in Judge Berne's trial of the previous week.

When Sam arrived at the courthouse, Nantel was waiting at the office door. "Double play, Monsieur le Juge, double play! Here is today's jurisprudence," he announced, proffering two clippings from *Le Journal.*

"Thank you. Bonjour."

Nantel walked off muttering to himself. "A new judge, and he makes a double play; yes, a double play!"

In *Le Journal,* a tabloid that specializes in reporting crime and sports, photos of the previous night's most sordid events are generally featured on its front page. The judge's name is mentioned in every courthouse report. Some avid readers actually count the convictions and acquittals of each judge, with a level of interest usually reserved for the win and loss records of goalies and pitchers.

When Jackie saw the clippings she shrugged. "Old news. Nothing here that I didn't know. Good thing *The Gazette* doesn't mention names, or I'd get calls from your relatives pretending to be concerned about your welfare. They really want some special scoop, and don't dare to phone you."

"If any members of my family call, tell them I am in splendid health. By the way, do you remember last November, when the Chief Justice distributed the list of books the government would buy for us? I ordered Gene Ewaschek's *Criminal Pleading and Practice* but it never arrived. Can you find out what happened? Six months should be long enough to get a book from Toronto."

"I'll call Renée, downstairs, and see if she's still in charge of book buying for judges."

"Thanks. It'll be useful when I prepare my charge in this case. Have you seen Linda yet?"

"I met her in the elevator on her way up to punch in. She told me she read *Le Journal* over and over on her way to work."

"I'm sure they forgot all about the hockey finals, to devote their full attention to bullfighting and crime," he said caustically.

"There was no game last night . . . .Don't forget the kids from

Hudson High are coming in today. They'll be very happy to meet a judge. What did Nantel say this morning?"

"Double play, Monsieur le Juge. Double play!"

"Ha! Would you like some coffee?"

"Yes, but don't tell *Le Journal*. Last week they featured a new scandal: the clerk was seen serving coffee to the judges in one of the smaller towns around Montreal."

"Big scandal! Last month, I saw a judge serve coffee to a clerk and two lawyers. You're probably the highest-paid waiter in the building. But don't worry; your secrets are safe with me."

"Didn't doubt it for a moment."

*　*　*

He went to the inner office, looked out the window and began to sip the coffee. Linda slipped through the partially opened door.

"Oh, Monsieur le Juge. Everyone in the subway was reading about our case. It's so exciting; I think I'll ask to be permanently assigned to the Criminal Division."

"And leave me alone when I hear civil cases?"

"Non, I meant permanently assigned, but only when you sit there."

"Thank you. Why don't you have a coffee before we go downstairs?"

Parent was waiting for them near the courtroom.

"Good morning, Constable. Is everything all right?"

"Bonjour. I'm not sure, Monsieur le Juge. One of our jurors hasn't arrived yet."

"Number twelve?"

"No. He showed up about five minutes ago. Number eight is missing. He's the older man who forgot to fill out the form for the sheriff on the first day."

"I remember. I was surprised they didn't challenge him. He looked kind of frail. Well, there's nothing to do for a while except wait. Please let me know when he shows up, and find out what delayed him."

"Yes, Monsieur le Juge."

*   *   *

Berne decided this would be as good a time as any to call *The Maintenance* about the leaky faucet. He confirmed that it hadn't been repaired overnight, then dialed Hubert Racine's office.

"Bonjour. Can I help you?"

"Bonjour. This is Justice Berne speaking. May I speak to Mr. Racine?"

"One moment please. I shall see if he has returned from his morning coffee."

After a long pause, a voice answered. "Racine, Hubert. Bonjour, Monsieur le Juge."

"Bonjour, Monsieur Racine, and a happy New Fiscal Year to you and all the employees of *The Maintenance*. I trust the old year ended successfully?"

"Oh yes, Monsieur le Juge! It's not easy, but we managed to complete all our projects within the budgetary limits established by the Treasury Board."

"As a taxpayer, I am delighted."

"Monsieur le Juge, we at *The Maintenance* manage many buildings on behalf of the government. It's not always easy, and few taxpayers are as sympathetic as you. We are always at your service—subject, of course, to budget limitations."

"I know, I know! Indeed, I was one of the lucky judges permitted to sit in a new chair purchased last week."

"Ah, you noticed! So rarely is our work appreciated by the members of the bench. We were most fortunate that I discovered the surplus money in the budget on time. One day later and—poof!—the money would have evaporated into the pockets of the Treasury Board and been lost to us forever . . . .What can we do for you today?"

"Roc . . . Hubert, it is not what you can do for me, but what we both can do for the taxpayers who pay our salaries."

Racine suspected a trap and waited expectantly for the next words. "Oui?"

"I have detected that water is leaking from a tap in the bathroom off the judges' office near Courtroom 3.01. If this matter is not repaired, there is danger it will continue to leak. The water of the taxpayers must not be wasted."

"So right, so right! I shall make a requisition to repair the tap immediately . . . .Monsieur le Juge, do you perhaps know if it is the cold water, or the hot water that is leaking?"

"The cold water," Berne replied with assurance.

"How do you know that?"

"Hubert, I anticipated your question and performed a simple scientific test. I placed my finger under the tap and felt the temperature of the water. It was definitely cold."

"That may be so, Monsieur le Juge, but I'm convinced it must be the hot water that is leaking. We at *The Maintenance* constantly test and review our procedures. The results of this monitoring have shown us that when a tap leaks, it is usually the hot water. Hot water is more corrosive than cold. Undoubtedly, it is the hot water tap that is leaking."

"But," Berne protested, "I felt the temperature of the water, and it was decidedly cold."

"I do not dispute your observations, Monsieur le Juge," Racine continued, as if he were explaining Einstein's theory of relativity to a young child. "When you place your finger under the tap the water feels cold, because it is indeed cold. But you must take into account that the tap is leaking slowly, so . . . the hot water, which is leaking, has time to cool before it comes into contact with your finger. Assuredly, it is the hot water faucet that is leaking. I shall mention that in my work order; otherwise the plumber will change the washer in the cold water tap. The water from the hot water tap would continue to drip, and one might conclude that we at *The Maintenance* had not done our job."

"Thank you. Your devotion to duty and budgets is exemplary, and your logic is impeccable. I shall verify tomorrow to see if it is correct as well. Bonjour."

Sam Berne left the office, somewhat numbed by the telephone encounter, and walked down to the jury room.

*   *   *

Constable Denis Parent was all smiles as he declared, "Number eight has arrived. He couldn't get into the parking lot across the street, so he had to find another lot. The jury's now complete."

"It's already ten to ten. Get the jury lined up and let's go," Berne said to Parent and Linda simultaneously.

When the court session began, Talbot announced, "Please call officer Nancy Grondin."

Nancy Grondin entered and advanced towards the witness box. She nodded to the detective beside Talbot, placed her hand on the Bible and responded "I do" as the oath was put to her.

Talbot rose and began the questioning. "What is your occupation?"

"Crime Technician with the Police Department of the Montreal Urban Community."

"How long have you been working in that division?"

"Four years."

"What professional or other training did you receive to qualify you as a crime technician?"

"I'm a graduate of the police college in Nicolet. I have taken additional courses in photography, fingerprint analysis, and the conduct of a crime scene investigation. I hold diplomas in these areas and, before assuming my present position, took a six-month practical course with the Sûreté du Québec. There are courses and seminars given on a regular basis which I attend."

"Thank you. Were you on duty on the night of October 7, 1991?"

"Yes."

"Were you called to the scene of a crime?"

"Yes I was. At approximately 3:35 a.m. I received a call to go to a bar called Le Wiz, at 1005 St. Denis, to take photographs and collect evidence. I arrived at 3:52 in the morning. By that time the street was quiet; only a few people were still hanging around. Sgt.-Det. Bob Caron, who is seated beside Maître Talbot, asked me to photograph the protected area and help search for evidence."

"What do you mean by *protected area?*" Talbot asked.

"When a crime occurs, the first police officers at the scene attend to the victim, keep the crowd back, and string a yellow ribbon around the area where evidence might be found. In this case the sidewalk and five feet of the road in front of Le Wiz were cordoned off. I have photographs with me—"

Talbot interjected, "We have a series of photographs taken by this witness the night of the crime which we'd like to produce as exhibits. There's an original for the court, and six copies for the jurors."

"Ladies and gentlemen," the judge said, "these exhibits are part of the evidence. When you retire to deliberate, you will have all of the exhibits, including the photographs in the jury room. It is your duty to examine all these exhibits carefully. Continue, please."

"In the first picture, you can see the sidewalk and part of the road in front of Le Wiz." Nancy Grondin leafed through the book and described the photographs, one at a time.

Great, just great, Rick Hayes thought to himself. They pull me out of the shop to sit in court and look at pictures of St. Denis Street. These people must live on the moon. I don't think there's a person in Montreal who doesn't go to St. Denis Street. Even the uptight snobs from the west end go there to eat in the restaurants, and to see *Les Miserables* at the St. Denis Theatre, across the road from Le Wiz. They say the bar was supposed to be called *Les Miz*, but the owner was afraid he'd be sued so he turned the 'M' upside down, and called it *Le Wiz*. Hey, a guy was killed, and these jokers have nothing better to do than show pictures of east end Montreal. No wonder trials last forever.

"Picture P-1M shows the street, and you'll notice the chalk circle at the top of the picture. That's where we found a shell. Now if you turn the page, you'll see a closeup of the circle and can identify the shell. After taking this photograph I picked up the shell, placed it in a plastic bag, and delivered it to the police laboratory."

"Did you find any other evidence at the scene?"

"Me? No, I didn't. Now, the next picture shows a chalk sketch where the body of the victim was found. I did not make the chalk marks; the victim had been taken to the hospital before I arrived. Sgt.-Det. Caron was present and asked me to take this picture."

"Is there anything else?"

"Yes. The last three photographs were taken several hours later at the hospital, and are pictures of Frank Lepine, the victim. I understand he died shortly after I took them."

"Anything else?"

"Yes, I have with me two pictures of Serge Tremblay taken at police headquarters after he was arrested."

"That's all, thank you."

*   *   *

At fifteen, Serge had left home and rented a room in a small boarding house on de Maisonneuve, about six blocks away. Weather-beaten signs proclaiming *Chambres* and *Touristes* adorned the front doorposts. *Touristes* was a dream, unless Montrealers living east of Papineau Street fell into that category.

Most of the guests were drifters and transients, who rented a room for a night or two to escape the tedium of daily life, or perhaps for a few hours of solace with a hooker or a compliant new acquaintance. Serge didn't really bother with the other residents. His room was on the top floor of the three-storey building, and rooms on that floor were rarely rented. Now and then he had a woman up to his room, but the experience was hollow and meaningless, totally unlike the scenes portrayed in porno parlours and cheap movie theatres. He spent very little time in the room, preferring the streets where he had raised himself.

He had no trouble earning or stealing thirty dollars a week for rent. Restaurants and stores constantly needed dishwashers, floor cleaners and delivery men. Much of his time was passed in the arcades that proliferated on both sides of Ste. Catherine Street. They were good places to find out what was happening, and to identify prospects he could attack later for a fast buck. He planned the muggings and purse snatchings carefully. To avoid capture by the police or reprisal by the victims,

Serge never knowingly robbed the same individual twice. Most were too drunk to identify the assailant anyway, and they rarely registered complaints. The authorities were busy with drugs and murders, and couldn't bother much with petty crime.

In the bars and taverns Serge became known as someone who didn't drink enough to contribute to the profit, but didn't cause any trouble either. It was known he could handle himself in a fight, and the other customers left him alone. If a scuffle became unavoidable, he protected himself efficiently, and his bloodied adversary withdrew quickly. Of course, the sober and the strong have a built-in advantage in barroom brawls.

After his few belongings had been moved to the rooming house, he almost never returned to Champlain Street. Encounters with his father were rare, because Serge didn't need him, and there were no other ties between them. It was doubtful that his father Marcel Tremblay even knew the address of the rooming house.

Serge's prized possession was a ten-speed bicycle which he had bought at a garage sale. He cleaned and polished it regularly, and never left it outside. Most bars in the east end were prepared to allow a bicycle on the premises, and it was so light that he could easily carry it up the stairs to his room. He didn't have a telephone; if he had to speak to someone, he would either cycle to their place or phone from a tavern.

Although the new independence was exhilarating, his lone existence was destined to deteriorate into violence and serious crime. It began a few days after his eighteenth birthday.

He should have never returned to the flat on Champlain Street. A bicycle spoke had broken, and he went to borrow a pair of long-nosed pliers from his father's toolbox. It would only take a minute or two and Marcel was working that afternoon—or should have been. How could Serge know that a rail strike had caused a backup of shipments that shut down the assembly line? Marcel surprised him in the flat and began ranting about his rotten ungrateful son.

Serge would have left then and there, but Marcel blocked his path and they began shoving each other. Father and son grabbed tools from the box and went at each other with hammer and screwdriver. Marcel lunged forward with the hammer in his hand, just as Serge struck an overhand blow, and the screwdriver was planted in Marcel's head. The hammer fell to the floor and slid under the couch. Serge didn't mean to stab his father; it just happened.

Panicking, he grabbed the toolbox and ran downstairs to make his getaway. The tall teenager carrying a toolbox and riding a racing bike attracted attention.

Neighbours who heard the scuffle called 911, and an ambulance brought Marcel to Notre Dame Hospital. He survived two operations but never recovered fully from the attack. His thought processes slowed, he developed a lisp, and his head always ached. The memory of that fateful day was erased forever from his memory. The hammer wasn't found during the perfunctory police search of the flat.

Serge was arrested and charged with attempted murder. Even his own lawyer didn't believe it was self-defence, and urged him to make a plea bargain. After all, a twelve-year sentence didn't seem that long. He'd be out in four years, and was lucky his father hadn't died. Murder would have cost him twenty-five years, firm.

The judge lectured him about ingratitude and the seriousness of the crime, before accepting the recommendation of the attorneys and imposing a sentence of twelve years. The court appearance lasted less than ten minutes, and the next day Serge was sent to the medium-security penitentiary in La Macaza. Now he was back in court—this time for murder.

4

After the cross-examination of Nancy Grondin, two other police technicians testified that the bullet removed from the body of the victim was given to them by the pathologist who did the autopsy, and that it matched the shell found in the street. They produced a pistol, and described the tests that were conducted to establish that it had fired the shell.

They explained how bullets and shells are examined under microscopes and compared with other bullets fired from the same pistol at the police laboratory. Sketches and photographs of the bullets and shells were shown to the jurors. Then the murder weapon was produced, and passed gingerly from one juror to another. When it got to Rick Hayes he kept it longer than the others. He had seen pistols before but never handled one. The trial was becoming more interesting. The decision by his boss to postpone his vacation and pay full salary for the duration of the trial transformed Rick's attitude.

The rest of the morning session was devoted to the pathologist's testimony. He filed a lengthy medical report with sketches of the body of the victim. The entry point of the fatal bullet was clearly indicated, but there was no exit wound. The bullet found in the victim's body had been placed in a small plastic bag and handed over to the police.

Frank Lepine had been in good health; clearly, the cause of death was the bullet fired into his chest. Although he had lived for several hours afterwards, death was inevitable. Some jurors were fascinated by the medical testimony, but most were bored.

Vincent Talbot, the prosecuting lawyer, sensed the sluggishness of the trial. He tried unsuccessfully to interrupt the thorough but tedious recital, but the pathologist could not be deterred. Spectators and reporters began to quietly leave the courtroom. It seemed to take an eternity.

*   *   *

The door opened and a group of forty or more young people flooded into the courtroom. The startled witness turned, and so did the lawyers.

Maître Edmond Anderson walked down the centre aisle of the room. "My Lord, I regret the interruption. I am here with the grade nine class of Hudson High School, and we request permission to spend a short while in the courtroom."

"Maître Anderson," Judge Berne answered didactically, "students, like other members of the public, do not need permission from me or anyone else to enter a courtroom. It's a basic principle of our legal system that the administration of justice be open, transparent. This contributes to the effectiveness of the system. I welcome you all, as do the attorneys and, undoubtedly, the jurors in this case."

Great! thought Rick. The boy scouts to the rescue. Where's the cavalry? Just when this case was getting somewhere, these kids decide to learn about courts on my time, and the judge talks like a professor. He leaned forward and said to number five, "Do you think they knew you were here, and came to see the best-looking juror in the courthouse?"

"Shh, everyone will hear you," she whispered. "Can't you see the mikes hanging from the ceiling? They record everything."

"Big deal. If I want to talk to you—"

"During lunch. We'll speak during lunch."

"Okay," said Rick, leaning back.

The students settled in and the trial resumed. Everyone in the court smartened up, reacting to the presence of the young audience. But despite his best efforts, the pathologist was unable to make his subject interesting. After a while he realized that his efforts were futile and began responding with brief answers. When his testimony ended, both the jury and the audience were relieved.

"Ladies and gentlemen," Judge Berne declared, "we will adjourn now. I invite the students to remain, so I can meet you and your teachers."

Parent opened the door and the jury departed. Marie-Lyse moved back to speak to her client for a moment before the guard led him back to the cell. Then she resumed her seat.

* * *

Judge Berne removed his gown and stepped down from the platform to talk with the students. "I'm pleased to see you here today. A jury is hearing the criminal trial in this courtroom.

"We can appreciate the nature of our legal system if we compare it with another way of doing things. Let's look at the time of Robin Hood. He lived almost eight hundred years ago, in the time of King John. The behavior of the government of the day—the king and his officers—was quite arbitrary; they did almost anything they wanted to. They could just come and take people's belongings, and keep people in jail without even holding a trial. The actions of the government didn't require any kind of approval by the people.

"Also, people charged with a crime had to prove their innocence. They didn't have to be proven guilty.

"That's how it was when the Sheriff of Nottingham taxed the poor and jailed them. The taxes were really a way of stealing, or confiscating their property. All the people could do was turn to Robin Hood for help. Robin, Little John, Friar Tuck, and all Robin's band fought to keep the poor out of jail and save them from arbitrary taxes.

"Well, the Sheriff of Nottingham wasn't alone in this business. King

John was as tough towards the nobles as the Sheriff of Nottingham was to the poor, and they decided to do something about it. They went to Windsor Castle in 1215 and asked the king to meet them in a field. When he arrived, they said they wouldn't fight for him any more unless he would make a contract, agreeing that they couldn't be thrown in jail without a trial; that the judges, sheriffs and other court officials study law, and that they get the right to be judged by their equals or peers. The king wasn't happy, but he signed the agreement, which was called the *Magna Carta,* or great charter.

Let me read you a paragraph from *Magna Carta* that I keep in my notebook:

> No free man shall be arrested or imprisoned or deprived of his freehold, or outlawed or banished, or in any way ruined, nor will we take or order action against him,except by the judgement of a jury of his peers and according to the law of the land. To no one will we sell, to no one will we refuse or delay right or justice.

This is probably the most famous paragraph in all of English law, and became the foundation for our legal system.

Not every country has a system of jury trials. It is part of what we call *the rule of law,* which means that we are governed by laws and not by the arbitrary whims of any ruler. Some legitimate body adopts laws, and the rulers are bound by those laws. This makes the law predictable. The person on trial in court today can only be deprived of his liberty if he is found guilty according to the law of the land, by a jury of his peers."

*   *   *

A young man entered and sat down near the door. Linda mouthed the words *Billy James,* pointing. Berne understood. Billy James was the teenager on trial for a triple murder in the courtroom down the hall. Vincent Talbot was about to leave the room to summon help, when Berne gestured towards him to be calm, and turned his attention again to the students.

There was an awkward silence, before one boy raised his hand and asked, "Who's winning this case here today? Will the guy get convicted?"

"I don't know. Did you ever hear of a baseball catcher called Yogi Berra? He said many things that sounded dumb but were really very intelligent. One of his sayings was, 'It ain't over till it's over.' That's as true of a trial as it is of a baseball game. You can't tell who's winning till you hear all the witnesses and all the arguments."

"But you're a judge," he persisted. "Don't you know?"

"I'm afraid I don't. We've only heard part of the case. The defence hasn't even . . . been up to bat."

"Ya!" an anonymous voice chimed in from the rear of the room.

"Can the prisoner try to run away?"

"He has chains on his feet, which are attached to a ring bolted into the floor."

"Really?"

"Yes. The judge worries about everyone in the courtroom, and the police tell him what's happening throughout the trial. I thought it was a necessary precaution in this case."

"Is there a prison in the building?"

"Sort of. There are cells in the basement, and there are cells behind some of the courtrooms."

* * *

Unexpectedly, Billy James now joined in the questioning, drawing on his experience in the courtroom during the previous weeks.

"Do you know anything about legal aid lawyers?"

"A little," Berne responded cautiously.

"Do they really work for their clients? Can you believe them? After all, they're paid by the government."

"They take their work and their clients very seriously. I've seen legal aid lawyers work as hard—even harder than—private lawyers for their clients."

"Are you sure?"

"I'm sure of what I've seen."

The students were now aware that they had been joined by a stranger. Judge Berne felt some comment was required. "The young man sitting on the side is interested, and asking questions about lawyers, because he's on trial for murder just down the hall. A jury is deciding if he is innocent or guilty just a few feet away. Am I right? Are you Billy James?"

"Yes, sir."

Eyes widenened and heads turned left with military precision. A few of the students shuddered visibly. One asked if it was difficult to make a judgement.

"It depends on the case. When the judgement won't have a major effect on the people involved, it's easier. When two large companies fight over a small amount of money, the judge does what he or she thinks is right, and quickly forgets about the case. But when the custody of a child or the future of a business, and above all when the freedom of a person is at stake, it's extremely difficult— sometimes agonizing—but decisions must be made."

"But you've no right to make judgements," said Billy, almost inaudibly. He covered his mouth with his hand. Then he held up the small book in his hand. "I read this Bible in the hall while I wait, and it says here that people can't make judgements; only God can."

The room was totally silent. Simply, politely, almost unintentionally, Billy had challenged the entire legal system in a public forum, and the visiting students were the jury. Talbot and the teacher exchanged glances, hoping the judge could extricate himself. The teenage jury waited expectantly.

Berne took a deep breath. "Billy, a judge or jury must consider all the evidence, all the facts, before deciding what to believe." He paused and looked around. "Well, it's the same with the Bible. You can't just pick out one or two sentences and make up your mind. You have to study all of the Bible. Keep reading and you'll find it says that a judge who is fair and unprejudiced, who listens to all the facts, can make a judgement because then it is God's judgement."

Billy rose and approached the front of the room, the Bible in his outstretched right hand, and asked without a trace of defiance, "Can you show that to me in my Bible?"

Talbot and Anderson locked eyes again. Anderson raised his shoulders and eyebrows simultaneously.

"Of course," Berne said as he took hold of the book and flipped through the pages. A year before he'd heard the sentence quoted at a colleague's funeral, and out of interest had checked the citation. "Here it is, in Deuteronomy, Chapter One:

> And I charged your judges at that time saying, "Hear the causes between your brethren, and judge righteously between a man and his brother, and between the stranger that is with him. Ye shall not respect persons in judgement. The great and the small alike ye shall hear. Ye shall not be afraid of the face of any man, for the judgement is God's."

Judge Berne returned the Bible to Billy, who quietly thanked him. The crisis had passed. Anderson stood and thanked the judge rapidly. He was not about to risk any more scenes like that one. The students stood and shuffled out of the room noisily.

"Billy," Sam Berne said, "you'll have to leave now, because I'm returning to my office and we're going to close this courtroom."

"Thank you, sir."

* * *

In the jurors' dining room Rick Hayes leaned back, balancing the chair on its back legs. Turning to juror number five, he said, "Parent calls this a private dining room, but I think it's a room behind the cafeteria with cold pizza and rubber chicken. I'd rather eat at McDonald's. How about you?"

"That depends who with," she taunted.

"With me?"

"Maybe."

"Maybe yes, or maybe no?"

"Maybe maybe."

"Do you think Tremblay's guilty?" he asked, trying to change the subject while he planned another approach.

"Maybe, maybe. Mustn't make up our minds too soon, according to the judge. What's your name?"

"Rick. Rick Hayes. Yours?"

"Lucy. Rick, why do you wear those sunglasses in court? You got a black eye or something?"

"No, I just like to. Do they make you uncomfortable? You feel uncomfortable talking to me?"

"No."

"You ever been in court before?"

"Once, fighting a ticket. Went through a red light and got stopped by a cop."

"You win?"

"Sure. The judge looked at me, and must've liked what he saw. Besides, the cop didn't show up so the judge threw the case out."

"I didn't think you were old enough to drive," he mocked.

"I'm old enough to do lots of things."

"Like what?"

"Like being on a jury," she said with a laugh. "Look at Parent at the end of the table, staring at us. First time he's opened his eyes today. How about that, a guard who sleeps while he guards! Not a bad job, lots of sleep, free food, and entertainment."

"You work?"

"Yes. I drive a canteen truck around construction jobs."

"You're kidding!"

"No. The guy I work for only hires women. Thinks the customers buy more that way. It's sort of like being a waitress at a bar, except I start early in the morning."

"How early?"

"I get up around six and drive the truck to the warehouse. They fill it up, and I get to the construction sites around seven, for breakfast . . . What do you do?"

"I work in a machine shop. I'm a lathe operator. Good steady work, and it pays pretty good. I've got no complaints. Where do you live?"

"Same place I park the truck overnight," she replied with a grin.

"Let's go, let's go!" Parent called. "It's after two, and most of you probably want to use the john before we return to the courtroom. We'd better hurry. Serge Tremblay is waiting for you."

The jurors followed Parent to the elevator. Rick moved ahead quickly to walk beside Lucy. He still didn't know her full name or address. She's special, he thought.

"You think we'll spend the weekend here?" she asked.

"No way!" he replied confidently. "Today's Thursday, and Talbot won't finish before the weekend. We haven't heard from the defence yet."

* * *

Before going upstairs, Berne checked the dripping tap again. Cold. The water was definitely cold, and so was the spout. He shrugged his shoulders. Who knows, maybe Rocket was right. After all, Einstein's theory of relativity wasn't universally accepted at first.

He could hear Jackie speaking on the phone.

"No, Renée. Ewaschek: E-W-A-S-C-H-E-K. Listen, this is not an ordinary request for books. You may classify this call as an extreme emergency . . . .Yes, an emergency . . . .Don't you read the papers or watch TV? This term alone, two murderers tried before him were declared not guilty. At this very moment they walk the streets."

She lowered her voice almost to a whisper. "Confidentially, just between you and me, he's presiding over another murder trial at this very moment, and if he doesn't receive the book, there's a chance another murderer will go free. Do you understand? This is an emergency! Immediate action is required. Money is no object in such situations. Bonjour."

"Bonjour," Sam called as he entered the office.

"Functionaries, civil servants!" Jackie mumbled to herself, in a voice loud enough for him to hear. "They don't function, they're not civil . . . and they don't serve!"

He was confident Jackie would solve the problem. She was probably the brightest secretary in the courthouse—over- qualified for the job. It was a lucky day when she accepted his offer to work, for less than she was worth in any law office. They had known each other for almost twenty years, and she was intensely loyal. She kept his ego within manageable limits by teasing and poking fun at him, but he wouldn't tolerate the slightest insult by others.

Berne leaned back in the reclining chair, letting the tension flow from his body. The window on his right offered an uninterrupted view of east end Montreal. With binoculars he could probably see the scene of the crime. It all looked so calm and serene, removed from the events being described in the courtroom, which seemed remote, unreal: a stage play, a new tragedy.

He felt that every jury trial contains the elements of both tragedy and comedy. The jury, police, lawyers and press form a permanent audience of thirty people. Usually others are present as well. In the smaller urban centres, groups of retired people, and even a few unemployed, become courthouse regulars. In Montreal they read *Le Journal* to find out which cases will be most interesting. After a while they get to know the judges and lawyers by reputation, and come to watch their favourites in action.

The Tremblay case was attracting the regulars. He didn't know if it was the crime or the performance of Juan Luis Torres, the would-be toreador, but they were playing to a full house. The presence of the audience, and especially the reporters, added to the pressure on the judge.

He thought of conducting a jury trial as being a bit like driving a tractor, pulling twelve trailers. From time to time the judge, as tractor driver, has to look behind to see if they're all still with him. Surprises appearing behind tricky curves may require quick reflexes . . . and there's no way to back up. Little time is available to think before deciding to admit or exclude evidence. A mistake can easily lead to a mistrial, or reversal in the Court of Appeal.

There was always the added responsibility of considering the welfare of the jurors. Fortunately this trial hadn't produced any unpleas-

74

ant surprises so far—unless you'd count the new chair incident—but one never knows. This jury seemed solid. Hopefully there wouldn't be any personal problems of the jurors intruding on the trial. So far, so good.

*   *   *

The elevator stopped at the third floor. Parent led his charges through the door marked *Civil Marriages,* between the desks, through the rear corridor and into the jury room.

"Denis," Rick asked, "What's this routine with the marriage office? You trying to tell us something, or mind someone's business?"

"I told you, I've been around since the building opened, about twenty years," he replied. "The architects who designed the building didn't know about trials and juries. They made special hallways and elevators for the prisoners and judges, but they forgot about the juries."

"What do you mean?"

"Some jurors get nervous when they see a camera, or a crowd in the hall. They think someone's following them. Well, the judges expect me to keep the jury away from the press and the public. They don't let the cameras into court, and *we* use special passages. Where they don't exist, we try to invent them." Parent added proudly, "I'm the guy who discovered that the fire exit through the marriage office can be used to get jurors to the elevators, without crossing the main lobby."

"Makes sense," commented Rick, "but when we come out of the marriage office with our guards, it probably looks like a shotgun marriage with the whole family watching."

"Hmm. Never thought of it that way," Parent commented. The jurors shuffled back into the jury room as he continued. "Another thing the architects forgot is windows. There are eight jury rooms in this building, and only two of them have windows like this one. Some people get pretty crazy after hours of meeting in a small room without any windows. You're lucky to get a room with a window."

"You ever use the gun in court?"

"Not yet, but if things get rough I know how. I take special training every two years."

*　*　*

The next witness, Oscar Cimon, was a friend of the victim, who was at Le Wiz the night of the murder. He was in his mid-twenties, medium height, and spoke well. The jury followed his testimony closely.

"Frank and I met at high school and were friends ever since. The night he died we weren't together though. It just happened that we were both at Le Wiz."

"Was he armed?"

"I don't think so. I didn't see a gun or knife. He didn't really need any. He was good with his fists, and looked tough: big, broad-shouldered, . . . hot-tempered sometimes too. Most people would back off if he just shouted and moved towards them."

"Continue, please."

"Well, this guy started to hassle a girl and Frank decided she needed help. He kind of liked to rescue women in trouble. So he got up and walked over to the accused, Tremblay, over there," he pointed, "and said something. I was too far away to hear. Then Tremblay gave Frank a push, and they started shoving each other. The bar was full, everyone was drinking, and some of those guys were looking for a fight. I don't think they came in to fight, but once the pushing started, things could get pretty bad. I got up and moved towards Frank, because I knew there'd be trouble. The doorman must have called the police, because they were there in no time and broke up the fight. Nobody was seriously hurt; they hardly had a chance to throw any punches."

"And?"

"And, the police pushed Tremblay right out the door. That was around midnight. After the fight I saw Frank look around for the woman, but she left without even speaking to him. She was probably upset at the whole episode."

* * *

Juror number seven, Kathy Johnson, envied the unknown woman in the bar. Kathy sometimes fantasized that she would be the object of a duel, a fleeting daydream. She felt cramped, in the position of juror number seven. It is the least comfortable seat, in the second row, crammed right against the judge's bench. The dining room was more comfortable, though the food wasn't very good. Tonight she would bake a cake for the jury, and perhaps send a piece to the judge. He was so patient and kind; she wondered if he was married.

She glanced at Rick and Lucy with a tinge of jealousy. It was a long time since anyone had asked her out, or even flirted with her, although she was only thirty-five and had no children. Kathy hardly went out at night. Some friends had dropped her at the time of the divorce, but that was a year ago, and now was the time to get back into circulation. She looked around. Bernard Richer (number eight), sitting next to her, was an old man—in his sixties. Nice but too old for her. No other likely candidates. Pasquin, the guy in the fancy suit sitting at the other end of the first row, looked like he had a wife and children.

Rick didn't attract her, and anyway he was hustling Lucy. They'd be in bed together before the trial ended. Can you imagine, driving around construction sites at six in the morning selling sandwiches to the workers?! Especially in the winter! Better to work in the accountants' office, typing at a computer terminal.

Betty Major looked approachable. A barbershop: that's a place to meet men . . . and hold their heads back against your chest.

* * *

"Did you see Tremblay again that night?" Talbot asked.

"Yes, he returned just before closing, sat down at the bar and had a beer or two. I was sitting with some friends on the side and had a good view of what was happening. Tremblay glanced at Frank's table a few times, but they never made eye contact."

The jurors appreciated the candour of this witness. Cimon had an excellent recollection of the events, and his steady voice and bearing added to his credibility. Rick Hayes looked ahead like a sphinx in a leather jacket. Next to him, Albert Rousseau scribbled furiously in his notepad.

"What happened next?"

"At around a quarter to three, there was the usual last call, and we all ordered drinks. At three the lights blinked, and we all started to pour into the streets. It seemed busier than usual that night; I don't know why. I saw Frank walk out to the sidewalk, where Tremblay was leaning on a car. Frank walked over and gave him a shove with his open hands; Tremblay sort of snuck away. A minute I later heard a voice call, 'Hey, big shot!' Frank turned around; I heard a shot, and he fell to the ground. The police were there in a flash."

"Do you know who called out 'Hey, big shot'?" asked Talbot.

"Not really. It could have been Tremblay, but I'm not sure. There were hundreds of people in the street. The road was blocked with honking cars and . . . I really couldn't say."

"And who shot Frank?" asked Talbot.

"It must have been Tremblay."

"No further questions. Your witness."

Marie-Lyse Lortie rose to begin the cross-examination. "I'm going to repeat the last questions and your answers."

"Yes, I'm listening."

Question: Do you know who called out 'Hey, big shot'?

Answer: Not really. It could have been Tremblay, but I'm not sure. There were hundreds of people in the street. The road was blocked with honking cars, and . . . I really couldn't say.

That's the end of the quotation. You really don't know who called out 'Hey, big shot!', do you"?

"No I don't."

"But, you thought it was Tremblay, because of what happened in the bar and in the street before the shooting?"

"Yes, that's right. I said I really couldn't say."

"So you did. And, you really didn't *see* who shot Frank Lepine, because there were hundreds of people in the street, and the road was blocked with cars?"

Cimon remained silent.

"Answer the question please," Lortie insisted.

"No, I didn't see the gun or the flash. I heard the shot and saw Frank fall down."

"And you thought it was fired by Tremblay, because of what happened before, in the bar and in the street?"

"Yes, I guess so."

"It's a guess that Tremblay fired the gun, and not a fact you observed?"

"Yes, but—"

* * *

Suddenly, every alarm bell in the building sounded. The jurors fidgeted in their seats, glancing at the exit. The look on the guards' faces left little doubt that this was a genuine alarm. Judge Berne knew he must discharge the jury immediately.

"Ladies and gentlemen, obviously we'll have to adjourn. Please leave the building as quickly as possible. I'll see you tomorrow morning at 9:30."

Parent had already opened the door, and the jurors rushed out. Marie-Lyse tried to speak to Tremblay as the guards hustled him through the door to the cells, but it was impossible. Within seconds, Judge Berne was alone in the courtroom, in his striped pants, vest, and black and red gown, hardly appropriate attire for a taxi, subway, or dinner party. His private office was twelve floors up.

He walked out into the public hall, where the alarms continued and people rushed about. In the distance, Rocket was holding a door so people could exit rapidly. Berne wondered whether Rocket would be the last to leave. Perhaps he'd stay aboard—noble captain on a sinking highrise building.

The elevators had all been closed down. Berne decided to take the stairs up to his office to retrieve his clothing. He waited till no one was looking, then ducked into the stairway, and began to wind up the twelve flights of stairs, moving upstream against the flow of people, like an overweight red and black salmon. He stopped on each landing, hoping his heart and legs were in good enough condition. He regretted not having taken the doctor's advice to lose fifteen pounds. Tomorrow he'd start a new diet.

On the sixth floor he met Judge Pierre Boyer.

"You also going in the wrong direction?"

"Yes, Sam. Maybe that's the story of my life."

"Did you get your verdict yet?"

"No, the jury was deliberating when the alarm sounded."

"What did you do?"

"Sent them off to the restaurant across the road. I'll hang around and see what happens later. You had a visit from Billy James this morning?"

"Un-huh." They had reached a landing and silently agreed to catch their breath before continuing. "Strange feeling, being questioned by a kid who's up on a murder charge. He seemed quite— well, ordinary . . just like all the other kids in the room."

"The other kids who were in the room aren't on trial for murder, Sam. This is my floor. See you later. This is probably one of those routine fire drills, and we'll be back in the courtrooms shortly."

"Not me. I sent my jury home for the day. By the time we'd get together again there'd only be a few minutes left. 'Bye."

On the twelfth floor landing, Berne met Jackie descending slowly. She demanded, "Why are you going up the stairs, when everyone else is going down? Can't you hear the bells? This is a real alarm. You're wearing a judge's gown, not a Superman cloak, so you'd better get out of the building. Come; we can walk down together. I'm on the security team."

"And, I'm on my way up to get my clothes, so I can make a meeting and dinner party tonight."

"We have to leave immediately. This is a real alarm. Forget your clothes. You're as stubborn during emergencies as you are in the office."

"That's known as grace under fire."

"Fire—a fire alarm, and we're just standing here. I'm leaving while I can."

"See you tomorrow. First thing, please find out what happened so I can tell my jurors."

"Oui, Monsieur le Juge," she answered with a forced grin. "I shall watch the news tonight, to see if you escaped safely. Sure you won't come down with me? Please!"

"Yes. Bonjour."

The bells sounded louder. Fewer and fewer people entered the stairwell to leave the building. Sam persisted, dragging himself up the remaining three floors to his office. He changed slowly into regular clothes and began the long descent to the street.

Rocket was still at his battle station, holding the door, but ready to leave at the slightest indication of real danger.

"Bonsoir, Monsieur le Juge," he called.

"Bonsoir, Monsieur Racine, and a good evening to you and your family."

The streets around the courthouse swarmed with people. Eight fire trucks were parked at the St. Antoine entrance. The command vehicles of both the fire and police departments arrived. Important-looking officials jumped out, joined the crowd on the sidewalk, and began shouting incoherent orders. Firemen unrolled hoses and ran into the building, followed by the bomb disposal squad in space-age uniforms, and the paramedics with stretchers. In the distance, police cars with sirens wailing escorted the blue windowless buses evacuating the prisoners.

Crime reporters and photographers who generally cover the trials were intently photographing the scene and interviewing each other in a desperate search for news. The crowd of curious onlookers, red and black gowned judges, and lawyers, clerks, ushers, secretaries, and witnesses milled about, waiting for news. A group of judges clustered on the sidewalk shared one common concern: how to get their cars out of the underground garage. Several briefcased young attorneys shuttled up and down the street wondering how to file their documents.

Jackie rushed over excitedly. "You're safe! I was worried. I thought you were the only person left in the building and perhaps the stretcher was for you."

"No, I'm safe, although my legs don't seem to be functioning well any more."

*   *   *

Kathy Johnson approached Francine Roux on the sidewalk. "What do you think about all this?"

"It's a crazy place. A fire alarm can happen anywhere in the building, and it's full of strange people. I must live a sheltered life. Not that I don't go to St. Denis Street now and then to see the comedy festival, and we often walk there on week ends, but this trial has its surprises for me. Can you imagine thousands of people in the streets at three in the morning?"

"Hardly," Kathy answered. "When I was married to Pierre, we went out quite a bit, like you, but we didn't go to bars. Now that I'm divorced, frankly, I'd be afraid to go to those places alone . . . and people don't invite me. What does your husband do?"

"He's a doctor, a neurosurgeon at Hotel Dieu Hospital. Treats a lot of accident cases. Did you know there's a killing almost every week in that part of the city? Some newspapers have cameramen and reporters on St. Denis Street every night, just waiting for something to happen."

"Really."

"Why don't you come with me for a cappuccino? Where do you live?"

"Outremont."

"Me too! We can drive straight up Park Avenue to the Patisserie Belge. I love the pastry there. It's just like in France. Ron, my husband, operated on their chef, and they treat me very well there."

It was a quiet afternoon. The two women sat at a corner table and ordered cappuccino.

"Have you been to court before?" Francine asked.

"Yes, for my divorce hearings. Came to this building three times last year. Getting a divorce is messy."

"Not as messy as murder."

"I suppose not," Kathy replied. "What do you think of the other members of the jury?"

"I don't know. That number twelve is a strange one, wearing sunglasses all the time. Bothers me, not to see his eyes—though it doesn't seem to bother Lucy."

"No, she's working on him full time, and he thinks he's chasing her! Kind of fun watching, don't you think?"

"Yes. I bet Hayes knows all about St. Denis Street bars at three in the morning."

"Probably. What do you think will happen tomorrow? Do you think the fire will delay the trial?"

"I don't know. It's probably nothing. Maybe the cafeteria kitchen caught fire. That might not be such a bad thing. The food there is boring, b-o-r-i-n-g," Kathy said.

"Hm, it's not quite the Patisserie Belge."

"No . . . .Well, I guess it's time to go."

Kathy didn't protest when Francine paid the bill, and the two women left.

5

The pungent odour of men's aftershave lotion wafted into the office, heralding the usher's arrival.

"Robert Grimard, Monsieur le Juge. I am replacing Linda today."

"Bonjour, I don't think we've met before. Is everything all right with Linda?"

"Yes. She had to take her daughter to the doctor. She'd have told you yesterday, but the fire—"

"I know."

"Monsieur le Juge, I was hired as an usher recently, and this is my first time in the criminal courts . . . but I have a paper with all the court announcements."

"Fine. Relax, Monsieur Grimard, you won't have any problems. I helped Linda through her first days in the criminal courts, and I'll do the same for you."

"Thank you, Monsieur le Juge."

Berne was unhappy about the replacement. He was a bit old-fashioned and had qualms about older men carrying books, opening doors, and running messages for him. Grimard appeared to be well into his sixties, if not his early seventies. Sam swore under his breath at the administration for recruiting court ushers among older retired men:

former policemen, firemen, and even bank employees, who became bored sitting around their homes or puttering in their gardens. Invariably they're polite, talkative, and wear too much aftershave lotion — an elixir to restore their lost youth.

Berne tried to organize his surroundings to minimize his work and provide maximum comfort, familiarity and predictability. New personnel disrupted the well-ordered world he had created for himself. Outside the courtroom he loved to tease, joke, and pun. It was his way of coping with the daily pressures. The greater the tensions and problems in the courtroom, the more outrageous would be his private behaviour. Jackie understood and was rarely insulted. She waited for him to return from court during the breaks; their repartee added spice to the tedium of office life.

The newspaper clipping from *Le Journal* caught his attention; Nantel had written *sizzling* above the headline and underlined it twice. The report was complete and concise, and as usual mentioned the judge's name in its final paragraph. Linda would be pleased; Jackie would scoff.

He hadn't seen Jackie that morning. Perhaps she was checking out the previous day's alarm. Throughout the evening he had listened to the newscasts but heard nothing of the fire and bomb alert. Jackie finally arrived and breezily greeted him with the news.

"During the search yesterday, they found a suspicious-looking package in the office of the prosecutors. Rocket said they should sound the general alarm, evacuate the building, and call the fire department and bomb disposal squad."

"And what," he asked, "was in the suspicious package?"

"Well, they took it to a safe place to explode it. It was full of chocolate bunnies that one of the prosecutors had purchased at lunchtime for his children."

At precisely 9:20, Berne put on his gown and walked out to the corridor where Grimard was waiting patiently at the desk beside the elevator. To avoid giving orders to an older man, Berne decided to perform the morning verifications personally. He counted the jurors as they filed into the hall. Then he pushed the buzzer and said to Grimard, "Let's go."

"Yes, Monsieur le Juge."

They entered the court, and Judge Berne remained standing till number twelve had taken his place. Then he whispered to Grimard, "Now."

Grimard stood rigidly at attention. His loud voice boomed. "The Superior Court, Criminal Division, is now open. Mr. Justice Sanborne is presiding. Please be seated."

Judge Berne closed and reopened his eyes slowly. Linda would return tomorrow. Most of the audience missed the slip, and only two jurors stifled a laugh. He explained that the fire alarm the previous day had been a minor incident and the jury need not be concerned. Marie-Lyse then indicated that she had no further questions for Oscar Cimon, and Talbot called the next witness.

*   *   *

The lady sitting in the first row turned and smiled at the audience before moving towards the witness box. Then she grabbed the Bible with both hands.

"Your name?" the clerk asked.

"Pauline Vinet. Some people call me Pauline D. Vinet," she gushed. "You see, I was a fortune teller, and I used to 'divine' the future, so they called me Pauline D. Vinet. It became my professional name, and I like it. Even today—I am retired—still, I often give my name as Pauline D. Vinet."

"Your age?"

"Do I have to tell?"

"Yes, madam."

"Fifty-three, . . . but I still have a lot of life left in me. Let me tell you that I have a young lover, and you would never know—"

"Madam," the judge interjected, "the clerk only asked your age. If the attorneys wish to know more about your activities, they will ask you in due course."

"Oh, I live on welfare, but I didn't always. I was a well-known fortune teller, the best in the east end. People called me *La fleur de l'Est*: flower of the east. That's a play on words, *fleur de l'Est*, sounds like *fleur de lys*. Pretty good, eh?"

"Yes," the clerk responded. "Your address?"

"1652 Visitation, corner Logan, right in the heart of the east end. The flower of the east has lived her entire life in the east end . . . . Do you know where Logan Street is? It ends right in front of my house on Visitation Street. It's just a few blocks long, between the new de Maisonneuve and Sherbrooke; runs in the same direction . . . ."

Serge Tremblay sat in the prisoner's dock, flanked by two policemen. He had shown no emotion whatsoever since the trial began, acting as though he were an accidental or involuntary spectator, attending a movie to please his friends. Now his eyes narrowed to conceal his hatred and disgust for Pauline Vinet. She was probably responsible for that fire yesterday. Pauline D. Vinet, Pauline 'damn' Vinet, Pauline 'devil' Vinet.

Judge Berne had noticed that, in a courtroom that was too small to contain them, Serge Tremblay and the witness engaged in intense silent combat. Betty Major sensed electrical currents—or was it sound waves at a pitch too high for humans to hear? She knew instinctively that they resented—detested—each other.

Talbot looked at the witness and began. "Madame Vinet, how long have you lived at your present address?"

"Since I moved there," she responded, turning around to look at the audience.

"Madam," Judge Berne interrupted, "please try to think a moment; then answer the question while facing the jury. Now, I believe Maître Talbot wanted to know how many years you have lived on Visitation Street?"

"A long time. Maybe thirty years. This isn't my first place on the street. I lived near Ste. Catherine Street till '76, close to my store on the corner of Ste. Catherine and Maisonneuve—the old Maisonneuve: the street they call Alexandre-de-Sève now. When Alexandre—that's my son—started school, his father and I moved up near Logan Street. It's quieter and we don't hear all the traffic. Of course, at that time I wasn't living with the same man as now. I couldn't, because in '77, my new man was a kid, only eight years old . . . , and what can you do with a lover who's only eight years old . . . ? I like young men, but—"

"So you've been living at 1652 Visitation Street since 1977?"

"Yes, it was farther away from my store, but I did it for my child!" she said, beaming at the jury and seeking approval for this unselfish sacrifice of her convenience.

"What kind of a store did you have?" Talbot asked. His face betrayed immediate regret at asking the question.

"I told you it was at the corner of old Maisonneuve and Ste. Catherine; you know, where the Bank of Toronto used to be. The Bank of Toronto closed, and they moved back to Toronto. The store was for rent, and it was a good location, almost across the street from Edgar Charbonneau's store where they sold jewellery and trophies. I think that everyone in the east end bought their engagement and wedding rings from Charbonneau. And that's where the hockey and bowling teams got their silver cups. You know, the ones with funny little men swinging sticks or holding bowling balls, that they give each other at the end of the year. Edgar was once a government minister. I said to myself, if people come to Maisonneuve and Ste. Catherine to buy jewellery, that's the place to open a jewellery store." She paused and asked, "Can I sit down please?"

"Yes, you may," Berne answered.

"I had a serious operation a few years ago. Where was I?"

"Buying jewellery from Mr. Charbonneau?"

"No," she chided with a smile, "I didn't buy jewellery, I sold jewellery. I opened a jewellery store and sold bracelets, bangles, and earrings. *La Divine Pauline*: that was the name of the store. It was on the same side of Ste. Catherine as the restaurant Le Carabin. Now, that was a busy restaurant and bar; lots of people went there. I tried to sell them jewellery, but they didn't want to buy earrings and bracelets. They wanted to know the future. Well, I had a lease for two years, and the customers wanted to hear their fortunes, so La Divine Pauline became Pauline the diviner of the future. I left some bangles in the counter, put a table and hung a curtain in back of the store, and began telling fortunes. Business was very good. But I learned it was dangerous to predict the hockey scores. The customers wanted me to tell them the scores, so they could go next door to Le Carabin and bet. I wouldn't; if I got it wrong they might have come back and beat me up."

Talbot sat down, and looked on helplessly.

"I only predicted things they couldn't check, or things that wouldn't happen for a long time. I used cards, and read palms and predicted the future. Those were wonderful times! I was young, and busy . . . but, why are you asking me all of this?"

"I'm not, madam."

"You must be too young to remember Expo '67. Those were great times, even in the east end. The subway was just finished, so people could go to the Expo Islands. We had the official Expo church near us. I think that's the church they tore down, and pasted on the front of the university building. Did they think it would make the students religious? Nobody goes to church any more. We had many churches in the east end. 'Course we needed them; there were so many sinners, and so much to confess. We did lots of things that were a sin—still do, but they're not a sin any more."

"Madam, madam," the judge interrupted, "You're getting carried away. I suggest that you give shorter answers, and allow Maître Talbot to ask the questions."

"Oh . . . .They told me to tell the complete story, and I don't want to leave out any important parts."

"I understand, but perhaps you can leave out one or two, and if the lawyers think it's important, they'll ask further questions."

She turned to the audience to see if they agreed with the judge's observations, before answering in a low voice, "I'll try."

Rick fidgeted in his seat, and stared through the witness at the audience. What a dingbat, he thought. Expo was twenty-five years ago, when he was only six. A few remnants of the 1967 World's Fair remain standing, like the amusement park, La Ronde . . . .That might be a place to take Lucy. He scribbled a note and passed it over her shoulder when no one was looking.

Number 5
Do you want to go to *La Ronde* this weekend?
                                    Number 12

She wrote *Maybe* at the bottom and returned it. Things weren't going as well as he wanted. Lucy could tease a man to death. It wasn't like him to allow a woman to lead him by the nose, but he felt intimidated by the court, the guards, and the judge. There was no privacy and no room to manoeuver.

"Does anyone live with you in the flat on Visitation Street?" Talbot asked the witness.

"Of course. My two children always lived with me, since they were born . . . which is more than I can say about their father. I haven't seen him for years—left after Caroline was born in 1980. Nice name, *Caroline;* rhymes with *Pauline.* I wanted it that way. It's nice when the mother and daughter's names rhyme. Pauline and Caroline, Caroline and Pauline,.. sounds good, doesn't it? My son's name is Alexandre; I got the idea from the street name, Alexandre-de-Sève. He's a good boy, but he's in prison now. Be out soon. I visit him all the time. He's twenty-two. Matter of fact he's the one who introduced me to Maurice."

*   *   *

Serge Tremblay squirmed. Maurice was the reason he was in court. Maurice had attached himself to Serge shortly after he arrived at La Macaza.

Serge had adapted to jail easily and found the routine comforting. Having never been accustomed to good food, he wasn't bothered by the monotonous bland meals. He didn't smoke or take drugs—habits he perceived as weaknesses and avoided.

All his previous life had been preparation for the prison experience. Serge didn't need anything from the other prisoners, and wasn't prepared to give them anything. After eighteen years of living without friends, relatives or women, the solitude of the cell was bearable.

People talked a lot about guns in prison. There were rumours that

90

some prisoners had managed to smuggle pistols into their cells. Serge thought they were just trying to protect themselves from possible attack. The guards would have found a gun during their searches.

He could defend himself with his homemade knife. The blunt instrument stolen from the kitchen had been gradually sharpened and hidden behind the loose mortar separating two cement blocks in his cell, for emergencies. There had only been one emergency during his years in the cell, and he had reacted quickly. Many of the inmates knew, but the guards never discovered who stabbed Tony Roland, or why. Tony never told them. Serge didn't really dislike Roland; he did it to protect Maurice Pomerleau.

Serge and Maurice shared a cell. At first Serge had ignored him, but it was impossible to do that for very long. Maurice was the incarnation of craven weakness, replete with faults and addictions. His mind was an encyclopedia of the needs of everyone in the yard knowledge which he used to satisfy his cravings. Maurice couldn't survive without the small quantities of drugs that he managed to wheedle or steal from other inmates. Now and then he offered his cellmate a joint, but Serge wasn't interested. Occasionally he'd accept a chocolate bar. Serge never asked what Maurice gave other prisoners in exchange. It wasn't his business.

When they went outdoors Maurice rarely strayed too far, for fear of the other inmates. Occasionally, when he did, he would get roundly beaten, and return to Serge cowering and moaning, but it became known throughout the prison that anyone who beat up Maurice would have to tangle with Serge.

Darkness scared Maurice. He would often wake up shivering and whimpering, and call out. Serge would ignore the noise, or grunt or hit the bed-frame so that Maurice would know he was there and feel assured for the night.

Maurice talked on and on about his exploits, and about his plans for when they'd get out. Sometimes Serge listened; at other times he just tuned out.

Serge never planned the future. He just drifted through life, detached, like a passenger on a train observing the scenery. Life on the outside wouldn't be so much different. He might pick up a gun or two after he got out. A clean pistol costs about four hundred dollars, but bargains show up, and a gun could be useful, though dangerous. The minute the cops pick you up with a gun, they check their computers and you never know what they'll find. A knife is a quieter, safer weapon, but . . . a gun could be useful.

From the beginning Maurice was like a loyal slave, cowering and fawning at every opportunity. Serge didn't encourage the relationship, but gradually he became accustomed to the idea that the other human being who shared the cramped quarters would do his bidding. Maurice felt secure around Serge, and was willing to serve in exchange for protection.

Most of the prisoners had visitors. There was no one to visit Serge. He had no family and had never been close to a woman. Maurice became his family, fusing the roles of servant and younger brother. Serge tolerated Maurice's friends, and ignored his enemies. The relationship grew imperceptibly. Sometimes he wondered how Maurice would have survived without him, but usually he just accepted the servile dependence, without betraying any sentiment. In time, Serge began to expect Maurice's attention, showing no sign of warmth or dependency—just expectation, in the same way that he expected meals to be served at designated hours.

When Maurice was sent to the hospital for a few days, Serge actually missed him. It was the first time in his life that he had missed anyone.

Maurice had met Alexandre at the detention centre before they were sentenced. Gradually Maurice found out more about him and decided that one day the relationship might be useful. He introduced Alexandre to Serge. Neither was interested in the other, and Maurice remained the sole link between them.

* * *

"Maurice, Maurice is my man, and he lives with me," Pauline continued. "We first met when I went to visit Alexandre. A few months later, Maurice got out and had no place to go, so he called and I invited him to stay for a night or two. Been living with me ever since. He doesn't pay any rent, but he's good to me." She smiled. "You know what I mean. And Alexandre—I don't think he minds if his friend stays in the house. Why should he mind? He's still in prison, like I said. So I live with Caroline, and Alexandre when he gets out of jail, and Maurice . . . and for a while Serge lived with us."

"Who is Serge?" asked Talbot.

"Serge, Serge, over there in the prisoner's place." Pauline pointed to Tremblay without actually looking at him.

"For the record, the witness is indicating the accused," interrupted Talbot.

"Yes, Serge. I didn't invite him, but he moved in anyhow. You see, Maurice and Serge, they sort of—"

"Sort of what?"

"Do I have to answer?"

"Yes."

"Sort of . . . sort of . . . .Well, they lived together before, and I don't like the idea of men who . . . .Oh, you know what I mean . . . .And Maurice has been straight since he moved in with me. I try to keep him busy, but it's not easy, because I'm getting older. Frankly I'm afraid to have Serge around, because it might give Maurice ideas. One day he'll find another woman, but . . . .

"I didn't invite Serge to move in. He just kind of showed up a few days before the murder on St. Denis Street. I didn't invite him, and I don't like him. Maurice must have invited him. He came and moved into Alexandre's room and stayed without my permission. Serge scares me and he's not good to have around Caroline. She's only twelve years old, and I don't like him around her. I feel much better since the police arrested him. I don't want him back. He's trouble, trouble, and more trouble." The witness was just warming up to the subject, but it was time for the morning break.

* * *

Berne followed the usher out of the courtroom, remaining a discrete distance behind to allow the odour of the aftershave lotion to dissipate. After closing the door to the back office, he had an uncontrollable urge to inspect the leaking bathroom faucet. He knelt on the floor and crawled under the sink. There were separate valves for each of the taps. First he closed the hot water valve, but the spout in the sink continued leaking. Then he repeated the procedure with the cold water valve, and the dripping stopped. Well, so much for Rocket's studies and impeccable logic. It was definitely the cold water that was leaking.

"Monsieur le Juge . . . Monsieur le Juge!" Parent called.

Judge Berne appreciated the incongruity of the situation: a Superior Court Justice, dressed in striped pants and a gown, crawling under the bathroom sink. He backed out silently, taking great care to not strike his head on the underside of the counter.

"Monsieur le Juge, are you sure you're feeling all right?"

"Yes, why do you ask?"

"But you're on the floor! Did you fall?"

"No, I was making a personal investigation of the . . . .You'd never believe it." He brushed the knees of his pants, and tried again to act as though he hadn't taken leave of his senses. "Why did you call me?"

"I wanted to know if I should make reservations at the restaurant," replied Parent, trying to conceal his surprise and stifle a laugh simultaneously.

"Yes, . . . uh, good idea. Call the restaurant," Judge Berne answered in a grave voice. "The jurors will undoubtedly appreciate a meal out." He could imagine the howls of laughter in the guards' lounge when Parent described the scene to his colleagues. "Please leave me alone. I must attend to an important matter."

"Thank you, Monsieur le Juge. I'll call Le Vieux Port immediately." Parent bowed slightly and left.

As soon as the door closed, Judge Berne phoned Rocket to describe the results of his scientific tests, and to inform him that cold water was still leaking from the faucet in the bathroom. Rocket was crestfallen, and sounded as though a law of physics had been repealed without his consent—and at a cost that exceeded his budget estimates.

* * *

After the adjournment, the witness picked up exactly where she had left off. "Every time I see him, something happens. You don't have to be a fortune teller to know that he'll always make trouble for himself and everyone around him. He looks calm and quiet—funny blank look on his face, but I know the look: trouble, just trouble. A few times I told Maurice, get rid of your friend, tell him to go away, but Maurice was afraid, 'cause he said nothing."

"When exactly did Serge Tremblay move into your house?" Talbot asked.

"The first of October. There was a meeting at Caroline's school. It was a Monday, I think. The day before, I got a lift and visited Alexandre in prison. That was on Sunday and the next day, I remember, I went to the school to see the teachers. When I returned, there he was, sitting in my living room like he owned the place. Maurice was in the kitchen getting some beer, and Serge was sitting on the couch—my couch— watching TV. I asked what he was doing, and he told me that Maurice said he could stay in Alexandre's room for a few days."

"How many rooms do you have in your home?"

"Three bedrooms. You know those flats in the east end. They're all the same. It doesn't matter where you live: Montcalm, Panet, old Maisonneuve, Visitation—all the same. Some face the street, with stairs that go up the outside of the building, and others face the courtyards, like my flat.

"There's a big wooden door to close off the courtyard from the street, and a small door in the big one. When the big door is closed, we go out through the small door.

"In the courtyard there are three or four buildings with stairs on the outside. My windows look into the yard. Many of the houses still have wooden sheds. I have a shed, where I store bicycles and things."

"In your house, where does everyone sleep?"

"Well, I have a bedroom for me . . . and Maurice, and Caroline has her room, and Alexandre has a bedroom too. But he's in jail now, and . . . Serge, Serge, over there, he slept in Alexandre's bedroom till they arrested him, but I didn't agree. I told you all that."

"Did anything special happen while the accused, Serge Tremblay, was living in your house?"

"Everything is special when he's around. Oh, I know what you mean. Yes, on October sixth he went out at night. Maurice and I went to sleep early. We woke up a little after three in the morning. I suggested we go to Dunkin' Donuts for a snack. They're open all night—always people there. It takes about fifteen minutes to walk down to Ste. Catherine Street. We went in and stayed for an hour or so."

"Did anything happen while you were there?"

"No. We joked around with some of the customers, and I had a donut: a chocolate one, twisted and not round. They call them donuts, but I think a donut should have a hole in the middle, like a tire or a lifesaver. You wouldn't call it a lifesaver if it didn't have a hole in the middle, would you?"

"No, I guess not," answered Talbot.

"So where was I? Yes, I had this straight twisted donut, and Maurice had one too, and then we went home."

"Where was Caroline at the time?"

"Sleeping. She's only twelve and you can't expect us to take her out at that hour!"

"And what happened next?"

"We went to sleep. It was late and we were tired."

"Madame Vinet, please think carefully, and tell me if you can, what time you went back to your home from Dunkin' Donuts."

"I don't know. Very late."

"What happened?"

"We went to bed. We talked for a few minutes and then I fell asleep."

"What's the next thing you remember?"

"I woke up."

"Why? Did something wake you?"

"He did. He did," she said, pointing at Tremblay."

"For the record, the witness is pointing at the accused, Serge Tremblay."

"He stood in my bedroom doorway, white as a ghost, and said 'Wake Maurice, wake Maurice. I have to talk to him.'"

"Did you wake him?"

"No, I didn't have to. He couldn't sleep with all that noise. Never slept well anyway. Maurice woke up by himself, and told Serge he wanted to sleep, but Serge just said 'Get up. Get up! We have to talk.'"

"And, what happened next?"

"We got up. What else could we do? I was afraid the noise would wake Caroline. So we got up, and sat down in the kitchen, and Serge talked wildly about a guy who had been shot on St. Denis Street. He said the guy might have been killed. He looked scared, really scared. Maurice started shivering and said he wanted to go back to sleep, but Serge wouldn't let him.

"Then Serge took out a gun from his belt, put it on the table and said, 'This is the gun—'"

"Was it a pistol or a revolver?" Talbot asked.

"Don't ask me. I'm a fortune teller, not a cop. Pistol, revolver, gun: they all shoot bullets, don't they? It was some kind of gun."

Talbot lifted the pistol from the clerk's desk and handed it to the witness. She recoiled, fumbled and dropped it on the floor. Officer Caron, who was seated beside Talbot throughout the trial, crawled under the table to retrieve it, and placed it in front of Pauline. She drew back in her chair, staying as far as possible from the weapon.

"Is this the gun you saw Tremblay holding that night?" Talbot asked.

"How should I know? They're all the same colour, and I'm afraid of them all. I hate guns."

"So you can't identify the gun?"

"No, I can't, and I'd be happy if you'd take that thing off the table, and put it where it belongs. Give it to the policeman!"

"What happened next?"

"Next? Next to what?"

"What was the next thing to happen in your kitchen?"

"Oh, sorry. You upset me with the gun. Next, Serge asked us, 'The guy on St. Denis Street, do you think he was killed?' And I said, 'Why ask us? We weren't there.' And it's a good thing we weren't. He kept asking, 'Do you think he's dead?' over and over, like a broken record. Finally I said, 'Why don't you turn on the TV or radio?'"

"Then what happened?"

"Caroline woke up, and came into the living room. She started crying. Serge shouted, 'Shut the kid up!' and he grabbed the gun from the table. Can you imagine all this, in my home? He didn't pay me rent or anything. I got scared and pulled Caroline back into the bedroom, and shouted that I wouldn't come out till he put the gun away."

"Did he? Did you come out?"

"Not for a long time. I told Caroline to go back to bed, and said I'd explain everything in the morning. I sat on the chair beside her, and finally she fell asleep. Then I returned to the living room, where Serge and Maurice were watching TV. I didn't want to see Serge, or that gun of his, so I went to my room to sleep. Most of the night I was awake with the TV noise. Finally I fell asleep."

The witness looked up and implored, "I'm tired. You know I had an operation. Can we stop now?"

"Yes," Judge Berne answered, "I realize it's hard to be a witness. We'll adjourn for lunch."

"Thank you."

I thank you too, Rick muttered to himself. How much of that loon could he take? She had an operation, but she sure as hell recovered well. One of the strongest talkers I've seen in a long time. That woman will never stop nattering. She's enjoying every minute and will try to drag it out forever. Where else will that windbag find an audience like this, at her age?

*   *   *

The jurors filed back into the jury room and began talking excitedly.

"Quiet! Quiet, please!" bellowed Parent, cupping a hand by his mouth to magnify his voice, "Good news!" When they settled down he lowered his hand. "I convinced the judge that it's time we went to a restaurant. Judges do it all the time and it's only right that you should eat in a restaurant too.

"We have a reservation at a place called Le Vieux Port, in Old Montreal. Leave anything you don't need here; Constable Harvey will lock the door."

"Let's hear it for Parent!" "Great!" "About time." Two or three jurors clapped. Parent beamed at the recognition and approval of his efforts. He loved to eat in restaurants.

I can see that he likes food, thought Rick. Look at his stomach, almost popping out of that shirt. Well, I won't complain— free meal in a restaurant, with Lucy. He moved in Lucy's direction and asked, "D'you wanna have lunch in a restaurant with me?"

"All right. I'm looking forward to this. You know, I usually have lunches in my canteen truck. The comfort of a restaurant will be a treat."

"Guess we're walking. It's a nice day. Hope it's not too far."

"What kind of food do they serve in your machine shop?"

"They don't. We go out to the places around the shop. You know—usual stuff."

"The streets in Old Montreal are beautiful. The Vieux Port. It's probably the judge's idea to send us there, and not Parent's. If the restaurant's nice, I'll send the judge a note."

"You're kidding."

"Why shouldn't I? Besides, if the judge thinks we like the place, he might send us back. Why should he care if we eat in the cafeteria or a restaurant? It's not his money."

Parent led the jurors through the marriage registration office, into the main lobby and out to Notre Dame Street. It was a bright April day, a harbinger of the summer to come. Rick was oblivious to the brilliant sun that was screened by his glasses. The other jurors, momentarily blinded by the light as they descended the stairs, reassembled on the sidewalk.

The streets were crowded. Occupants of the surrounding buildings took full advantage of spring's first nice day. The jurors, in pairs and threes, followed Parent across Notre Dame and down the narrow street beside an imposing grey building with grecian columns. The constables accompanied them.

"What's that building?" Rick asked.

"New courthouse," replied Parent. "It used to be the criminal courthouse till they built the one we're using now. The other building, beside the one we're in, was the old courthouse and this one was the new courthouse. Well, for twenty years we've been in the building where we are now, and they don't use the old courthouse—the old new court-house—any more."

"Come again?" Rick asked.

"Never mind. The two buildings facing each other were court-houses and now they're used for other things by the government. See the little building ahead on the left?—the one with the sign *Claude Postel?* It's a restaurant now; used to be the coroner's offices and the morgue. I remember—In those days I worked for the police. Didn't have a lot of jury trials. People couldn't afford them before legal aid."

"Is Marie-Lyse Lortie a legal aid lawyer?" Rick asked.

"I don't know."

Rick turned to Lucy. "There's the place. You can see the wooden sign hanging at the corner."

The owner greeted Parent with a vigorous handshake and a slap on the shoulder. He led the group to the rear of the restaurant and pointed to a long table.

Rick manoeuvered next to Lucy. "Don't say I never take you out to restaurants."

"Not bad!" she commented. "Not bad."

"Attention! Attention please!" Parent called. "Choose your meal from the middle page of the menu, that says *midi*, the one where all the meals are under ten dollars. We still have to stay within the budget—and you can order a glass of wine or one beer."

"Big sport!" Rick whispered to Lucy.

"No worse than you."

"What do you mean?"

"You offered to take me to La Ronde on the weekend."

"I did, and I meant it. You said, 'Maybe, maybe.'"

"La Ronde is still closed for the winter. They won't open for a few more weeks, till the weather gets warmer."

"Damn! Can we go somewhere else?"

"Maybe."

"Maybe maybe?"

"No, just one maybe," she said. "I think I have less doubts about you. Just one maybe."

"What are you eating?"

* * *

When the jury returned from lunch, Parent walked over to Judge Berne's office and handed him an envelope. Berne the entered the courtroom, the door closed, and after the usher had asked everyone to sit down, he opened the envelope and read the note out loud.

Monsieur le Juge,
Thanks for the lunch. It was SUPER!
Juror number five, Lucy

"I arranged for the jury to eat outside the building today. This is a note of thanks from one of the jurors. I request the clerk of the court to show the note to the attorneys and the accused, and then to produce it as exhibit J-1." He felt uncomfortable reading the note out loud, but preferred a little embarrassment to speculation and suspicions. "Bring in the jury please."

When they returned to the courtroom, number five flashed him a smile, and Judge Berne nodded acknowledgement. He couldn't help noticing that she was cute—reminded him of Linda. Although it was

101

Friday afternoon the jurors showed no sign of impatience or boredom, awaiting the rest of Vinet's story.

"Under the same oath," the clerk intoned.

"Yes."

"Madame Vinet," said Talbot, "before lunch you described the night of October seventh. The last thing you said was that you fell asleep, and Serge and Maurice were in the living room watching TV."

"That's right. I don't know how Caroline got to school the next day. You see, I slept in, and when I woke up she was gone. I guess Maurice helped her, or she left all by herself. I didn't see her in the morning. Worried all day. That's not the only thing I had to worry about. Serge just stayed around the flat and watched TV. He wouldn't leave me alone! I told Maurice to get rid of him, but Maurice was—you know—afraid. Serge kept the gun with him all the time. He watched TV and played with that damn gun . . . . I almost never went out."

"How long did that continue?"

"Two weeks. A few times I went out, but Serge told me that if there was trouble or anything, he'd make sure I didn't forget about it. He looked at Caroline when he said that and I was scared. I wanted to call the police, or somebody, but you know, when you have a young daughter . . . . Maurice was no help at all. He spent hours talking with Serge, and I started to worry if I could trust him. I don't know if he was afraid of Serge, or if he and Serge knew something I didn't. Too bad Alexandre was in jail! At least I could have talked to him, and maybe he would've had an idea."

"Then what happened?"

"I knew I'd have to do something. For a while I thought I'd take the gun and shoot Serge when he was sleeping, but I'm afraid of guns and he didn't seem to sleep—and Maurice, well . . . ." She shrugged her shoulders. "So I decided I couldn't do anything myself, and there was no one to help me, and I'd have to call the police."

"Did you?"

"It's not that easy. In the east end you don't just call 911 and invite the police to your home. They ask all kinds of questions, and besides

Serge was always there. I had to make a plan to contact the police. Then I remembered Coco—"

"Coco?"

"Yes, Coco. Coco Martin, the cop."

"Does officer Martin have another first name besides Coco?" asked Talbot.

"Of course he does," she answered with a smile. "His real name isn't Coco. It's Claude but we all call him Coco, and I've known him a long time."

"What was your relationship with Officer Martin—Coco?"

"What are you suggesting? Coco was just a good friend. I told you how I used to have a jewellery store where I told fortunes, on Ste. Catherine Street near old Maisonneuve, next to Le Carabin."

"Yes."

"Well, across the street from my store was a clothing store."

"Across old Maisonneuve?"

"No, that's where the Happy Home Tavern was. I mean across Ste. Catherine Street. Right across Ste. Catherine street was this clothing store, St. Onge. Their address was 1495 Ste. Catherine East and my address was 1490 Ste. Catherine East. We were right across from each other, and Coco worked there."

"I thought you said that Coco was a policeman."

"He was, but he also worked in the clothing store."

"I don't understand. Was it a large store? Did this Coco work as a guard?"

"No. The only big store in the East was Dupuis Frères, and they closed long ago. You should know that! None of the other places was big enough to have a guard. Coco was a real cop, he worked for the police, like that guy sitting beside you and all the other cops walking around this building."

"But you said he worked in the clothing store?"

"I did. He did. Coco worked in the store even though he was a cop."

"Would you explain how Coco could be a cop, and work in the clothing store?" Talbot asked.

"Like I said, Coco was a cop, but you have to remember it was a long time ago and the police weren't like now. Well, the police only worked four days a week . . . but they worked hard: ten or twelve hours a day.

"Coco was single and young, and never had enough money for clothes, so he got this other job working in the clothing store. They paid him whenever he came to work and he bought his clothes cheap. He tried not to work as a cop on Fridays and Saturdays because that was the best time to work in the clothing store, especially around Christmas."

"What has this to do with the case?" Talbot asked.

"You'll see. Now where was I? Yes, I had my store, across from St. Onge next to Le Carabin. All the people who worked around there got to know each other. Coco used to eat at Le Carabin and sometimes came to see me. Didn't believe in the fortune telling, but he used to drop in to my store, and you know, . . . we were the same age, almost, . . . and we got to know each other. A few times in the back of my store, he and I kind of . . . ."

"I'm still not sure what this has to do with the case."

"Well, you might say we became friends. That was a long time ago, when I had the store. So now that I was in trouble I decided to try and call Coco. I hadn't seen him for years but I knew he was still with the police force."

"Did you call him?"

"I didn't call 911, but I looked up the number of the police in the phone book. When I went out I called and asked for him but he wasn't there. I called two or three times and finally got him. I said I was in trouble. He told me to meet him at Le Carabin. It's still there on Ste. Catherine Street. We met and I told him everything." She slouched in her chair, obviously tiring. "Are you feeling all right?" the judge asked.

"Yes, it's just that every time I think of what happened I get frightened and tired all over again. You know, it happened months ago, and now when I have to think about it all again . . . .But I want this to finish. I can answer more questions. Thank you, you're nice, and—"

"That's quite all right. Maître Talbot, ask the next question, please."

"Did anything happen as a result of your conversation with Coco?"

"No, it was all over between us a long time ago, and we were just friends. Besides, he didn't look the way he used to, and I'm sure that I don't—especially since I had this operation. Coco is married now, has children, and doesn't live in the east end any more. Moved to Ahuntsic."

"I meant concerning the case," Talbot said.

"Oh, the case. Yes, well, Coco told me he needed a day, and I should go home and I'd get a call when it was all arranged—to arrest Serge. Y'see, it wasn't easy because he didn't want to take chances with Caroline and me. When everything was ready I was supposed to get a phone call from a woman who'd say she was Coco. That was pretty smart, wasn't it? Serge wouldn't be suspicious of a woman's voice if he answered, and no one in the house knew about Coco and me—it was such a long time ago."

"Did you plan what you'd do when the lady Coco called?"

"Yes, that meant the police were watching the house and were ready to arrest him. They told me to keep Caroline in the house and they'd arrest Serge when he came out. I described what he looks like, his clothes, how he walks. Coco said I didn't have to worry because he'd call the SWAT team to make the arrest. Would you believe that he was a detective, a big shot in the police force?"

"Did you receive a call from Coco?"

"Not right away. I thought they'd call as soon as I got back home. I stayed in the house waiting for the call and pretending nothing had happened. Maurice didn't know anything, because I didn't trust him. I was afraid to tell Caroline, too, so I was the only one in the house who knew this terrible secret. When Serge looked at me, I shook inside and tried not to show it. This went on for a day and a half. I kept praying they'd call. Every time the phone rang I practically jumped through the ceiling. Can you imagine what it's like?"

"I don't know," answered Talbot, mesmerized by his own witness.

"Serge went out a few times but nothing happened. Then I got the call. Would you believe that Serge answered the phone? He said someone called Coco was calling me. I almost died when I picked up the phone and a lady's voice said it was Coco. It was four in the afternoon and I wanted to ask what had taken so long, but I couldn't say a thing. I let on it was from the Welfare. After that I waited for Serge to go out.

"Finally he decided to go for cigarettes, and asked Maurice to go with him. The fool, he said okay. Then Caroline came in from school, and asked if she could go with them to buy a chocolate bar! Maurice said yes, and my heart dropped; I could have killed him. Now, both Maurice and Caroline were going out with Serge! How would the police know what to do? It'd be my fault if something happened to Caroline. I said that she couldn't go, and that chocolates were bad for her teeth, but Maurice joked and said I was being a mean old mother, and she could go with him. Well, what could I do? I was afraid to make Serge suspicious, so I said nothing.

"I watched the three of them go. Serge had the gun tucked in his belt, like always. I sat down in the living room with my eyes closed and waited, and waited. It seemed like hours, while I sat, alone . . . waiting.

"Finally I heard Caroline shouting, 'Mummy, mummy, they arrested Serge! The police came and took Serge away! We were in the back lane, and I stopped for a minute 'cause I saw Marjo out playing. That's when it happened. Five or six men in baseball caps jumped from all around us. They had machine guns like on TV, and all of a sudden they were holding Serge down on the ground. They stuck handcuffs on him and took him away! Ask Maurice if you don't believe me. Ask Maurice. He was there too.'

"I didn't ask anybody. I just sat and cried."

"No further questions," announced Talbot. It was 4:30.

"Ladies and gentlemen," Judge Berne said, "the cross-examination of this witness will be held on Monday morning at 9:30. Once again, please do not discuss the case with your friends or relatives. And please don't try to make a decision before the evidence and arguments have been completed. Thank you for your attention to the evidence in this case. Have a good weekend. The court is adjourned until Monday morning, at 9:30."

* * *

Marie-Lyse wanted to talk to Tremblay before the guards took him back downstairs. She moved back a few steps and whispered, "Tell me something I don't know about that woman. You lived in her house for three weeks."

"There's not much to tell. She's a screwy old bitch who threw a spell over Maurice. He thinks she's the Madonna of the east."

The image appealed to Marie-Lyse. A fifty-three-year-old retired fortune teller with a bad heart—and a young boyfriend. It would be a few years before Madonna reached that age, and who knows . . . ? "Look, this is a murder trial, your neck is on the line, and you're holding back information from me, your lawyer. Can't you give me anything to help? If we lose, you go to jail, not me."

"It's not the time."

"You said that before. It's not the time. It's not the time. You don't control time. When you make up your mind to help, it'll be too late."

"It's not the time."

"I heard that twenty times since we met. Will there be a time before this ends?"

"I think so, but I can't be sure."

"Did you see those jurors today? They soaked up every word. They believe Pauline. Are there other men in her life? Is she two-timing Maurice?"

"Are you kidding? I don't know how the witch caught Maurice. She'd never find two blind men at once."

"You hate Pauline, don't you?"

"That's no secret."

"Why?"

"Why? You heard her. Do you love her?"

"No, but I'm not on trial, and I don't have to love or hate her. I just want to cross-examine her. Give me some material: some dirt the jury doesn't know."

"Not now."

"It's the weekend. Will you think about it?"

"Yeah. There isn't much else to think about, except Pauline, and Maurice, and this trial, and—"

"Look, Serge, you've got to come up with something, or else," she challenged.

"You're not paid to push me, just to defend me."

"I'm not paid by you, but by legal aid. And they're getting their money's worth from me, but you're not doing your job. You're not helping. Don't you know what will happen if you don't help? Think of that before it's too late! I'll try to come see you on Sunday. Maybe you'll change your mind by then."

" 'Bye."

"Oh, Serge, have you heard from your father since . . . since you got out of jail?"

"No, why d'you ask?"

"I don't know. See you Sunday."

Serge Tremblay stood in the prisoner's dock watching the people leaving the courtroom. His gaze lingered on Marie-Lyse's retreating figure. She had a double name beginning with Marie, but was very different from all the other women in his experience. The women who'd visited his father's flat had been fearful, tired, hardened, often bitter. Some were sneaky; others were really simple, but none had the brains and the drive of Marie-Lyse. She had a toughness and determination in going after her goal that surprised him.

The guard got up. "Let's go downstairs. It's Friday night and I'm not going to spend the weekend in this building." He nudged Tremblay towards the door to the cells. "Maybe you've got nothing to do, but me, I have plans for the weekend."

6

Marie-Lyse's heart pounded as she hurried up the stairs to the central recording office on the fourth floor. She had been nervous all week. Serge's persistent refusal to cooperate was disturbing, but she was determined to win her first murder trial, even if she had to do it all by herself.

*   *   *

The police testimony was routine. Torres had entertained the jury but had done little harm. Oscar Cimon was an impressive and crucial witness, present throughout the night of the murder. She had listened to him with trepidation, on the edge of her chair. He couldn't identify Serge as the person who shot Lepine, and had been too honest to offer his suppositions and conclusions as facts. Her fears had been groundless; the police had not found an eyewitness who could identify Tremblay as the person who had fired the fatal bullet.

The Crown's case rested on the murder weapon seized when Tremblay was arrested, and the testimony of Pauline Vinet and her friend, Maurice. If Vinet's credibility could be shaken, there might be a doubt in the mind of the jurors, or at least some of them . . . .Maurice would be a weak witness; his record was enough to destroy the value of his testimony.

Fortunately, the Crown's examination of Pauline Vinet had lasted all day, so she would have the weekend to prepare the cross-examination. The technicians in the central recording office had promised to make tapes of the day's proceedings for her. She would go over them and find something, anything. A witness who talks so much is bound to make mistakes.

The recording office wasn't usually cooperative but Marie-Lyse had worked as a clerk in the courthouse for two years and could ask a favour. She entered the office breathless from her race up the stairs.

The technician smiled and handed her five cassettes. "Here you go. We don't do this for everybody. Usually when we get an order from a lawyer it takes four or five days to make copies."

"I appreciate the favour."

"You're welcome, but don't ask us too often. There are limits to how much we can do—even for friends."

She raised her shoulders and grinned.

"Good luck!" he continued, "Don't work too hard on the week-end."

"Thanks. You're a dear. When it's over and my client is free, you'll be glad you helped."

"I don't know. We don't have a clue what's going on in your courtroom, and don't care. We record eighty-seven courtrooms, all day long. What the people say is none of our business. For all we know this could be the tape of a sidewalk fall, a malpractice case, a divorce—almost anything. Enjoy yourself! Me, I'd rather watch the hockey game Saturday night."

"Not me. Bye-bye!" Marie-Lyse left the room as quickly as she had entered. Landing this trial had been pure luck. Most of the work at the Laurier Legal Aid Clinic was alimony claims, nonsupport cases and minor criminal trials. Good cases showed up rarely, and senior lawyers on staff usually grabbed them. This was her break and she'd make the most of it.

She chuckled, recalling the comments of her friends and the clinic lawyers when her name had appeared in *Le Journal* that week. They read *Le Journal* every day, but pretended to subscribe to the more intellectual *Le Devoir*.

The case would be won with or without Serge! All of her past would work in her favour. As a child, Marie-Lyse had lived in the east end of Montreal, and knew those streets and alleys inside out. She had grown up at Panet and de Montigny (now Maisonneuve),very close to Visitation and Logan.

She remembered Charbonneau the jeweller, and St. Onge. Le Carabin was still in business; long ago Marie-Lyse had eaten there. She tried but couldn't conjure up the image of the fortune teller's store.

She resolved to visit the area on the weekend and refresh her memory. Maybe she could walk around on Sunday morning before going out to the detention centre to visit her client. She might see something she could use to pry information from him.

The scene of the crime was familiar too. She'd studied at l'UQAM—the University of Quebec at Montreal—at the corner of St. Denis and Ste. Catherine. They weren't easy years. She'd been a serious student with a passion to succeed. The law school diploma would be her ticket out of the east end. Students at l'UQAM didn't have rich parents to pay for their education. They borrowed all they could from the government, and worked whenever they could find a job. Success doesn't come easily to people from the east end.

During her student years she lived on St. Louis Square, about seven blocks north of the university. She began working when she entered law school. It was pure luck; there was a shortage of clerks and ushers in the courthouse, and the government hired students.

She couldn't hold a full-time job during the school year, but managed to convince the people at Judicial Support Services let her to share the job with her roommate. Friends thought they were crazy, but in the end it paid. The two kept the job for four years, and learned how the courthouse worked. The practical experience and friendships from this period would be valuable. Now, her background, the years at university, and experience in the courthouse would fuse and work for her . . . and for Serge Tremblay.

A number 55 bus was parked on St. Laurent, near the side door of the courthouse. The driver was gone but had left the door open. She got in, put away her bus pass and went to the second seat from the back. That was her favourite place to sit; it faced forward and had more leg room.

A clock projecting from the corner building across the street read a quarter past five. The bus wouldn't start to get crowded till it reached Chinatown. Court employees usually leave around 4:30 on Fridays, and few lawyers use the bus.

It was the easiest way back to the clinic. The bus would weave its way up St. Laurent, and stop opposite the wonderful old fire station at the corner of Laurier. It was a fifteen- minute trip, and another five or ten minutes' walk to her office. Some days she would dawdle, as she looked in the boutique windows. That was one of the nice things about working at the clinic. It was in the midst of chic restaurants and stores, close enough to court, and she could live in Outremont.

She closed her eyes and concentrated. What a difference between pleading before a judge and pleading before a jury! With a judge there's only one person to convince. The judge can be patient or abrupt, interested or bored, smart or not too smart . . . but a *jury*: one word that meant twelve people with different backgrounds, outlooks, work histories, and who knows what else.

She would try to reach out to each of the jurors in one way or another. She had seen experienced defence lawyers establish eye contact with several jurors during the trial, and use body language to communicate with the responsive ones. They pitched their arguments towards the two or three receptive jurors. One or two hold-outs could mean an acquittal. Most jurors prefer to acquit. It's not easy to send someone to jail for years, or a lifetime. If a few jurors hold out, the majority might come around eventually and agree on acquittal. If they don't, a hung jury and a mistrial isn't the worst result for the accused. It's harder to convict at the second trial, and time usually benefits the defence—usually, but not always.

It's unusual for jurors to identify with an accused, because even if they aren't convinced the accused is guilty, there's always some suspicion that the police wouldn't arrest someone without reason. They can relate more easily to the attorney for the accused, the defence lawyer. This can be helpful to keep in mind in pleading the case. Defence lawyers know this; they used to be called criminal lawyers, but the title suggested they were engaged in criminal activities, so now they call themselves defence lawyers. Regardless, everyone else calls them criminal lawyers.

Marie-Lyse was determined to work on all the jurors. She thirsted for victory. She tried to remember their names, or at least their numbers, and faces. Juror number one, Henri Lanctot . . . seemed ordinary. Looked about forty. His exact age would be in her notes on the selection process.

She pulled the yellow notepad out of her briefcase. Why do lawyers always use long yellow paper, as if it were more legal? When you start, these trappings are adopted as a badge of the profession. They become habits which only the creative or eccentric bother to alter.

Henri Lanctot worked for the Standard Life Insurance Company. Couldn't be too high up in the company, or he'd have requested an exemption. He looked as though he worked in accounting or underwriting. Had an indoor office look.

Number two was a young female student—perhaps at l'UQAM. It might be worthwhile to find an excuse to mention the university. That wouldn't be hard because Berri-UQAM was the closest Metro station to Le Wiz.

Number five was also a young woman. Lucy Morin. Canteen operator? She wondered what that meant. Obviously number twelve was interested in her. He'd passed her notes and constantly managed to be near her.

Number five may control two votes on the jury, her own and number twelve's. Rick Hayes. Nobody chose him; he just happened along in his leather jacket and sunglasses, when it was too late to make a challenge. She never would have accepted him. How can you convince a man of anything when you can't see his eyes?

How about number eleven, sitting next to him? Sometimes jurors are influenced most by the person next to them . . . .No way; number eleven doesn't talk to any of the others. He just writes more and more notes. Albert Rousseau, high school teacher. That explains why he's making notes: for his students. Too bad the jury was sent out before the judge spoke to those kids from Hudson High School. Wonder what he teaches? Not that it matters much. Can't imagine him getting along with Hayes, but you never know. He won't have a chance to get close to number five, sitting in front of him; Hayes will see to that.

There's the old man, number eight, the one who couldn't find a parking space. It might be worth paying him some attention now and then. He may be old, but he can still look, and dream, and—

"Laurier, Laurier," announced the driver as he guided the bus away from the curb at St. Joseph, and nudged through the Friday traffic. Marie-Lyse put the yellow notepad back in her briefcase. She slithered through the crowded bus and got off.

She crossed St. Laurent and walked briskly up the street. She'd have loved to sit around and talk with the other lawyers in the clinic, but it was close to six when she reached the office and they were gone. She checked her phone messages and the mail. Her desk was a mess of papers, but who cared? At the moment, nothing was more important to her than the trial.

The adrenalin was still pumping. She had to slow down and pace herself. The trial was far from over and there'd be time tomorrow and Sunday to prepare for the week. Her portable cassette player protruded from beneath the papers. She dropped it in her briefcase and left the clinic.

Walking slowly up Laurier, she read menus pasted on restaurant doors, and admired the profusion of clothes and gourmet foods. The tension eased from her body, opening her to a sensuous awareness of the sights, sounds, and people around her. She turned left on Querbes, walked a short block and entered the squat brick apartment building at 453 Edward-Charles. Home.

*   *   *

BY A JURY OF HIS PEERS

After a week in the courthouse, Albert Rousseau was anxious to be home. He sat in his Honda, stuck in the Friday afternoon traffic on the Ville-Marie expressway. No use getting excited; traffic was heavy at this hour, and the road crews seeming preference for rush-hour repairs invariably made things worse.

He'd never dreamed that he'd be chosen as a juror. It happened so quickly. One moment he was in the high school teaching math; the next, he was no longer Albert Rousseau, teacher, but juror number eleven for a murder trial.

This was the most exciting thing that had happened to him in a long time. He had never paid attention to crime reports in the papers, and knew very little about criminal law and its enforcement. In the world of math and logic, absolute certainty existed; the laws of nature cannot be disobeyed or altered. As a juror he was thrust into a world of ambiguity, where a man's right to freedom was being weighed.

He could identify with the judge. After all, he spent five hours a day in front of the class, and the judge sat in front of the court guiding jurors. Yes, he thought, there's a lot of similarity in their roles. Rousseau had expected the trial to last a few days only. Obviously trials take much longer in real life than on TV, but surely two or three days should have been sufficient. Apparently they weren't, and this trial could last two or three weeks—maybe more.

Rousseau's car was boxed in, traffic hadn't moved more than half a kilometre in the past fifteen minutes, and he just needed to get home, read his notes to Diane, and tell her about Pauline D. Vinet, fortune teller, *la fleur de l'Est*. Diane had worried when he was chosen to be a juror in a murder trial, but she got over her fears when he explained the elaborate security arrangements. Fortunately, the school board contract guaranteed he wouldn't lose any salary.

After eight years of marriage, Diane was pregnant, expecting their first child next month. Albert loved the way she looked, the glow on her face, and the funny strut that had recently developed in her walk. A few weeks earlier she had stopped working at the bank and now was home awaiting the baby's arrival.

They weren't rich but their home in Laval had increased in value substantially. He hadn't felt comfortable with the idea of a child until there was financial security. They had calculated their family budget many times before making the decision.

After the pregnancy was confirmed by their pharmacist, they talked of little else. The unborn child preempted all other interests. Imagine!—he, a teacher, was actually rushing to prenatal classes and enjoying every minute of it. They spent hours convincing each other that all the best, most beautiful, healthiest babies were breast-fed. His copious notes, from the prenatal classes and from all he read, were piled neatly on the coffee table, and reviewed each evening before the six o'clock news.

An overhead sign announced the exit for the Decarie Expressway. It would be hopelessly blocked at this hour; Highway 13 would be a better bet. He wouldn't be home for another half hour. How do people do this every day? Better still, why do they do it, when there are homes and jobs in the suburbs? Perhaps Laval didn't have all the excitement of downtown Montreal, but it didn't have Montreal's traffic problem or its crime rate, either.

People say it's unlucky to fix up a room and buy baby furniture before the birth, but neither of them was superstitious. They waited until the very end of the after-Christmas sales when prices were cheapest. February fifteenth, the day after Valentine's Day, they began shopping for the baby. Every Thursday and Friday night they visited shopping centres in search of bargains, and gradually accumulated furniture, clothing, and boxes of rattles, toys, games, posters. The child wouldn't be able to use many of these things immediately, but February was the best time to shop for toys, and the variety at Toys R Us was irresistible. Albert Rousseau Junior would have everything . . . almost everything.

In the distance he saw the bridge that joins the island of Montreal to the island of Laval. Cars continued to merge into the expressway. Friday was always worst, because the cottage-owners joined the rush out of town and headed north to the Laurentian Highlands. The atmosphere was permeated with the hot exhaust fumes of thousands of automobiles crawling along the concrete roadbed. Once he crossed the bridge, the air would smell better.

Denise saw the car turn into the driveway and came to greet him. "How are you? It's late and I can imagine what the traffic was like."

"Usual Friday night mess. I sure wish they'd build another bridge, or do something. Doesn't matter. Wait till I tell you what happened today. But first, how's the baby? Did Junior kick today?"

"He's just great. Here, feel." She took his hand in hers and placed it on her stomach. "I can't wait much longer. Next week I'll be in my ninth month, and after that it could happen any time . . . .Gosh, what if I go into labour while you're in that court?"

"Don't worry. There are phones all over—even on the clerk's desk. It doesn't ring often but I'm sure they'd reach me in an emergency."

She kissed him on the cheek and pulled his hand. "Come in, come in. I want to hear what happened today."

"You will," he promised as they entered the house together. "We ate in a restaurant in Old Montreal. Great little place. I never thought the government would spend the money. Even gave us each a drink with the meal. Not a bad job, being on a jury." They sat down in the living room. He pulled out his notes and referred to them from time to time as he spoke. "Tremblay, Serge, moved in with this couple a few days before the murder. They live on Visitation Street in the east end. Any idea where that is?"

"No, but it must be somewhere near Lafontaine Park."

"Lower, south of there, not far from Maisonneuve. The woman was, of all things, a fortune teller. She's about fifty, dresses kind of funny, and thinks she's still sexy. Doesn't look it to me, but she does have a young lover, Maurice, who's twenty-two or so."

"That's kind of romantic."

"Think so? She's fifty, and he's the same age as her son."

"Well, if they don't bother anyone, it's no one's business."

"In any case, now that there's been a murder it's everyone's business."

"Tell me more."

"Well, Tremblay was a friend of Maurice, and he moved in with them. Seems like a rotten type. The woman is scared of him and I can't blame her. She wanted Tremblay to leave but couldn't throw him out.

Her boyfriend, Maurice, didn't do anything about it. Come to think of it, that fortune teller was a brave woman; crazy as a loon, but brave."

"You're so lucky, and I'm proud of you. Think you have an appetite for dinner?"

"With you? Always."

*   *   *

Marie-Lyse slept late on Saturday morning. She hadn't done so for a long time but the week's activities had been exhausting. It was ten o'clock when she put on her jeans and T-shirt, raced down the stairs and jogged over to the bakery on Laurier. Sipping cafe au lait and munching on a fresh croissant at a window table was her weekend luxury. She hoped someone she knew would wander by, preferably a colleague from the legal aid office, so she could discuss the week's events.

The testimony of the witnesses echoed in her head as she tried to find some elusive clue. She was convinced something was hidden on the tapes of Pauline Vinet's testimony. She'd spend the afternoon listening to them till she found that needle in the haystack.

There was something she couldn't fathom about that peculiar trio of Pauline, Maurice and Serge. Pauline had a charm of her own, but it was hard to tell if she was naive or shrewd. Was this an elaborate plot to get Serge out of her house and life?

Serge was so stubborn in his silence; it was really annoying. Perhaps he didn't quite get it—what was going on in the courtroom or in his life. At first he'd seemed guilty as hell, and the case was just one she'd plead for experience. But Serge was beginning to grow on her. She admired his strength and his stoic silence, while at the same time resenting the lack of cooperation. What kind of man remained silent while a case was built up around him? Why wouldn't he talk about the night of the murder? He'd told her about other things in his life. At first he just looked at her with that impenetrable gaze, as if she were some creature from a foreign planet. It wasn't easy to win his confidence, but slowly during their repeated meetings he began to unfold and told her about his childhood. She couldn't visualize a home without some love. She'd been raised poor in the east end, but had a caring mother and father.

Everyone in the east end knew poverty. Few of the men had steady jobs, and the shrinking petrochemical industry and manufacturing base had hurt the east more than any other part of the city. The paternalism of the old industrial enterprises had disappeared. Aging and obsolete manufacturing facilities had had to choose between imminent bankruptcy and a move to the suburbs, where lower taxes and new facilities would enable them to compete. The procrastinators lost their choice and went under.

Marie-Lyse had learned these things first-hand. Her father had been laid off or fired frequently, and her family lacked the initiative or the courage to break out of the east and follow the jobs to the South Shore or the West Island. Moving from the east end was almost like leaving your country of birth and travelling to a strange new land.

Marie-Lyse had determined to break out, succeed in her new career, and have it all. The first step had been accomplished when she was admitted to the bar. Now, three years later, she was experiencing the ultimate, pleading a murder case before a jury. True, it was a Legal Aid case, but it *was* a beginning.

She'd been lucky to get any job in this economy. Some of her classmates were actually unemployed, or working in hotels and restaurants as waiters and dishwashers. In a few years she intended to apply for a position as prosecutor in the crown office, where she'd make contacts and gain experience. Then she could return to private practice; perhaps to join one of the large legal offices and get involved in other kinds of litigation. With her brains and ambition, she'd make it to the top. There's always room at the top, she thought. Only the base of the pyramid is crowded.

One day she'd marry, and have a child or two, and money, a career, holidays in the Caribbean and Europe, a Lexus—everything. That's what life was all about, having everything all the time! That's what she left the east end for: to live and grow, succeed, acquire and enjoy. But first she had to win this case, establish a reputation. She must penetrate the barrier erected by Serge Tremblay and find the ammunition to destroy the credibility of Pauline D. Vinet. The case had to be won in the cross-examination of Pauline and Maurice.

It might not be possible for Serge to testify in his own defence. The criminal record of the accused can only be mentioned if he chooses to testify. If Serge remained silent, the jury would know nothing of his fight with his father — but if he testified it would come out. The jury would conclude that a man who almost killed his own father wouldn't hesitate to kill a stranger . . . .But what if the ground was prepared in advance? What if Serge's father came to court and sat in the audience to support his son? She could tell the jury the incident with his father had been an accident, and even his father cared what happened to him . . . .But where was Serge's father? Could she find Marcel Tremblay?

She was getting ahead of herself. She'd spend the afternoon listening to the tapes and speak to Serge later. It was only Saturday morning and there was plenty of time before seeing him on Sunday.

She spread jam on the croissant and bit into it. As she blotted the jam from her upper lip with a napkin, a man peered into the bakery window. She returned his smile, and then looked down at her scribbling on the paper place mat. She must win this case before there would be any time for social life. One more week or two.

She re-entered her apartment and put the cassette into the recorder. The sound quality was poor and scratchy, but every word was intelligible. The jokes weren't quite as funny the second time around. The third time she heard Pauline call herself *la fleur de l'Est,* Marie-Lyse groaned. But she persevered, and replayed the description of events the night of the murder.

"On October sixth he went out at night and we didn't see him until much later. Maurice and I went to bed early. We woke up a little after three in the morning. I suggested we go to Dunkin' Donuts for a snack. They're open all night—always people there. It takes about fifteen minutes to walk down to Ste. Catherine Street. We went in and stayed for an hour or so."
"Did anything happen while you were there?"
"No. We joked around with some of the customers, and I had a donut: a chocolate one, twisted and not round. They call them

120

donuts, but I think a donut should have a hole in the middle, like a tire or a lifesaver. You wouldn't call it a lifesaver if it didn't have a hole in the middle, would you?"

"No, I guess not."

"So where was I? Yes, I had this straight twisted donut, and Maurice had one too, and then we went home."

"Where was Caroline at the time?"

"Sleeping. She's only twelve and you can't expect us to take her out at that hour!"

"And what happened next?'

"We went to sleep. It was late and we were tired."

"Madame Vinet, please think carefully, and tell me if you can, what time you came back to your home from Dunkin' Donuts."

"I don't know. Very late."

"What happened?"

"We went to bed. We talked and fooled around for a few minutes and then I fell asleep."

"What's the next thing you remember?"

"I woke up."

"Why? Did something awake you?"

"He did, he did."

"For the record, the witness is pointing at the accused, Serge Tremblay."

"He stood in my bedroom doorway, white as a ghost, and said 'Wake Maurice, wake Maurice, I have to talk to him.'"

The timing, the timing . . . .Pauline Vinet was unable to fix the time of either her departure for Dunkin' Donuts or her return. Marie-Lyse replayed the key answers once again.

> "On October sixth he went out at night and we didn't see him until much later. Maurice and I went to sleep early. We woke up a little after three in the morning. I suggested we go to Dunkin' Donuts for a snack."

That's too vague. "We woke up a little after three o'clock in the morning. I suggested we go to Dunkin' Donuts for a snack." *A little after three* could be just vague enough to give Maurice time to get back to the apartment

121

after the murder. If the clubs closed at three, and the shooting occurred at ten after three, or 3:15, Maurice could have returned home by 3:30—in time to go with her to Dunkin' Donuts. When did she return to the flat? Once again Marie-Lyse played the reply.

> "Madame Vinet, please think carefully, and tell me if you can, what time you came back to your home from Dunkin' Donuts."
> "I don't know. Very late."
> "What happened?"
> "We went to bed. We talked and fooled around for a few minutes and then I fell asleep."

They woke up "a little after three" to go to Dunkin' Donuts, and returned "very late". She never said what happened before they went there. That sounds vague. The time was never clearly established. Marie-Lyse made a note to avoid asking questions about the timing. Maybe it was just an oversight or ambiguity. Further questions would allow Pauline to strengthen and clarify her testimony.

What if she was intentionally vague? Where was Maurice earlier that night? He doesn't have an alibi. Doesn't need one, because he's not on trial. What if he fired the fatal shot? Could he have? Only Maurice and Serge knew. Would either one tell her? She'd have to wait till tomorrow, when she could talk to Serge at the detention centre.

She got tired of Pauline's voice and decided to do something else for a while. Her thoughts returned to Serge's criminal record. The attempted murder of his father—What had she thought about over breakfast? Prove it was an accident. Find Marcel Tremblay and get him to come to court, and show he forgave Serge for the accident of four years ago. Find Marcel Tremblay.

She walked to the kitchen, reached into the cupboard and took out the phone book. Eleven pages of Tremblays, fifty-three Marcels, and five columns of M. Tremblays. This would be more difficult than she'd expected! She decided to call the Marcels in the central area only. It might not be appropriate to ask if this was the home of the man whose son was convicted of trying to murder him.

What was the name of the furniture company where Marcel had

worked? . . . Fapco. She'd ask for the Marcel Tremblay who had worked at Fapco Industries . . . .There might be an easier way. Fapco must have a personnel department. She looked in the phone book but Fapco was no longer listed. In any event it was Saturday, so even if she found their office it would be closed.

She began calling. "Bonjour, I'm looking for Monsieur Marcel Tremblay who worked at Fapco Industries . . . .It's not you? . . . Would you know him? . . . Thank you."

A few of the people were irate at being disturbed from their sleep. Some didn't respond, and a few tried to be helpful. No one had heard of him. She'd try another way.

It was early afternoon when she slung a light sweater over her arm and walked to the corner of Laurier and Park. An empty bus was approaching from the north. People had deserted the transit system, preferring to walk, cycle, or just stay home on the beautiful April day. Minutes later she stepped into the Metro, travelled a few stops, and emerged at the Beaudry station in the heart of the east end. She ran up the moving exit ramp and walked east along Ste. Catherine, stopping at each of the neighbourhood taverns to enquire if they knew Marcel Tremblay.

Le Carabin was still open. She ordered a coffee. The waiter knew a few Marcel Tremblays, but none who worked at the furniture factory. Most people who go to restaurants and taverns are known only by their faces and first names. And there are so many Marcels.

As she approached Champlain she stopped at convenience stores too. No luck. She climbed the winding stairs to the flat on Champlain. The woman who answered had moved in the previous July, and no, she didn't know a Marcel Tremblay who worked in the furniture factory. The previous tenant was a Dufour.

*   *   *

There's little difference between weekend and the weekdays in a high-rise prison. In Parthenais Detention Centre a break from routine is significant, and any visit is a major event. Serge found it hard to return to the monotony of his cell. For the first time in his life he was anxious to see a woman. He actually looked forward to seeing Marie-Lyse on Sunday.

Two women were crucially important in his life at this time. The wily, nutty, absurd Pauline Vinet was struggling to push him over a precipice into oblivion, while Marie-Lyse tried to pull him to safety. He felt paralysed, inert, distant, as the two women struggled to determine his fate. This was his life and freedom, and he must rouse himself and become involved in the conflict. Round one was over, and the combatants had returned to their corners, but the battle would resume Monday.

Perhaps he'd been anesthetized by the trial—or had he been hypnotized by Maurice? No, that was ridiculous. Maurice was weak, dependent and vulnerable, while he was strong and protective. He had moved into Pauline's flat a couple of days after leaving La Macaza. He could have stayed longer at the Salvation Army shelter, but Maurice had persuaded him. That was seven months ago, and things hadn't worked out. He had spent three weeks at Pauline's flat, and six months at Parthenais after his arrest. Now there was a good chance he'd spend most of his life back in prison.

The girl at Le Wiz didn't want to dance with him. He hadn't especially wanted to dance with her either. He couldn't even remember why he asked her to dance.

It seemed that women surrounded him, that policewoman who called herself a crime scene technician, half the jury, Pauline, Marie-Lyse. Women—suddenly invading his life? None here in Parthenais.

He'd better open up a bit and help Marie-Lyse. She wasn't like the others; she was trying to help him. Why did she ask about his father? He hadn't seen Marcel since the accident, when he stabbed him with the screwdriver. Marcel never visited him at La Macaza.

Marie-Lyse wanted him to think about Pauline. But what could he remember? She was an aging, conniving, devilish sorceress, who clung to any man who passed. How could anyone take her seriously? Even if they did, she didn't really say much in court except that she wanted to be rid of him and spend the rest of her life in bed with Maurice. Pauline could have Maurice. He had lived without Maurice before they met in jail, and could live without him now. Maurice never did anything except blather, snivel, and make plans that never happened.

The name Maurice evoked confusing thoughts in his mind. Serge deplored his weakness, yet he felt compelled to protect him from Pauline, from all the others, from his senseless plans, from himself.

The time passed slowly. Friday dinner, Saturday breakfast, lunch. The hot meals Marie-Lyse had requested in court for him were better. Saturday dinner, Sunday.

Serge clutched the cell bars and peered down the long hall at the clock; 2:30 and she hadn't arrived. She hadn't said exactly when she'd come, but she knew Sunday visiting was only from two to five o'clock. Not enough guards available for weekend duty to have longer visiting times.

Each time he heard footsteps and the jangle of keys he thought the guards were coming to take him downstairs. Four times he'd been disappointed, as other inmates received visitors. Something important must have delayed her. Serge trusted her; his turn would come. The other bench in the cell was unoccupied, so he didn't have to put up with an enquiring cellmate. He squeezed the bars until his knuckles turned white. This was the first time he trusted a woman and he feared disappointment. The footsteps came closer.

"Serge Tremblay."

"Yes."

"Your lawyer's here. Follow us." A key clicked and the door slid sideways. Serge followed the two guards down the hall, past a window. The afternoon light was brighter than he expected.

Marie-Lyse sat on an oak chair across the table from him. The interview room was bare and windowless.

"I waited for you. What happened?" Serge asked.

"There was a slowdown at the control counter downstairs. I've been here half an hour."

The guard closed the door so they could talk freely. Every few minutes he glanced in through the window. There were rumours that cameras and mikes were hidden in the interview rooms, but Marie-Lyse didn't believe them and Serge didn't care.

"Why did you ask about my father on Friday?" Serge asked.

"I don't know. I just had an idea we might find him and he'd help. I even looked for him yesterday."

"What?"

"I went looking for him but got nowhere. I walked along Ste. Catherine, dropped in to a few bars and restaurants, but no one knew anything. Do you know where he lives?"

"Probably still on Champlain Street."

"No, I went there and he must've moved a few years ago. There's a new tenant who never heard of him."

"What can he do anyway? I haven't seen him in years. And, why would he want to help after all this time?"

"I don't know, but I had to try. If he'd only come and sit in the audience, the jury might think of you as a person—not some monster killer who scared the daylights out of Pauline Vinet and her daughter."

"You want him to sit in court while Pauline testifies?"

"Why not, if we can find him?" For a moment Marie-Lyse thought she saw a strange expression disfigure Serge's face. "You just made a funny face. Did your father know Pauline?" She saw the expression again.

"What makes you ask?"

"The look on your face. Tell me, did your father know Pauline Vinet?"

"Could be."

"What kind of an answer is that? Did she ever come to your flat?"

"No."

"Did he ever mention her name to you?"

"No."

"To anyone else when you were around?"

"No. Hey, you're cross-examining me!"

"Yes, answer the question. Why in the world do you react when I mention your father and Pauline at the same time?"

"I dunno."

"But you reacted; there must be something. Did they go out together?"

"No, I don't know. I think—but I don't know—that they might have met."

"Serge, what's going through your head? Please tell me. There isn't much time before I question Pauline tomorrow, and I need something to go on. Please tell me."

He answered in measured tones. "They just . . . might have met. I never saw them together and she never came to our place, and I never heard the name Pauline Vinet till I met Alexandre at La Macaza." He paused, closed his eyes and leaned the chair back till it rested against the wall.

Marie-Lyse waited, then took a deep breath. "Think. Think hard," she whispered. "Your father and Pauline Vinet, Pauline D. Vinet, the fortune teller."

"Pauline D. Vinet. Fortune teller . . . .I think she told my father's fortune before the accident. She predicted we'd have the fight . . . and what would happen."

"How do you know that?!"

"He used to go to the taverns and bars."

"Le Carabin?"

"No, the Happy Home. It was across the street from Pauline's salon. The beers were cheaper at the Happy Home, and guys from the factory went there often. A few times, I looked in the window and saw my father drinking with his friends."

"Did you ever see Pauline's fortune telling salon?"

"I knew about it. The kids told stories about her."

"What kind of stories?"

"Kid stories. Made-up ones."

"Did you ever see your father go there?"

"No, but I know he thought about it."

"How?"

"He used to say one day he'd go there before a hockey game, and find out who would win."

"Did he mention her name?"

"He said 'Pauline Devine'."

"Yes?"

"I don't remember exactly when, but something happened."

"What? Tell me."

"Something happened, a long time ago." He rocked the chair back again and continued. "Do you know why I left my father's flat? When I was sixteen he said something weird—really weird. It's all coming back."

Marie-Lyse took a yellow pad out of her briefcase and began taking notes. "How did he make you leave?"

"She made me leave."

"She? But Pauline never came to your house . . . ?"

"No, I don't even know if it was Pauline. But someone, some 'she', told his fortune, and warned him there would be an accident. She told him."

"How do you know?"

"He came home one day, in the summer when he wasn't working. He started shouting and called me a little killer. I didn't know what he was talking about, and then he called me a 'mother killer' and shouted I would be a 'father killer' too."

"What happened?"

"I don't know. I didn't understand what got into him. I sat there sort of stupid like, till he tried to hit me. Then I took off and he shouted, 'I'll get you first you, you mother killer, I'll kill you first, and prove she's wrong. She don't know nothin'.' I escaped from the house before he could catch me. He was drunk."

"And—"

"And nothing. I was sixteen, I left. Never wanted to see him again and still don't want to."

"Why did he call you a 'mother killer'?"

"I don't know."

"Did you ever know your mother?"

"No."

"Ever see a picture of her?"

"No."

"Do you know her name?"

"Marie something. All the women were called Marie, like you."

"You have a birth certificate?"

"No."

"Were you born in Montreal?"

"Uh-huh."

"When?"

"February—February 23rd, 1969."

"Anything else you want to tell me about your father or mother?"

"Not really."

"What about Pauline? Did you move in because you wanted to get even for what she told your father?"

"No, no. I never thought of it until now."

"Why did you suddenly remember?"

"I dunno. Maybe because of you—because you asked so many questions."

"And Maurice—Where did you first meet him?"

"La Macaza."

"Did he ever talk to you about Pauline at La Macaza?"

"Only just before he left. Said he didn't want to stay at the Salvation Army and that Alexandre said it was okay to stay with his mother for a while. Alexandre was trying to be nice. He didn't expect Maurice to hop into her bed."

"Did you?"

"No. If I had, I wouldn't have moved in for even one night."

Marie-Lyse heard the knock on the window and looked at her watch. Time to leave. "Keep cool. I'll see you tomorrow morning."

"Thanks for coming." The door opened and the two guards signalled for Serge to follow. He looked at Marie-Lyse a last time, and left the interview room.

*   *   *

She returned to her apartment and reached for the legal directory. Inside she found several loose typed pages with the addresses and home telephone numbers of crown prosecutors, distributed for emergency use. She found Vince Talbot's number, hesitated, and then dialed.

"Vince?"

"Yes."

"Marie-Lyse Lortie. Sorry to bother you at home on a Sunday, but I'm preparing for tomorrow and there's some information I need."

"Don't you ever stop working? I know this is your first murder trial, but take it easy or you'll burn yourself out."

"Thanks Vince, but there's something I want to know."

"M-hmm?"

"Marcel Tremblay, Serge's father. Where is he?"

"I don't know what this has to do with the case."

"Maybe nothing."

"One minute. Let me check my notes. I think he died . . . .Yeah, here it is. He died a few months after Tremblay was convicted of attempted murder. The doctor felt it was a direct result of the blow to his head, but Tremblay had already pleaded guilty to attempted murder, so the file couldn't be reopened. Your client's damned lucky he wasn't convicted of murder."

"Why didn't you disclose that before?"

"Didn't think it was relevant."

"And you were waiting to ambush him if he testified?"

"No, I wouldn't do that. You know we can only question him about the conviction and not about what happened months later."

"Sorry. Can I ask one more question?"

"Sure."

"What about Serge's mother? Do you know anything about her?"

"No. Should I?"

"I don't know, but something's bothering me. Can you run a check on her?"

"What's her name?"

"Marie, I think."

"Maiden name?"

"I don't know."

"What can I check? There must be two thousand Marie Tremblays in the country."

"Start with the hospital records. Serge was born February 23rd, 1969. He lived in the east end all his life, and must have been born at Notre Dame Hospital. They should have her maiden name."

"I'll see what I can do. Get some sleep before tomorrow. You'll want to look your best for the jury."

"Thanks, Vince. I hope you don't mind my calling you at home."

"No. See you tomorrow. I'll let you know if I find anything. 'Bye."

7

Pauline D. Vinet captured the imagination of the journalists and their weekend readers. The front page of *Le Journal* featured a large smiling picture of her, with the caption 'Flower of the East in Court'. The story on page three described the ordeal suffered by the flower of the east and her young daughter, when they were forced to share their home with Serge Tremblay.

In addition to a review of all the facts of the case, the reader was treated to Vinet's life story, and a colour photograph of the exterior of the vacant store where she had worked as a fortune teller. The article glossed over her relationship with Coco, because the reporter didn't want to risk offending a policeman who might be a source of information in the future.

A beaming Nantel handed the clippings to Judge Berne. "Jackpot, Monsieur le Juge, Jackpot! Look at these papers, *Le Journal, Allo Police, La Presse*, The Gazette. You made every one of them! This will fill up an entire page in my scrapbook."

"Thank you, thank you. I am honoured by the attention from the newspapers, and from you."

"This is real jurisprudence, Monsieur le judge, the real thing. In my younger days as a boxer living in the east end of Montreal, I visited all the places mentioned in the article. St. Onge . . . St. Onge has been closed for five years. Used to buy my clothes at St. Onge. They always treated me well."

He lowered his voice to a conspiratorial whisper. "Their prices were lower than Dupuis Frères, and whenever I bought a suit they gave me a free tie. If I bought a coat, they gave me a scarf. I used to joke with them, Monsieur le Juge. I would ask, 'What do you give me if I buy a pair of underwear? Don't you have something extra for a good customer?'

"The boss would answer, 'I gave you the suit at cost, and threw in a tie. Now you buy a pair of underwear for two dollars, and you want a bonus? What else do you want?—My mother-in-law?'

"Once I answered Yes. Do you know what he did? He reached into his shirt pocket, and gave me a picture of an old woman. Said it was his mother-in-law! We had a good laugh, Monsieur le Juge, a really good laugh. Those were the good days in the east end, when everyone knew each other—not like today. In those days when you bought a suit it was theatre, pure theatre. Monsieur le Juge, if you have any problems with your case, just ask me. I'm an old guy from the east."

"Thank you. I appreciate your offer, and I'll keep it in mind. And thank you for the 'jurisprudence'. Au revoir, old guy from the east."

"Have a good day, Monsieur le Juge."

*   *   *

Jackie was already at her desk when Berne finally entered the office. "You and your press reports! My friends want to know why they write so much about that woman. Even had her picture on the front page of *Le Journal!* And you—they only mentioned your name once."

"I take it you do not approve of fortune tellers."

"I don't approve of that fortune teller. Can you imagine!—her living with a twenty-two-year-old kid who was straight out of jail?" She shrugged her shoulders, "At the same time that he—Maurice Pomerleau—lived and slept with her, he probably did the same with your accused, Tremblay. What kind of people do you invite into this building?"

"All kinds—but I don't invite them. They just . . . seem to show up. What else is new?"

"The constable, Parent, called. He has a note for you."

"Ask him to come up. Perhaps I can deal with it before court this morning. Have you seen Linda?"

"She's at the water cooler, filling the coffee pot. Here she comes now."

"Monsieur le Juge, how could you let all this happen on the day I was absent?!" Linda asked.

"Don't worry; it's not over. This morning you'll hear Marie- Lyse Lortie cross-examine Pauline. There'll be more excitement."

"But I missed so much!"

"It was fully reported in the Sunday *Journal.* Here's the 'jurisprudence' from Nantel. You can read about it."

"It's not the same as being there."

"No, I guess it never is. Would you watch for Parent? He phoned earlier and told Jackie he has a note for me."

"I wonder what it is. Can't be the verdict."

"No. Something must have happened to a juror over the weekend. Send Parent in as soon as he arrives."

"Oui, Monsieur le Juge. I'll get you a coffee."

"Thank you."

Berne saw Constable Parent a few minutes later. "Oui, Constable. What do you have for me today?" Parent smiled and handed him a small irregular foil package. "What's this?"

"Number seven asked me to give it to you, when she arrived this morning."

"Number seven?"

"Yes. Kathy Johnson."

"Jackie!" he called, "Come in, and bring Linda too. I need a witness."

"I'm a secretary. They don't pay me enough to double as a witness . . . .What's that?"

134

"I don't know. We're about to find out now." The crumpled foil contained two large pieces of homemade coffee cake.

"She's falling in love with you," Jackie observed caustically. "The newspapers will love this! I can see the headlines, JUROR FALLS IN LOVE. JUDGE TAKES THE CAKE. MISTRIAL ORDERED AND MURDERER RELEASED. Now what do you do? File the cake in the court record and embarrass her in front of the whole court?"

"The law doesn't really require me to go to that length." He handed pieces to Linda and Jackie, who ate enthusiastically.

"Fast thinking," Jackie observed. "It's a good thing we ate the cake. It would have messed up the file. Still, the law says any gift valued over two dollars must be reported to the government and handed over to an official."

"But I shared the cake with both of you. That makes you an accessory, or an accomplice."

"You're lucky. I won't say anything this time. Besides, the cake wasn't worth that much."

"Thank you, Madame Escoffier."

"Who's she?"

"The wife of a famous chef. I'm going down to court."

"But Monsieur le Juge," protested Parent, "I have an envelope for you too."

"Who from?"

"Number two, Rita Belleville. She's the student who sits in the first row right near you." He handed Berne a grey envelope, and remained standing in front of the desk.

"Why don't you go into the outer office and join Jackie and Linda for a coffee, while I read the note?"

Parent was disappointed at the suggestion that he leave, but couldn't think of a good reason why he shouldn't. Sam Berne opened the envelope.

Monsieur le Juge,
During the weekend I heard that my Marketing class at Concordia University will have an exam next Thursday. I won't have

time to study, and don't know if you will allow me time off to write the exam. This is my last year, and I'm worried. Do you think you can give me a note for my professor?

Rita Belleville
Juror number two

P.S. I would concentrate much better if you can give me a note today.

The note had been prepared with care and typed. Judge Berne decided to respond immediately. He called Jackie and dictated a letter to Rita's professor. When it was ready, he handed it to Parent and directed him to go back downstairs, show a copy to each of the lawyers, and if they approved, to personally hand the letter to juror number two. Bolstered by the confidence placed in him, Parent left to perform his assignment.

* * *

Until the previous year, Roger Lebrun had lived in the suburbs and knew very little about the east end of Montreal. As an engineering student at McGill University, he had attended classes in the heart of the city, but rarely ventured east of St. Denis Street. After graduation Roger worked in the property management division of the Bank of Montreal, supervising the construction of new branches in shopping centres. It was interesting work, and kept him in touch with real estate developers, architects and engineers, as well as the people in Operations.

Roger didn't intend to spend his life working for the bank, but felt that it'd be a good place to learn about construction and development. Ultimately, he planned to start his own real estate development company, but this wasn't the time.

In 1990 when the recession began, shopping centre construction faltered and then stopped completely. Roger worried about rumours that the bank would scale down its property management division. Several of the senior people were offered early retirement and others were laid off. The bank decided to not build more branches till the recession ended, but hundreds of branches around the country needed renovation. This was the best time to do it, with contractors and skilled labour readily available and materials plentiful.

He was assigned to the team responsible for renovating branches in the area south of Sherbrooke, and personally supervised work on the Ste. Catherine Street branch, three blocks east of Alexandre-de-Sève. The job was completed a few weeks before he was summoned as a jury candidate. He remembered the corner building, which retained traces of the bank branch, the original occupant. His new familiarity with the east end helped him to relate to the events in the trial.

"Is the letter from the judge okay?" he asked Rita.

"It's what I need. I didn't expect an answer so fast, but I'm glad. The exam isn't till next week, but I don't want to take chances. This is my last year and I'd hate to fail, or have to write an exam in September. Now, the professor will give me a special exam after the trial is over."

"So you graduate in June!"

"Uh-huh."

"Any plans?"

"I was thinking about working for a while. Then, I might apply for the MBA program. But these days it's hard to find work."

"I know; even the bank has started to cut down, but you never know. I can ask a few people at the bank. No guarantees, but maybe there's something."

"Will you?"

"Sure . . . .How do you like being on a jury?"

"It's cool. Better than I expected. They take pretty good care of us, and I was surprised to get a cheque last Friday. It isn't that much, but when you're a student it helps."

"You ever visit the east end?"

"Sure, I go down to St. Denis Street now and then. They used to hold the Jazz Festival there, and I went to the St. Denis Theatre last year for the Comedy Festival. It was fun."

"Yeah, but have you been to the real east end?—You know, between St. Denis and Papineau?"

"No, I don't have a reason for going to Visitation or Alexandre-de-Sève. You've been to those places?"

"I worked there for about six months, supervising the renovation and remodelling of the branch a few blocks from where the fortune telling parlour apparently was."

"That should help you understand the case."

"You want me to give you a tour?"

"Would you?"

"Sure. Let's go after court today."

*   *   *

Judge Berne entered the courtroom alone. It felt strangely empty without the jury. After everyone sat down he announced, "I received a note from juror number two. The note and my answer have been shown to the attorneys, and will be filed as Exhibit J-2."

After the note was read, Linda opened the door and called to Parent, "The jury, please."

The audience stood once again as the jury filed in.

"Good morning ladies and gentlemen," Berne said. "I trust you had a good weekend." They mumbled 'good morning' in unison. Rita, in the second chair, just to the left of the judge, mouthed a silent 'thank you'.

"This morning, Maître Marie-Lyse Lortie will cross-examine Madame Vinet. Maître Lortie."

"Madame Vinet," Lortie began, "I know it must be difficult for you to be here, but you understand, I am obliged to ask you a few questions."

"Yes."

"You described yourself as a retired fortune teller?"

"Yes."

"And by that you mean that you tell people what to expect in the future?"

"Sort of."

"Did you have any special training or education for that profession?"

"No. there's no school for fortune tellers."

"Did you learn by working for another fortune teller?"

"No. That's not the way you become a fortune teller."

"How do you?"

"How do you what?"

"How do you become a fortune teller?"

"Well, it just sort of happens, . . . or at least it just sort of happened to me. Everyone wants to know about tomorrow! We all think about the future, and make guesses. If the guesses are almost right, or sometimes right, people start to think you can see the future and ask you all sorts of questions. That's what happened to me. I didn't always tell fortunes for money, but like I said yesterday—no, Friday—when I couldn't sell my jewellery and needed money, and people offered to pay me to predict the future, it just sort of happened."

"Did you use cards, tea leaves, crystal balls, or any other objects to help you tell the future?"

"Oh, I tried them all. People feel better when they see that you have something like that. It looks scientific, but really those things don't help much. The best help was when I just looked at the customer and listened. After a while I'd lean back, close my eyes and think. Then it would happen."

"What?"

"Something would come into my mind and I would start to talk. I always spoke slowly when I told fortunes. It makes people stay longer, and sounds more serious. Then they pay more money. It's sort of like lawyers: the longer the customer stays in your office, the more you get paid."

"Please return to the fortune telling."

"It was easier if I knew something about my customer. That's why I used the cards and the crystal ball. I would talk to the customers and see what they had to tell me, while I stared at the ball or played with the cards. After they told me something about themselves, I'd pretend to go into a trance and predict the future."

"Did you always predict good things?"

"I tried, because it made them happy, and they pay more for good news than bad news. But sometimes . . . . "

"Yes?"

"Sometimes bad news would just pop into my head, and come out of my mouth, almost by itself. I always felt funny after that happened, tired, very tired."

"Did you ever predict that someone would die?"

"Sure, people often came to ask about sick relatives they knew were dying. I would predict what they said was going to happen, and when it did, they were impressed."

"What if the patient didn't die?"

"I could always say it would happen later. Everyone dies some day."

"Did you ever predict that someone who seemed well and healthy would die young?"

"No . . . .I don't remember . . . no . . . .Yes, now I remember; it happened once or twice by accident."

"What do you mean, *by accident?*"

"It was one of those times when I closed my eyes and this just popped into my head."

"Did you predict someone would be killed by his child?"

"Who told you??"

"Answer the question please."

"I don't remember."

"You do remember. Answer the question."

"No."

Turning to the judge, Marie-Lyse Lortie asked, "Would you please order the witness to answer the question?"

"Madame Vinet," Judge Berne said, "do you remember this kind of incident?"

"Yes."

"Then you must answer."

Pauline Vinet breathed heavily and remained silent for a minute. Then she began speaking in a monotone. "Years ago, a man came to see me, and talked about his son. I remember because customers usually talked about hockey games and business, and jobs, and their girlfriends. They almost never talked about their children, but this man did. He said that his son had killed his mother and now he was afraid he'd do the same to him."

"Did you ask how old the son was when this happened?"

"No."

"Did you ask any other questions?"

"No, I was too scared. If the son had killed his mother, the father must have been in great danger. I told him to protect himself, or something terrible might happen. I remember that I was very frightened because I didn't quite understand what was happening."

"And?"

"The man became angry. He ran out and didn't even pay me!"

"Did he ever come back?"

"Never."

"Had you seen him before that day?"

"I don't know."

"Can you describe the man?"

"No, except he made me feel . . . uneasy."

"What was his name?"

"I don't know."

"Was it Marcel?"

"I don't know. It could have been almost any name. My customers didn't tell me their names."

"Was it Marcel Tremblay?"

"No. I don't know. Stop, please stop. I don't know." Pauline began crying softly. She reached for the glass on the table in front of her, and sipped slowly.

"Are you able to continue, Madame Vinet?" the judge asked.

"Yes, I think so. I think so." She sniffed.

"Do you want me to adjourn the court for a few minutes?"

"No, I just want to get this over with. I'm okay now."

"Continue."

Marie-Lyse had pushed this line of questioning as far as she could without arousing the jury against her client. She decided to change topics. "Let's talk about the fortune telling salon. How was it furnished?"

"Like I said last week, there was a counter with some jewellery in the front, and in the back there was a curtain, and a table and chairs."

"Yes, that's what you said. I don't want to be indiscrete, but please, when you had sex in the salon with Coco, did you do it on the chair, on the table, or perhaps on the floor?"

"What do you think? We used the couch."

"The couch?"

"Yes."

"But," Lortie persisted, "you told me that there was a counter in the front, and there was a table and chairs, and a curtain in the back. You didn't mention a couch. Was there a couch as well?"

"Yes."

"So you didn't tell the complete truth when you said there was only a table and chairs in the back. Why didn't you mention the couch when you were first asked?"

"Well, the customers were only allowed in the front of the store, where the counter was, . . . and in the part of the back where there was a table and chairs. They couldn't see the couch because I hung the curtain a few feet from the wall, and put an old couch I brought from my flat behind the curtain. It wasn't for the customers and you couldn't see it when the curtain was closed. It was private, for me to take a rest when I got tired, and not for customers. That's why I didn't think of it as part of the store or the salon."

"So you used the couch to take a rest, and to have sex with Coco. Was it used to have sex with any of the other customers? Did you sell them the right to have sex with you on the couch?"

"What are you saying?! Who do you think you are, asking me such questions?! I'm not on trial here, and the men I sleep with are none of your business."

Talbot rose, saying, "My Lord—"

"Just one minute," Judge Berne said. "I suggest that everyone calm down. Madame Vinet, Maître Lortie has the right to ask you these questions because the subject of the fortune telling salon is relevant. You must answer the questions." He turned towards Lortie before continuing, "And I am sure that Maître Lortie will not ask any more questions than are necessary to protect the interests of her client . . . .Now Maître Talbot, I believe you were about to make an objection?"

"Thank you, My Lord, your comments make the objection unnecessary." He sat down.

"Continue please."

Marie-Lyse Lortie pressed on. "Did you sell men the right to have sex with you on the couch in the back of the store?"

"No. I'm not a whore, and I resent what you're saying."

"Did you have sex on the couch with any men other than Coco?"

"In the store? "

"In the store or in the salon."

"Yes, but not for money. I never slept with a man for money in my life, I only did it with men I loved—well, liked."

"Please, I'm asking about the salon. Did you have sex with men other than Coco on the couch in the back of your store?"

"Yes, but I won't tell you their names."

"Did you have sex with Marcel Tremblay?"

"No . . . I don't remember. I told you I don't remember that name."

"Do you remember the names of any of the other men?"

"Some, maybe, but I don't have to tell you."

"It's not necessary, but would you please tell me the circumstances? Were these friends, like Coco, who just happened to drop in? Or were they jewellery customers, or neighbours?"

"Well, I told you that I was a fortune teller, and some of the men who came to see me were so lonely, and I felt badly for them, . . . and when I felt bad and . . . .They were young . . . .Sometimes I opened the curtain and they'd see the couch and then we . . . ."

"Had sex?"

"Yes, but I was really just helping them, and I like to help people and—"

"And you always like to be with men?"

"As a matter of fact yes . . . and I'm sure you do too!"

"My Lord!" Lortie said, "would you please tell the witness not to make personal comments about the attorneys."

"Ladies and gentlemen, please disregard the last comment. Madame Vinet, I appreciate that this is difficult, but try to answer the questions and not make comments about the lawyer."

* * *

Now what the hell does that mean, Rick wondered. Does she or doesn't she? Only her boyfriend knows—if she has one. Marie-Lyse really isn't bad looking. If it wasn't for Lucy I could be interested. That Marie-Lyse is tough, fights like a tiger. Fun to watch. This trial is developing into a real good show. Too bad Lucy's sitting in front and not beside me. Thought about her all weekend. Just didn't know how to reach her. Don't even know her last name—yet.

He turned to the side. Look at this guy, Rousseau. Takes notes constantly. What does he think he'll do with all those notes, write a book? After a witness stops talking, he still writes for two or three minutes. Different strokes for different folks. The judge just said it's time for a break; time for Rousseau to rest his fingers and get another notebook.

* * *

As they entered the jury room Phil Pasquin stood at the end of the table looking at his fellow jurors. He did up the button on the inside of his double-breasted jacket, straightened his shoulders and returned to the corridor. He approached Parent.

"Officer, the members of the jury chose me as their foreman, and my first job is to arrange to have lunch again at Le Vieux Port. How do you think I should approach the judge?"

This initiative to choose a foreman must have been influenced by television. Normally a judge instructs the jury to select someone for the role at the end of the trial, but in this case it wouldn't be necessary.

"Approach the judge! Is that what you just said?"

"Yes, sure. How else can I talk to him? Look, I've been in business for more than twenty years, and the first lesson I learned was, If you want something, ask the person who can give it to you. Nothing like the direct approach."

"Monsieur Pasquin, this is a court and not a business. Even though you're the foreman, there are only two ways to communicate with the judge. Either you tell me and I do it for you, or you write him a note and put it in an envelope, which I deliver. The judge doesn't speak to jurors in private."

"I see. No wonder everything takes so long to accomplish in the courthouse. If I had to write notes to everyone in my business, I'd never have built up Mondo Uomo. You've heard of Mondo Uomo, haven't you? Best little chain of exclusive men's boutiques in the city. Built it all by myself. You ever been in one of our stores?"

"No."

"Well, Parent, next time you need a suit, call and I'll give you a special deal. Here's my card. Just call and I'll get someone to take care of you at the boutique of your choice. Now, the members of the jury are counting on me; how do I arrange the lunch?"

"Monsieur Pasquin, I have a lot of experience in these matters. It's too late for today, but I'll speak to the judge and see what I can do for tomorrow. When were you chosen foreman?"

"This morning, just before we started. Can you tell the judge?"

"No problem. I'll let him know."

"What about my place? I think it would be better if I changed places with number three. That way I'd be in the centre of the first row. Right now, I'm at the end, near your chair."

"Sorry, but jurors don't change places. You were chosen as number six and that's your number and place till the end of the trial."

"Okay, but don't let me down on tomorrow's lunch." Funny place, this court, Pasquin thought. They don't know how to get things done. Rigid, overstaffed. Could use a good entrepreneur to whip things into shape. He was proud the jury had chosen him foreman. He considered himself a leader and tried to dress and act like one. That's how he built his business, and that's the way he'd expand when the recession was over.

Many of his competitors had gone under in the past year and a half, but not Mondo Uomo. Pasquin had seen problems coming and made the right moves. The company had drastically reduced its purchases of imports from Italy and Germany. He had gone to Europe, selected and bought cloth, and had the suits manufactured to his specifications by a local contractor. They were sold under the Barcello label.

The contractor was paid twenty dollars a suit more than he asked but Pasquin insisted on top quality work. He inspected the first order personally, and rejected about a quarter of the suits. The contractor got the message, and now things were in good shape.

It was the right move. The market for imported suits had collapsed. Few people were willing to pay a thousand to fifteen hundred dollars for a Canali, Belvest, or Brioni suit. The volume just wasn't there. The customers wanted cheaper suits—five hundred dollars or less—and the Barcello label was right for the times. Of course, he knew the difference and continued to wear Canali suits. The boutiques maintained a small inventory of imported garments for special customers. It was important to keep lines to foreign suppliers open. Markets change and recessions don't last forever.

He'd learned a long time ago not to fight the weatherman or the customers. There's no real spring season in Montreal, winter ends and summer arrives the same day. Business was always slow at this time of year so he didn't mind being on a jury. Now that he was foreman—

"I'm glad you were chosen. I'm Bernard Richer. Be good to have a businessman in charge."

"What do you do?" Pasquin asked.

"Oh, I'm retired now. Used to have a small business of my own — typewriter sales and maintenance. Couple of salesmen, and servicemen out on the road. I sold out ten years ago. Once computers took off there was no way to compete, and I was getting tired. I'm sixty-eight; could have been exempted, but I thought it would be a good experience. After all, I have the time."

"I made the time," Pasquin boasted. "When you run a business you have to know how to manage time. Made the time in order to be a good

146

citizen. My father would have been proud. He came to this country with nothing. Antonio Pasquini. Worked hard all his life, as a tile man. He managed to give us a good education. 'Be your own boss,' the old man said. 'That way you can't be fired.' I took his advice, and look where I am today. Three boutiques: Place Montreal Trust, Place Bonaventure and Galleries Rockland. He'd be proud that I'm foreman of a jury."

"How long do you think the trial will last?"

"Hard to tell. We're all new at this. Maybe the judge will tell us soon. If he doesn't, I'll send him a note . . . .Guess it depends on the defence. I think the Crown is almost finished."

"You're right. Did you do anything about the meals?"

"Sure did. Spoke to Parent and told him what to tell the judge. I'd speak to him myself, but it's not permitted. They have these rules. Must spend their lives writing and studying rules. Don't have to worry about the bottom line like businessmen."

* * *

"You said that you had an operation," Marie-Lyse Lortie repeated to the witness. "Can you tell us when that was?"

Pauline touched her hand in a feigned dramatic gesture. "Five years ago, at the Cardiology Institute. It was a serious operation, a bypass. You know. They explained it: first they cut me open like a lobster, and then they change the pipes to my heart like a plumber. I laugh now, but it was very serious. For months I was sore and didn't go out. Alexandre was home when it happened, and he helped me. Caroline was only seven at the time. But now, I'm good again."

"What happened to your business while you were in the hospital, and after, when you came home?"

"I closed the salon. I was too sick to work. There was no one else, and no money for the rent for the store. The landlord didn't bother to sue me. That's when I started to get money from the Welfare. We had no money and I had to do something, so I asked the Welfare and they gave me some money. Alexandre brought things home once in a while,

147

like a television set and a VCR, but the money from the Welfare was what we used to buy food. It wasn't easy after the operation."

"Was your relationship with men affected?"

"Hey, it was my heart that was broken, not my . . . .Yes, it was not the same after. You know, I'm fifty-three now, and at the time I was forty-eight. Men don't like the older women. Besides, I was sick and I had two children. Men didn't find me the same. I didn't have a regular man . . . until Maurice came to live with me."

"Do you love Maurice?"

"I don't know if I love him, but we live together and he's good to me, and—"

"Do you worry about losing him?—that he'll go away,or—"

"I guess so. He's not the best man, but he's a man, and like I said, he's good to me. And you know, it's not easy at my age to get a young man, especially when you're not well and had a heart operation—and also Caroline."

Phil Pasquin fidgeted in his seat. First that woman boasts about her exploits as a young woman, and now as an old whore. The way she talks about Coco! No wonder they have problems in the police force, with women like her tempting cops away from their work. Still, give her credit, she went to work. Tried to be an entrepreneur, opening the jewellery store. Didn't have a chance to succeed, but at least she tried. She got into all this trouble because of sex. Couldn't keep her eyes off that cop.

Not that he was a prude or didn't believe in sex, but Pasquin just couldn't understand why people talk about it in public all the time. Why involve the whole world in their private affairs? Sex should be private, and at the right time and place. That's how it was in his family.

" . . . so you must have been very happy when Maurice moved in."

"Yes, I was."

"When Serge moved in, were you worried it might affect your relationship with Maurice?"

"When Serge moved into my house, I was worried about everything. He's nothing but trouble."

"And you hate him?"

"I don't know, but I sure don't like him."

"And you would do whatever is necessary to get him out of your house?"

"I had no choice! He was trouble, for me and Maurice and Caroline. I had to call the police and get him arrested!"

"Madame Vinet, can you tell me why you left a display case with a few articles of jewellery in the front of your store, when you weren't able to sell any?"

"I thought I'd sell some, especially in the beginning."

"And in the end?"

"Well, after a while . . . the jewellery business wasn't for me, and like I told you, I became busy with the fortune telling."

"Precisely. So why didn't you get rid of the jewellery counter, and make a more comfortable salon for your customers? Why did you continue to display jewellery in the window?"

Rick turned restlessly in his seat. Come on, Marie-Lyse, he thought to himself. What do you expect a fortune teller and hooker to put in the store window? Stop being naive and underestimating the jurors. We weren't born yesterday. Get on with the case. You were doing so well earlier, but now you're slipping.

"Some people don't like fortune tellers," the witness continued, "and I thought it'd be better if it looked like a jewellery store."

"Were you trying to hide your business from the police?"

"No, no. I told you, Coco knew all about me, and he came to visit."

"Did any other policemen visit you?"

"Sometimes . . . not often. Sometimes they were going to do something dangerous, and wanted me to tell their fortune. They never told me, but I knew."

"Do you have a criminal record?"

"No, of course not. Do you think I would do something not legal?"

Lortie ignored the rhetorical question. "Why is your son Alexandre in jail?"

"He was convicted of armed robbery. Mind you he wasn't guilty. He was with friends and they held up a grocery store. Alexandre was in the car, and didn't even go into the store, but when they were caught, the police made a charge against him, and he was sent to jail."

"Do you know if Maurice was involved in the robbery?"

"No, he wasn't. Alexandre met him in jail. I don't think they knew each other before."

"Do you know why Maurice was in jail?"

"He said he was in a fight or something. I don't know."

"You seem to know more about people's futures than you do about the past."

"I don't predict the past. I only know what people tell me."

"And you believe them?"

"Not always."

"Did you always believe Maurice Pomerleau?"

"No. He tries to tell the truth, but sometimes—"

"No further questions."

"Madame Vinet," Judge Berne said, "thank you for coming to court . . . .Can we release this witness?" Both attorneys nodded agreement. "You are now free to go."

"Do you mean that I don't have to come back and answer more questions?"

"Yes, it's over. You can leave."

"Thank you, thank you," she said with a smile. She gathered her purse and sweater, and walked to the back of the room. Just before leaving she turned again and called, "Thank you, thank you. If I ever need a lawyer, Mr. Talbot, I'll come back and see you!" Then Pauline D. Vinet disappeared into the hall.

* * *

As they returned to the office upstairs Sam asked Linda, "Would you like Pauline D. Vinet to predict your future?"

"No. I don't go to people like that. She's just like . . . like *Le Journal* said."

150

Jackie heard them talking as they walked down the hall. "How's the trial going?"

"A little slow, and not so easy, but . . . not bad. It's a pleasure to have Linda back. At least she knows my name."

Linda smiled. "And a lot more than that! I haven't been working with you for four years for nothing."

"You're right . . . . Jackie, where in the world is that book I'm waiting for? Did you call downstairs again?"

"Relax, relax. You sit quietly in court all day long and convince everyone you're calm and patient; then you come up and go crazy over some book . . . . .I got you a present. It's in your office."

It was a framed certificate inscribed in large print,

DEAR GOD,

TEACH ME TO BE PATIENT,

AND . . . DO IT QUICKLY!

The trial would unfold at its own rhythm, and the book would arrive when Judicial Support Services wished; there was little he could do.

8

An expectant air permeated the room as Maurice Pomerleau entered. The jury had been looking at the accused since the beginning of the trial, and had spent a day and a half listening to the testimony of Pauline D. Vinet. Now they would see and hear the last member of this unlikely threesome.

Maurice was slim, of medium height, with short light blond hair and slouched shoulders. As the clerk administered the oath he stood in the witness box, eyes lowered, without the slightest acknowledgement of the presence of other people in the courtroom. Judge Berne gestured with the open palm of his right hand for Maurice to remain standing.

Talbot began to question the witness. "Do you know Madame Pauline Vinet?"

"Yeah."

"How long have you known her?"

"Not long."

"What is your relationship with her?"

"Live together."

"You share a flat?"

"Yeah."

"And a bed?"

"Sometimes."

"Who introduced you to her?"

"Alex."

"Alex who?"

"Vinet."

"So, Alex Vinet introduced you to his mother, Pauline?"

"Yeah."

"When?"

"Last year."

"Where?"

"Where what?"

"Where were you introduced to her?"

"Jail."

"Was Pauline Vinet in jail with you?"

"Naw. Visiting Alex."

"Do you work?"

"No."

"Are you looking for work?"

"Naw."

These young people!, Bernard Richer thought. Not like years ago. In those days if you didn't work, you'd starve. When I quit school and went to work at the office furniture company, I started in the shipping room. After a few years they saw the potential, and gave me a course in typewriter repair. Worked there almost twenty years before I started my own business. We knew what it meant to work.

These kids live off welfare, unemployment insurance, stealing, drugs and women. In my day we had a word for men who lived off women. Don't know what they call it today, but it's still not right. If Maurice was on trial, I'd know what to do with him! I was married at twenty-three. Soon Isabel was pregnant. God I miss her; it's hard to believe two years have passed since she died. She was sixty-five, and had just started to receive her pension cheques. Here I am, alone in Montreal—kids have moved west. It's not easy to live alone and retired. The worst thing is the loneliness. I'm glad they chose me for the jury; it's good being with people, eating together and talking—darn good.

"Mr. Pomerleau, do you know the accused, Serge Tremblay?"
"Yeah."
"How long have you known him?"
"Few years."
"Where did you meet?"
"Around."
"Did you ever go out together?"
"Yeah."
"Where?"
"Places."
"What kind of places?"
"I dunno . . . .Bars and places."
"So you would meet in a bar?"
"Think so."
"Which one?"
"Dunno."
"Do you remember the street where the bar was?"
"Maybe St. Denis. Maybe Ste. Catherine . . . ."

I can see why he gets along so well with Pauline, Rick thought. She never shuts her mouth, and he never opens his. Great couple! Maybe that's why she says he's good to her: lets her speak all she wants, and doesn't mix in. The good news is that the trial won't be delayed by this guy. Says so little that for the first time since the trial began, Rousseau has a chance to look up from his notes! The bad news is that we have to listen to him at all. 'Yeah, Naw, No.'; should add a *Maybe* to spice things up. Where do they find these losers? They give the east end a bad reputation! I don't see why people should be taken away from their jobs to listen to these nuts.

"Did you see the accused on October seventh of last year?" Talbot asked.
"Yeah."
"Explain the circumstances, please."
"He came home late; woke me up."
"Did he say anything?"
"Yeah, he said a guy on St.Denis might have been killed."

"Which guy?"

"A guy. He didn't say."

"Who did you think he meant?"

"I dunno."

"Did he say anything else?"

"Don't remember."

"Where were you when this happened?"

"In bed."

"Where? At what location?"

"Bedroom."

"In what house, or place?"

"Pauline's, Visitation Street."

"Who lives there?"

"Pauline, her kid Caroline, me."

"Anyone else?"

"Sometimes Alex."

"Anyone else?"

"No."

"Do you know where the accused, Serge Tremblay, lives?"

"Think he's in jail."

"And, where was he before he moved to jail?"

"Slept at Pauline's a week or so."

"Is that all?"

"Two, maybe three, maybe more. I dunno."

"And, you live with Pauline Vinet, don't you?"

"Yeah."

"Once again, what did he say on the night of October seventh?"

"He said a guy on St. Denis might've been killed."

"And where were you on the night of October seventh?"

"In bed, like I said."

"Before going to bed?"

"Dunkin' Donuts. Went late at night. Pauline couldn't sleep so we had a donut. Anything wrong with that?"

* * *

He's scared, Francine Roux thought, scared out of his wits. That's why he won't look up or speak much. I know; see it all the time in Ron's office. He's like those people who find out they need an operation. Either they babble like Pauline, or they clam up like Maurice. I wonder what the others on the jury think. Of course they may not have the same experience with fear. Doctors deal with these situations all the time, but businessmen, students, the others— they don't live with death the way Ron and I do.

Ron wasn't happy when I got the subpoena for jury duty, but I wanted to do it. Said he needed me in the office, but really, he only has office hours two days a week. He's so busy at Hotel Dieu Hospital. So many accident cases there, with the fights and shootings that happen, especially on St. Denis..

I understand Pauline's fixation about street names changing. In '78, after Ron became known as a neurosurgeon and we bought our home in Outremont, the city changed the name of our street. Fortunately we didn't have to change Ron's stationery because we had a corner lot with his office entrance facing Lajoie, but it was a nuisance. The children got all mixed up, and some people thought we had moved. There are enough problems in life without street names changing all the time to confuse people.

Pauline has bigger problems than street names though. Imagine!—no job, a daughter of twelve, a lover who's thirty years younger, a son in jail, and a murderer moves into the house and scares everyone half to death. What a life. Funny—they live on Visitation and receive an unwanted visitor.

* * *

"Do you have a criminal record?"

"Yeah."

"What crimes were you convicted of?"

"Assault, robbery—the usual."

"Can you be more specific, dates, years?"

"I don't remember everything."

"My Lord," Talbot offered, "if the defence wishes, we'll produce a computer printout of the witness's record. Maître Lortie already has a copy."

"The jury will also want this information," Marie-Lyse indicated.

"Maître Talbot, please continue."

"No further questions."

After the jury had withdrawn for the afternoon break, the judge asked, "Maître Talbot, how much longer do you expect the Crown's case will take?"

"I have one more witness: Sergeant Claude Martin. He won't take long."

"Maître Lortie, if you intend to call witnesses for the defence, please arrange to have your first witness available tomorrow. I expect the attorneys to be ready with their closing arguments to the jury the day after the hearing of witnesses is completed."

"Yes, Monsieur le Juge," they answered in unison.

"Thank you. We'll adjourn for fifteen minutes."

* * *

Francine walked over to talk to Rita Belleville and Roger Lebrun. "Betty told me you got your letter from the judge. You really don't have to worry. My husband teaches at the University of Montreal Medical School, and I know they would never penalize a student for serving on a jury. What are you studying?"

"Commerce. I'll be graduating in June. Roger thinks he might be able to help get me a job. Do you know Roger, Roger Lebrun?"

"Of course. He sits right in front of me. That's good of you, Roger."

"Well, there's no guarantee they'll offer her something, but I can get her an interview."

"Do you think Tremblay will testify?" Francine asked. "Remember, the judge said he doesn't have to."

"Hard to defend yourself with your mouth shut," Lebrun replied. "Like building a house without tools: possible, but not easy."

"We'll know soon," Rita said. "I can only say that Maurice, our last witness, sure is a creep."

Phil Pasquin walked over and joined the group. "Just wanted to thank you personally for choosing me foreman. You hardly know me; in fact we all hardly know each other. It's like a cruise. People from different places are together for a week or so. The twelve of us sit in court, eat at the same table, and who knows what else . . . ." He left off in mid-sentence and glanced overtly at Rick Hayes and Lucy Morin in the corner of the jury room.

"C'mon Phil," Francine admonished him. "We elected you foreman, not chaperone. Really, in this day and age . . . ."

"It's like business," Pasquin said. "You don't get involved in everything, but if you know the facts, it's easier to make the right decision."

Rick Hayes could feel Pasquin eying him up and down. "Who the hell does he think he is?" he asked Lucy. "We made a mistake electing that jerk foreman. Acts like he owns the courthouse. Look at him, staring like he wants me to unpack a box of ties. We would've been better off with Francine Roux. She's smart, knows what she wants, and doesn't bother me. Betty Major would have been good too. But that fancy clothing salesman will drive us crazy."

"Rick," Lucy taunted, "are you trying to say you'd be happy with a woman foreman? What about me? I'm a woman, and you didn't want me . . . as foreman."

"Cut it, Lucy. We're going to have to live together for a few days."

"You and me?"

"No, the jury, all of us. And that jerk Pasquin is not going to give me orders. There's trouble ahead if he thinks he's going to decide this case for me; watch out. Pasquin may know how to manoeuver inside a fancy shopping centre, but he wouldn't last too long on St. Denis Street. One look at that fancy suit, and they'd steal his wallet."

"Rick, you're jealous."

"Of him?"

"Yes. Maybe you wanted to be foreman and give orders?"

"No way! I do my own thing. Still, I think either Francine or Betty would've been a better choice."

"I don't. Pasquin will be okay. You'll see."

"Maybe," Rick said reluctantly. "Lucy, I wanted to call you on the weekend. I still don't know your number. Don't even know your full name! Lucy . . . who?"

"Lucy Morin," she replied.

"And your number?"

"791-3043."

* * *

Parent was hovering around the courtroom entrance awaiting the judge's return. "Monsieur le Juge," he said excitedly, "I know who the foreman is."

"Not number twelve?"

"Non, it's number six, Phil Pasquin. Sits at the end of the row, and wears a new suit every day."

"Did he tell you?"

"Yes, and he wants a favour."

"What is it?"

"They want to eat at the restaurant tomorrow. He thinks it'd be good for his position if he's able to get the favour from you."

"And you told him you'd try to convince me, and it would be good for your standing as well?"

"No . . . ." He broke into a smile. "Yes, Monsieur le Juge. It would help, and you know, it's no more expensive than eating in the cafeteria."

"Call the restaurant and make a reservation for tomorrow . . . and tell the foreman you had a tough time with me."

"I will, I will. Thank you Monsieur le Juge," he said. bowing slightly.

* * *

159

"Constable Parent is signalling us," Lebrun said, "to go into the hall. I'm curious to see Lortie work on Maurice."

"Me too," Pasquin added as the jury filed back into court.

Marie-Lyse Lortie began the cross-examination. "Mr. Pomerleau, you said you were twenty-two years old?"

"Uh-huh."

"And you left school relatively early?"

"Uh-huh."

"Monsieur Pomerleau," the judge interjected, "the microphones around the courtroom are recording everything you say. Please answer yes or no and not *uh-huh*. Otherwise, after it's typed, they won't know if you said yes, or no. Do you understand?"

"Uh-huh . . . .Yes."

"Continue please, Maître Lortie."

"At what age did you leave school?"

"Fifteen."

"And have you been working since that time?"

"Sometimes."

"Please tell the jury all the jobs you've held during the past seven years."

"All?"

"Yes, all."

"I worked now and then delivering things for a pizza place, and a drug store. Worked on construction one summer when I was seventeen, and once I worked in a store but they laid me off."

"You left school when you were fifteen and you are now twenty-two. That's seven years. You haven't described much work for a seven-year period. Just how many months or years did you work during that period?"

"I dunno. Maybe a year or two."

"Are you sure?"

"Naw. Didn't count. Why should I?"

"What did you do the rest of the time? How did you earn money to support yourself?"

"I was in prison part of the time. Maybe two years or so . . . .I sort of did things."

"Illegal things? Like holding up small grocery stores and selling drugs . . . and robbing people?"

"Do I have to answer those questions?" he asked the judge.

"Yes, you do. Your testimony can't be used against you in a criminal prosecution. So answer."

"I forgot the question."

"I asked you," Marie-Lyse repeated, "whether you had held up small grocery stores and robbed people and sold some drugs."

"Yeah, but not hard drugs."

"So most of the time since you left school, either you were in prison or you supported yourself by committing crimes?"

"Not always. I worked sometimes, and sometimes I got paid by the Welfare—and then there's unemployment insurance."

"And sometimes older women took care of you, and let you live in their homes?"

"Objection," Talbot called out.

"I withdraw the question."

*   *   *

Phil Pasquin tried to stare into the eyes of the witness, but Maurice avoided eye contact by looking down at the table in front of him. Pasquin felt insulted. That punk can't give a straight answer. Can't even look a man in the eye. He wouldn't last ten minutes in my business; I'd kick his butt and throw him out. He's not even good enough for Pauline Vinet. Bad influence on her kid, Caroline, sponges off Pauline's welfare payments, and invites Tremblay, the accused, into the house . . . .Better get used to calling him *the accused*. The foreman of the jury should use the right terms, . . . just like business. You have to know what you want, and use the right words to ask for it, or you end up with something else.

Phil Pasquin wasn't bothered that Maurice and Serge were gay. There are millions of gay people in the world, especially in the prisons.

What do people expect when all those men are locked up together? Some jurors might want to find Tremblay guilty because he's gay, but as foreman Pasquin wouldn't let that happen.

As for Maurice, it'd be hard to respect him, the way he lived off other people and couldn't do anything for himself. Anyhow, Maurice isn't on trial; Tremblay is—and we don't know a thing about him! Well, he'll probably testify later and the jury will get a chance to size him up.

*　　*　　*

"In your examination by Maître Talbot, you said that on occasion you met Serge Tremblay, the accused, in a bar?"

"Yeah."

"What bar?"

"I said I don't remember."

"Please try to remember. It's important."

"Can't remember. Some place on St. Denis."

"Was it Le Wiz?"

"Naw. Didn't start going there till after I got out of jail."

"When was that?"

"September."

"Did you ever go to Le Wiz with Tremblay?"

"Maybe."

"What does that mean? Either you went with him or you didn't."

"I said maybe."

"*Maybe* isn't good enough; I want an answer."

"Yeah, I went with him once or twice."

"Once, or twice . . . or three times?"

"Maybe three times, but not more."

"Did Pauline go with you to Le Wiz?"

"No."

"Did you go to Le Wiz with the accused after you were living with Pauline?"

"I think so."

"I want a straight answer. Did you or didn't you?"

"Yes, I did."

"Does Pauline know that while you were living with her you went to Le Wiz with the accused?"

"Serge wasn't living with us. He just sort of spent a night or two."

"That's not what I asked you. Were you living with Pauline Vinet when you went to Le Wiz with Serge?"

"Yes."

"Do you go to St. Denis Street bars often?"

"Not like I used to."

"What does that mean?"

"I used to go a lot, before I was sent to jail. After I got out I moved in with Pauline, and now I don't go out so much at night."

"What do you mean when you say you don't go out much at night?" Lortie asked.

"I mean I don't go out much—like, to bars and places. With Pauline—we only go out to eat, but hardly ever for drinks. She doesn't drink, you know."

"Monsieur le Juge," Lortie said, "it's almost 4:30, and I am about to change subjects. May I suggest that we adjourn now?"

Pomerleau turned sideways and looked in the direction of the accused. For the first time since beginning to testify, his eyes fixed upon Tremblay. The two faced each other, frozen by a strange hypnotic spell, oblivious to the people in the courtroom. Pomerleau's lips moved slightly, as though he were about to speak. An eerie oppressive silence permeated the courtroom, till Constable Demers touched the prisoner's elbow. Tremblay looked down at his arm for a second. When he looked up again, Pomerleau had turned his head and started to leave. Only a few of the jury members noticed the silent exchange.

*　*　*

Phil Pasquin felt it was time to establish a relationship with Rick Hayes. After all, a foreman had to work with all of his people, including those he didn't like. From the corner of his eye he'd seen Lucy Morin go into the washroom and decided to make a move while Rick was alone.

"Just thought you should be the first to know: I sent Parent to speak to the judge, so we can eat in the restaurant tomorrow."

"Good! It's nice to get out....Why you telling me like this? Is there something you want from me?"

"No, I just thought you might want to know, because you and Lucy—"

"Me and Lucy what?"

"You and Lucy seemed to enjoy the last time we ate out."

"Are you watching us? Why the hell are you minding our business?"

"I'm not. Just doing my job as foreman and trying to make things a little more pleasant for everyone. Look, I don't like being here any more than you do, but I'm here, and I intend to make the best of it and do my job properly."

"Look, Pasquin, you're one of the twelve of us—no better, no worse. They made you foreman because you were wearing a fancy suit, but that doesn't give you the right to mind my business, or anyone else's. This is a trial, not a business owned by you. So leave me and Lucy alone. Understand?"

"I was only trying to be friendly."

"Friends don't meddle in my life."

"Rick, Mister Pasquin," Lucy interrupted, "did you see the way Pomerleau and Tremblay looked at each other as we left the room?"

"Yeah," Rick answered, "like old boyfriends."

"Like boyfriends? What happened?" Pasquin asked.

"It was different than I expected," Lucy continued. "Do you think maybe Pomerleau knows something he isn't saying about the murder? Remember, Pauline said that Tremblay and Pomerleau spoke a lot the night of the murder. I wonder—"

"Lucy," Rick said, "you're acting like a TV lawyer! Are you sure you drive a canteen truck?"

Pasquin muttered to himself, "I didn't see a thing! Must have been thinking about tomorrow's lunch," as he moved towards the head of the table. "Ladies and gentlemen," he announced, "attention please. Before you leave for the night I want you all to know that I sent Parent to speak to the judge, and he has arranged for us to eat at Le Vieux Port tomorrow!"

There was a murmur of approval. Bernard Richer walked over. "I knew you were the right person to be foreman. Choose a busy person, if you want something done. That's the way I ran my office equipment business, and it's still true."

"Thank you; I'm glad someone appreciates my efforts."

"We all do," Richer replied, bobbing his head up and down.

"Well, I'm not so sure about number twelve over there. All he seems to appreciate is Lucy."

"Forget him. They still don't have women in machine shops, and he might be pretty glad to be here for that reason. Spends all his time at a lathe, or in a welding booth with a metal mask over his face. Come to think of it, that could be why he wears sunglasses. Welders always wear glasses at work, and he probably feels undressed without them."

"Hey, you're pretty observant. I think you're right! . . . Did you notice the way Tremblay and Pomerleau looked at each other when the court adjourned? Very significant. Judge said we should keep our eyes open throughout the trial."

"I didn't see anything. What happened?"

"They looked at each other kind of funny. I'm not sure what that means, but it's important. We'll have to hear what the other jurors think."

"I guess I'm not concentrating enough. I'm getting older and sometimes my mind wanders."

"Don't worry about it. There are twelve of us, and me—I don't miss much! Learned in business to watch for things the other guys don't notice."

"I see why you built such a big business. If I'd been younger when computers were invented, I might have done the same thing, but after a certain age it's hard to change. Good thing I sold my business."

* * *

Francine Roux and Betty Major had been talking in the corner. Now they sauntered over and interrupted the conversation between Pasquin and Richer.

"What are you businessmen hatching?" Francine asked. "You look like you're about to make an offer to buy the Montreal Expos. Better hurry up; the opening ball game is in a few days."

"We're discussing the evidence," Pasquin said. "Very strange how Pomerleau and Tremblay looked at each other a few moments ago. What do you think?"

"I think we're dealing with a very strange group of people," Betty replied. "I spend all my time speaking to men, and those two are the pits."

"What do you mean, you spend all your time talking to men? What do you do?"

"Mr. Pasquin, don't you recognize me?"

"Oh, of course! . . . but, maybe you should tell the others what you do . . . .It's hard to describe."

"You don't remember me, Betty!" she chided. "And it's really not so hard to describe. I'm a hair stylist in the barbershop at the Four Seasons Hotel. I've seen you there several times. But you're always so busy you don't notice us."

"Well, I—"

"I know. You big businessmen don't have time to notice people working in a barbershop. You come in all worried about your business problems, and the only thing you notice is the *Playboy* magazine you pick up and start reading backwards the moment you enter."

"Betty, I'm sorry. I just didn't recognize you here. I'm sorry."

"It's all right. I'm glad we met like this. There's something I wanted to ask you."

"Shoot."

"Why do you read *Playboy* magazine backwards?"

"What?"

"Why do you always read the *Playboy* magazine backwards when you get your hair cut? The whole barbershop wants to know, and no one has the courage to ask you."

"I don't read it backwards. I just start at the end and thumb through towards the front, because I like the cartoons and they're in the back half."

"What a simple answer," Francine interjected. "And what an original way to read a magazine!"

"I never thought it was original—only convenient," said Pasquin.

"Well, it is," commented Francine. "I'm going to ask Ron, my husband, if he reads *Playboy* backwards when he has his hair cut."

"First, you better find out if he reads *Playboy*. He may be the *Penthouse* type," Betty teased.

"My husband?!" Francine exclaimed in mock horror. "Ron thinks *Penthouse* is a magazine about real estate."

"Ron? Ronald Roux, the doctor—is he your husband?" asked Betty.

"Yes. Have you heard of him?"

"Heard of him! The eminent neurosurgeon . . . with the brown hair and ever-so-small bald spot on the . . . top right-hand side of his head?"

"You know him?"

"Of course I know him. I cut his hair the first Tuesday of every month. He doesn't read *Playboy* or *Penthouse,* just lies back and closes his eyes while I cut his hair. I guess he's thinking of you, Francine."

"He'd better," she answered with a grin. "Anybody want a lift towards Outremont?"

* * *

Marie-Lyse rushed from the courtroom down to the basement where prisoners are kept till a busload is ready to return to the detention centre. Time was running out and important decisions had to be made. Some guards recognized her and smiled acknowledgement; others just glanced curiously. There isn't much privacy when six or more prisoners are crowded in a cell. Lawyers and their clients must huddle in a corner, to exchange whispered comments through the steel bars.

"What's going on between you and Maurice?" Marie-Lyse demanded.

"Half the jury saw the look you gave each other. What are you holding back?"

"I told you everything you have to know. I didn't kill Lepine. I swear I didn't."

"Were you on St. Denis Street the night of the murder?"

"Sure."

"At Le Wiz?"

"Uh-huh."

"Did you have a fight with Frank Lepine?"

"Yeah, in the bar. It wasn't much. Out on the street, he started pushing me again."

"You didn't fight back?"

"No."

"Why not?"

"I just didn't."

"Were you armed that night?"

"Yup. I had a knife, big kitchen knife. I made a sheath out of newspaper, and tucked it into my waist. It's dangerous to go to clubs without protection."

"But you didn't use the knife?"

"No."

"You just ran away?"

"Yes."

"Did you have a gun with you that night?"

"No."

"Do you own a gun?"

"Sure."

"The one in court?"

"Yeah, it's mine."

"Where was the gun that night?"

"It must have been in the hiding place at Pauline's."

"So how did a bullet get from the gun at Pauline's into Lepine's head?"

"I can't say."

"You won't say?"

"Same thing: can't say, won't say, don't say. It wasn't shot by me and that's for sure."

"Even if I believe you, what do I tell the jury? I have to tell them something. Was Maurice with you? Did he shoot Lepine?"

"I don't want to talk about Maurice. He's not on trial. I am."

"He's not helping you."

"He does what he has to."

"And you?"

"I do what I have to."

"How can I advise you to testify or not if you won't tell me the whole truth?"

"I told you the whole truth. I didn't do it."

"What will you say when they ask about your criminal record, and the death of your father?"

"I didn't kill him. He was only hurt, and it was an accident . . . .Did you say the death of my father?"

"Yes, he died a few months after you were sent to jail."

"Who told you?"

"Talbot. It's in the police files."

"They never told me, and I'm his son."

"Did you ever ask about him, or write to him?"

"No. Hey, what else do you know about me?"

"I know about your mother, Marie Tremblay. She died in the hospital three days after you were born."

"Talbot tell you that too?"

"Yes."

"How come?"

"I asked him to do me a favour and check the hospital records."

"That's what Marcel meant by *mother killer?*"

"I guess so. You didn't kill her."

"I didn't kill no one. And that's why you asked Pauline if she told Marcel's fortune?"

"Yes, but she didn't remember."

"I don't believe her. She made Marcel attack me like that. She made all this happen with her crazy prediction."

169

"I'm not sure."

"She turned my father against me even more than he was before, and you know what came of that. She took Maurice too. Now she's getting the jury all against me, and that'll really do me in."

"There's not much time to stop her from putting you away forever. What can you tell me about Maurice?"

"Nothing you don't know."

"Did you see him the night of the murder?"

"Sure. I saw him in the middle of the night when I woke him up."

"Did you see him earlier that night on St. Denis Street?"

Serge didn't answer. Marie-Lyse repeated the question.

"Time's up," a voice called. "Bus is going to Parthenais. Everybody has to leave now."

"Did you see Maurice earlier that night?" Marie-Lyse persisted.

"'Night." Serge replied. "I'll see you tomorrow. Maybe we can talk before the court opens."

"'Bye, I'll see you tomorrow." Marie-Lyse turned and muttered under her breath, "I could kill that man. Like my father used to say, he could drive a saint to drink."

9

Judge Berne was surprised to find a noisy gathering of secretaries huddled around four cardboard boxes marked COMPUTER: HAN-DLE WITH CARE on the floor in front of Jackie's desk. He knew some by name, and recognized others by appearance.

"Ladies, mesdames, what are you all doing here, in my office at 4:30 in the afternoon? Planning a birthday party? a strike? Organizing a petition to the administration about poor ventilation in the building?"

"Non, Monsieur le Juge," a voice replied, "we came to see the new computer."

"But all you can see are four cardboard boxes."

"It doesn't matter. Jackie has a new computer and we came to see it."

"Jackie, Jackie," he called, "are you there in the crowd?"

"Yes, but this is not a crowd. These are my friends and they came to welcome the new computer."

The voices all jabbered simultaneously.

"Is it a colour monitor?"

"How many Ks?"

"How many bytes?"

"Is it an IBM clone?"

"Jackie, have it checked right away. There's a new virus called Michelangelo going around. The computer factories are infected."

"You sure it's not called Botticelli?"

"No, I said it was a virus, not a Venus."

"Monsieur le Juge, do you know if it's true?"

"Ladies, ladies!" Judge Berne called. "Come back tomorrow morning, when the expert will unpack the boxes and answer your questions. Tomorrow Jackie will provide coffee, and I will be in court."

They left, calling reluctantly, "Bonsoir; bye-bye; lucky," and "au revoir."

Jackie followed him into his private office and demanded, "Why didn't you tell me?"

"Tell you what?"

"What, what! Tell me that you bought a new computer."

"I wanted to surprise you."

"Surprise me? You almost scared me to death," she gushed. "You said you'd never spend your judge's allowance to buy me a computer and—" She stopped in midsentence, walked over and put her hand on his shoulder. "Thanks. I appreciate what you've done."

Sam Berne blushed. "By the way Jackie, how did all you friends find out so quickly?"

"Oh, Monsieur le Juge, there are no secrets here in the courthouse. Cecile was in the elevator when they brought the computer up. She told Diane, and Diane shares an office with Jocelyne. Jocelyne is Debbie's best friend, and Debbie met Irma and Danny in the hall. Danny called Lolita, and Françoise and Gaby are in the office next door. They started calling me, so I invited them to come up. I knew you wouldn't mind . . . .Do you?"

"Not at all. I'm flattered by the attention, though I think they're more interested in the computer than they are in me."

"Oh, Monsieur le Juge," she assured him, "I am interested in you, and I am even more interested since the computer arrived."

* * *

172

During his ten years working in the crown office, Talbot had pleaded hundreds of cases, many before juries. Much of the work was routine: meeting police officers, interviewing witnesses, drafting written briefs, and the inevitable waiting for cases to be called. The pay didn't compensate for the long hours, but jury trials provided the excitement and notoriety that made it all worthwhile, and he was addicted to the pressure and drama of the courtroom.

The role of crown attorney is not easy. Unlike his dramatic counterparts in the media, he does not seek victory and conviction at any price. It is his duty to present all relevant evidence before the jurors, so they can determine if it is sufficient to convince them, beyond a reasonable doubt, that a crime has been committed by the accused. He is a public official who does not win or lose cases. The acquittal of an innocent person is a victory for the defence, but the Crown has not lost. Conviction of the guilty person is not a victory, but evidence of a society's failure to mould the character of the person who has turned to crime, and to protect its citizens.

Talbot knew full well that public perception of his position does not always accord with these lofty ideals, and it is not easy to adopt a dispassionate, even-handed approach to the work when the public is aroused and the investigating police officers zealously seek vindication of their theories and efforts.

He liked this case. The witnesses were more flamboyant than usual. Marie-Lyse Lortie was a strong adversary, but she had an uphill climb. He wondered what she was doing.

*　*　*

Marie-Lyse spent a restless night. Only a few hours remained for her to decide if the defence would present any witnesses. So far the jury didn't know anything about Tremblay's conviction for the attempted murder of his father, and so long as he remained silent the judge and attorneys couldn't comment on his past. If Tremblay testified, the Crown could cross-examine on his record. Why kid herself? Serge Tremblay can't take the stand because of his criminal record. She remembered the look on the faces of the jurors when Talbot asked Pomerleau about his criminal record. They were almost ready to find him guilty of murder, or at least of living off a helpless woman—which some consider just as bad.

To the jury, the facts of the case were really quite simple. Just after midnight on October sixth, Serge approached a girl at The Wiz. Lepine intervened on her behalf, and a fight erupted. The police arrived before any serious damage was caused. After the bar closed, Serge and Lepine fought again on the sidewalk outside Le Wiz. Seconds later, Lepine was gunned down, but there were no eyewitnesses to identify the murderer.

The gun carried by Serge at the time of his arrest was a problem. Well, it had been in Pauline's home, and perhaps the jury could be made to realize the gun was accessible to both Serge and Maurice. If they thought it was a possibility, and that Pauline Vinet would go to any length to get rid of Serge, maybe, just maybe, they would have a doubt and acquit him, even if he didn't testify. It was a long shot, but there might be a chance.

Is it possible Maurice was at Le Wiz, saw the fight and shot Lepine later in the street? Would Pauline know? Could she be covering for Maurice?—or does she just hate Serge and want to get him out of her house? Could the jury be convinced that Pauline and Maurice may have concocted the story to protect Maurice, or to get rid of Serge? After all, Serge had moved into her flat without permission, and Pauline hated and feared him, as a bad influence and a competitor for Maurice's attentions.

Would the jury believe that? Would they have a strong enough doubt to acquit the accused? It wouldn't be easy. Not a single witness placed Maurice on St. Denis Street on the night of the crime. He denied it and Serge won't testify against Maurice.

There was that scene at four in the morning when Serge talked about a guy being shot on St. Denis Street. Why wake them to make this announcement? If there's no other plausible explanation the jury will conclude that Serge killed Lepine. Could she convince the jury that Serge never made the statement? If Maurice were the only witness to say he heard Serge, his testimony might not be believed, and Serge might be acquitted without saying a word. But there was also Pauline Vinet, outrageous but attracting sympathy. If the jurors doubted her testimony, Maurice confirmed it, albeit weakly.

Marie-Lyse still wasn't absolutely sure herself that Serge hadn't fired the fatal bullet. He denied it, but his refusal to tell her everything made it more difficult for her to believe him. He couldn't testify anyway because of his record. If the jurors did not hear both sides of the story, they'd feel cheated and conclude he had something to hide.

Marie-Lyse got out of bed and switched on the light, but found it too bright and extinguished it immediately. She groped her way to the living room, where the VCR digital clock read 2:15. Soon after nestling into the old armchair she fell asleep.

With the arrival of the early morning light, she awoke, stretched lazily and smiled before looking around the room. The VCR now displayed 5:33 — hours before her normal waking time. She wriggled out of the chair and went to the kitchen. Some coffee would wake her up.

Her briefcase lay askew on the blond oak desk in the living room corner near the window. She glanced out at the parking lot, filled with the familiar cars of neighbours in the older buildings. It was unusually silent, but then she wasn't in the habit of rising so early.

She filled the coffee maker with boiling water, inhaling the aroma, then took a mug of coffee over to the desk. Although the room was getting lighter by the minute, it wasn't yet bright enough for reading. She switched on the gooseneck lamp, pulled out the notepad and began to read the list of jurors.

1. HENRI LANCTOT, 43, married, clerk, Standard Life Insurance Company. He looked pale, nondescript—the kind of person she could easily forget. Sitting in the first row by the judge's bench, he seemed to disappear into the woodwork.

2. RITA BELLEVILLE, 22, single, student. She wrote that note to the judge about her exam. Concordia University student in commerce. Young, attractive, same age as the accused and Maurice. Others on the jury might listen to her.

3. ROGER LEBRUN, 28, engineer, single, Bank of Montreal. What do engineers do working for a bank? . . . Talks with number two when they leave the courtroom.

4. BETTY MAJOR, 37, men's hair stylist, single. Why hadn't she paid her more attention? She looks almost motherly, auburn hair, attractive. Surprising she didn't ask for an exemption; she'll probably lose a lot of tips. Pleasant open smile. Seems interested in everything going on in the courtroom. Didn't show much emotion when Pauline Vinet testified.

5. LUCY MORIN, 25, canteen worker, single. She couldn't care less about the trial. Spends all her time sending signals to number twelve. Probably works at the airport washing dishes or something like that. She'll vote with number twelve.

6. PHIL PASQUIN, 48, executive, Mondo Uomo, married. He's the foreman. Dresses up in a new suit every day. Mondo Uomo: they have a nice store in Place Bonaventure—probably where he gets his own suits. Looks aggressive. He'll probably influence two or three others. Must be cultivated somehow. How can a story about clothes and a clothing store be worked into the closing summation?

7. KATHY JOHNSON, 36, secretary, divorced. She appears a little lost, and may have been recently divorced. She'll be on the lookout for a friendship with someone, probably a man—but who knows? She'll tie up with another juror, and is unlikely to follow an independent path. Not worth particular effort; convince her leader, and she'll follow.

8. BERNARD RICHER, 68, retired, widower. He's over sixty-five and could have had an exemption, but didn't request one. Probably happy to be with people. Hard to say which way he'll jump. He'll be objective because he won't like Serge, Pomerleau, or Pauline.

9. FRANCINE ROUX, 44, medical secretary, married. She lives in Outremont on one of the nice mid-level streets near the park. Medical secretary? Probably married to a doctor and runs his office. That's the style these days. Gives the doctor a chance to control his expenses and transfer part of his earnings to his wife. She has that Outremont look, confident, comfortable. Wonder if she was born in Outremont? Looks smart, dresses just right; probably shops around the corner on Laurier. She'll be a powerhouse in the deliberations.

10. CLAIRE SAVARD, 59, housewife, married. Hard to read women like her: different generation, stayed home. I know nothing about her.

11. ALBERT ROUSSEAU, 34, high school teacher, married. That's the fellow who records every word in his notes. If the jury gets stuck on what someone said or did, he'll have it there. Of course, the jury could ask to rehear the tapes of one or more witnesses. They usually do. I wonder if he makes notes on the romance between number twelve and number five.

12. RICK HAYES, 30, machinist, single. There's the mystery man, with his eyes concealed. At least he took off that stupid cap and stopped chewing gum. Rick Hayes, the mystery man who's hustling the ass off Lucy, the canteen worker. Too bad there were no challenges left when his name was drawn.

Serge Tremblay, this is the jury of your peers that will decide if you're guilty of second degree murder.

It was six o'clock. Marie-Lyse shut off the lamp and rubbed her eyes. The sun was up, but there was time to sleep another hour. She returned to bed, and started to review the jurors again, Henry Lanctot, . . . Rita Belleville, . . . Roger Lebrun, . . . and she fell asleep.

*   *   *

Sam Berne smiled as he recalled the office scene of the previous day, with Jackie's friends converging to welcome the new computer into the public service. The timing of the new arrival was propitious. He had awakened early to prepare a rough outline of the charge, the instructions to the jury. Jackie could enter his notes in the computer and test the miracles of modern technology.

He rose from bed, put on a bathrobe and went down to the dining room, where he took a black notebook and several files from his briefcase. He became completely immersed in his handwritten trial notes, compiling lists of the witnesses, important dates and times, key phrases used during the trial; cutting and pasting together sections of the law and excerpts from previous charges; and adding notes of relevant facts. It was painstaking, meticulous work.

Preparing a charge is a bit like walking a tightrope. Judges must tread a narrow path, favouring neither the Crown nor the accused, conscious of the jury's need for a simple and understandable charge while complying with myriad changing legal requirements. Each word is recorded and may be scrutinized by a higher court.

It was 6:30, too early to drive to the office but too late to return to bed. A leisurely walk to the courthouse in the crisp spring air would fill the time perfectly. It would take about an hour and a half, providing an opportunity to admire the flowers and look into the Sherbrooke Street store windows.

He was pleased with the rhythm of the trial. Delays and adjournments cause a loss of momentum and concentration. If the defence didn't present witnesses, the attorneys could make their closing arguments Wednesday morning. He would then give his charge that afternoon, and the jury could start their deliberations. With luck the trial would be finished before the weekend. However, if there were witnesses for the defence he wouldn't have to give his charge until the following week.

Sam walked along The Boulevard admiring the daffodils emerging beside imposing stone residences. An unfamiliar flag fluttered from a distant flagpole. The early morning peace was interrupted only occasionally by a passing car or bus headed downtown. His thoughts transcended the immediate issues of the trial.

A jury is comprised of twelve randomly selected ordinary people, equipped with various skills and diverse experience. Initially the jurors treat the experience like a school outing, and mistakenly consider the thanks and flattery by the judge and attorneys as an attempt to persuade them to favour one side or the other. They underestimate the magnitude of their task; it is not easy for one human being to judge another.

Details of the crime unfold; unfamiliar names assume reality and personality; the initial resentment dissipates; faces are transformed with smiles and joking, and the jurors adapt to the courtroom atmosphere. They identify with the witnesses, and participate in the fear that grips both victims and accused. This is not a theatrical performance, to be followed by a return to reality. The trial and its outcome have consequences that will change lives forever.

The jury system is a window between society and its justice system, allowing knowledge and experience to circulate freely in both directions, and assuring that the laws and their application remain rooted in the local environment. For hundreds of years juries have brought a sense of reality, grounding the legal system in the morality of the times.

A car horn sounded. Ahead, the Trafalgar Apartments rose from a concrete island amidst a sea of traffic, and beyond it the outline of Mount Royal appeared. The road curved gradually along the ridge, passed Marianopolis College, and descended to Sherbrooke Street. There, many charming buildings remain from the beginning of the century, and few new towers offend by their height or facade. Exclusive boutiques, galleries, and hotels invite passers-by to linger and enjoy.

When the Four Seasons Hotel loomed, his thoughts returned to the trial. Didn't one of the jurors work in the hotel as a men's hair stylist?: Betty Major, number four. She sat front and centre in the jury box.

Walking east on Sherbrooke past a series of more modest hotels, he noticed the statue of Queen Victoria across the street, reminding citizens to observe the dictates of restraint and good taste, a stricture not always heeded in her time or ours.

On St. Laurent he headed south, past a succession of camera and video shops, fast food restaurants, sex shops, porno parlours, and finally the special sights and aromas of Chinatown, to the courthouse.

The building was still calm when he took the elevator to the fifteenth floor. Jackie was sipping coffee, gazing with admiration at the computer.

"Jackie, when was the computer unpacked and set up?"

"The man was here at 7:30. He phoned last night after you left, and I agreed to meet him early. Coffee?"

"Please. Any calls?"

"The coordinating judge called about the meeting to distribute next week's trials. If you can't make it you should call her."

"I don't know where I stand. This case might run into next week.

I'll ask to be placed on standby next week. With luck, I'll have a verdict by Friday evening, but I could be here during the weekend."

"Is there anything you want me to type on the new computer?"

"Yes. Could you enter these notes I prepared? But please keep my handwritten notes. I don't trust electric impulses hidden in vinyl boxes . . . .Did Renée mention anything about that book I'm waiting for?"

"Be patient. It's only six months since you ordered it. You know that it has to come all the way from Toronto. I'm borrowing one. Lolita will bring me her judge's copy this morning."

"Thank you."

"There's a surprise to go with your coffee. It was delivered just before you arrived."

"What is it?"

"Here." She removed her shawl from the table with the flair of an experienced magician about to display a missing object to an incredulous audience. "This glittering silver package was sent up from the jury room. There's no note but I recognize the distinctive wrapping paper. The spirits have told me the Johnson woman's falling in love with you. The commercial could now become 'Say it with tinfoil.'"

"Jackie, one fortune teller is all I can handle at a time. Please unwrap the package."

She removed the foil as if she were detonating a bomb, then studied the mound of white cake. "Well, well! The daily special is . . . vanilla cake with slivered almonds. I read in *National Geographic* that in the remote areas of Tibet vanilla is used as an aphrodisiac."

"Jackie, what do you think I should do about these daily offerings from juror number seven? It's getting uncomfortable."

"Send her a note you're on a diet."

"And file a copy in court? No thanks. What else is new today?"

"There's a letter from the Chief Justice announcing the date of the annual badminton tournament for judges."

* * *

Parent hovered at the entrance to the courtroom like an expectant father. "Bonjour, Monsieur le Juge."

"Bonjour, Monsieur le Constable. Is everything in order? Have all the jurors arrived?"

"We're still waiting for number eight, Bernard Richer, the older man who had trouble parking last week. I called his home and there's no answer."

"Let's hope he arrives shortly. Anything else?"

"I made a reservation for lunch at Le Vieux Port. The foreman, Monsieur Pasquin, was very happy."

"Good. Please tell me when number eight shows up. Is the prisoner here?"

"Yes, he's in the cell behind the courtroom."

Time passed slowly till Linda announced the arrival of the missing juror. Sam nodded to the jurors in the corridor before entering the courtroom. After everyone was seated he began.

"Good morning, ladies and gentlemen. Once again I welcome you and express my appreciation for your efforts, and your attention to the witnesses. I believe it necessary to mention the importance of everyone being on time. As you have seen, this court can only function when all of the required people are present. We work as a team, and the trial cannot proceed unless all members of the team are present . . . .When we adjourned last night, Maître Lortie was cross-examining Monsieur Maurice Pomerleau. Maître Lortie, I invite you to continue."

Pomerleau went to the witness box.

"Monsieur Pomerleau, yesterday you testified that while you were living with Pauline Vinet, you went to the Wiz with Serge Tremblay."

"Yeah."

"How often?"

"Like I said yesterday, two or three times."

"Did you ever see a fight at the Wiz?"

"Sometimes."

"Did you see any knives or guns there?"

"I don't know."

"What do you mean, you don't know? Did you see a gun at Le Wiz, ever?"

"Maybe; I'm not sure."

"Do you own a gun?"

"Not now."

"Did you ever own or possess a gun?"

"Yeah, but not now."

"What do you know about guns?"

"Not much."

"Do you know the difference between a pistol and a revolver?"

"Yeah."

"Explain the difference, please."

"Well, they sort of load differently. A revolver has this round thing that turns where you put in the bullets. When you load a pistol there's a thing in the handle that comes out, and you load the bullets into it."

Lortie leaned forward and asked the clerk for the pistol which had been filed as an exhibit. She gave it to Sgt.-Det. Caron, seated beside Talbot, and asked him to check that it wasn't loaded, then handed it to Pomerleau. "Is this a revolver or a pistol?"

"Pistol."

"Could you please show the jury how it is loaded?"

"Don't have any bullets."

"I know, but please go through the motions. Show us how you remove the magazine from the handle."

Pomerleau took the pistol and deftly removed the magazine. He pretended to insert several bullets, reinserted the magazine, and placed the pistol on the table in front of the clerk. "There."

When Pomerleau took the pistol in his hand and started to manipulate it, Albert Rousseau looked up from his note-taking. He had seen policemen and armed guards carry guns, but never an ordinary person. It wasn't loaded, but nonetheless he felt uncomfortable when Pomerleau picked up the pistol and pointed towards the jury.

This was even more exciting than TV. How did a high school math teacher end up in this strange place? What if they hadn't removed all the bullets? He'd be a father soon, and Diane and Albert Junior needed him. He squirmed and glanced down the upper row of the jury box. Even Francine Roux, who always acted as though nothing could frighten her, seemed uncomfortable. Why does the judge allow this sort of thing?

"Did you ever see this particular pistol before?" Lortie asked.

"I don't know."

"Did you ever see this pistol in Pauline Vinet's house?"

"I don't know."

"Did you ever handle it before?"

"I don't know. Look, this pistol is like all the others. There's no name on it, and they all look the same. How do you expect me to recognize it? By the little paper tag hanging from the trigger? I didn't put the tag there and never saw it before. Okay?"

"Can you swear that you've never seen or handled this pistol before today?"

"No."

"Did you handle it often?"

"Not so often."

"Let's return to the night of the murder. Did you go to St. Denis Street?"

"At what time?"

"At any time."

"No."

"Did you go into Le Wiz that night?"

"No."

"Did you see the fight between Serge Tremblay and Frank Lepine?"

"No."

"Did you shoot Frank Lepine?"

"No."

"Did you see Serge Tremblay shoot Frank Lepine?"

"No."

"Didn't you shoot Frank Lepine?"

"No. No!" Tremblay called involuntarily from the accused's dock. Marie-Lyse turned and glared at him. Her cheeks flushed and anger darted from her eyes. At that moment she was ready to kill him to save his life. After that outbreak, she could do no more with this witness. As she turned back to face the jury, the angry look gave way to a forced smile. "No further questions."

"The court will adjourn for fifteen minutes."

Marie-Lyse watched the jurors murmuring and gesturing to each other as they left the room. Then she whispered hoarsely, in a voice loud enough for the police guard to hear, "Whose side are you on? The moment I make a little headway, you start calling from the dock. Maurice the weasel Pomerleau is trying to put you away for the rest of your life, and you yell 'No, no.'"

"It sort of came out. Look, you're only the lawyer and this is my trial, my ass. I told you over and over this isn't Maurice's trial, so get off his tail. He's got no choice."

"And what's that supposed to mean?"

"That's supposed to mean lay off him."

"If I don't lean on Maurice, you're going back to La Macaza. The only way to create a doubt is to make the jury think that maybe he did it. Do you have any other ideas? Do you think they'll believe Pauline shot him with a crystal ball? Or Caroline? You want me to convince them that Lepine was shot by Torres the clown, or Oscar Cimon?"

"Who's he?"

"The other witness who saw you in the Wiz and on the street. The jury won't forget he saw you at the scene of the crime. You're damned lucky he didn't see you pull the trigger."

"I didn't."

"I know. You didn't, Maurice didn't, the man in the moon must've done it. I've a good mind to ask the judge to let me get out of this case right now. I stay up nights trying to think of a way to get you off, and you yell 'no, no' the moment I get somewhere. The jury will forget everything Pomerleau said, and remember you and your 'No, no.'"

"Calm down and I'll cool it."

"No more interruptions from the dock?"

"No more. Will Maurice testify again?"

"No, witnesses testify once, unless the judge gives special permission to recall them."

* * *

Rick Hayes waited for Lucy to catch up with him. "You ever hear such a crock?"

"What do you mean?" she asked.

"All that stuff about Pomerleau. The guy's as chicken as they come. He wouldn't have the guts to kill a mosquito."

"How do you know?"

"I can tell. I watched him carefully when he was a witness. The guy's scared and putting on a show. I don't believe a thing he says, but that doesn't make him a killer."

"What if I don't agree with you? I see plenty of men around the construction jobs—probably more than you see in a machine shop. When they come for a sandwich I look into their eyes and smile. Tips are better when I do that. Well, I looked into Pomerleau's eyes, and that man can kill. I've seen the look before."

10

Officer Martin advanced towards the witness box as Talbot announced, "The next witness for the Crown is Sgt.-Det. Claude Martin."

"Your name?"

"Sgt.-Det. Claude Martin, badge 4982, Montreal Urban Community Police."

"Address?"

"775 Gosford Street, Montreal."

"Your age?"

"Forty-eight."

"Sergeant Martin," Talbot began, "do you have another name or nickname?"

"Yes. Some people used to call me Coco."

"How long have you been a police officer?"

"Twenty-seven years."

"What section are you attached to?"

"Crimes Against the Person."

"For how many years have you been in that section?"

"Eight years."

"And what is the major portion of your work?"

"Investigating murders and attempted murders."

"Were you assigned to the investigation of the murder of Frank Lepine, who was shot on October seventh, 1991, in front of Le Wiz on St. Denis Street?"

"No, I was not. That investigation was conducted by Sgt.-Det. Robert Caron, who's sitting beside you."

"Were you involved in the arrest of a suspect in that case?"

"Yes I was."

"Please explain how you became involved."

"I knew about the murder because detectives work together and we talk about our cases, and there was a lot of talk about this one. I knew it happened after a street fight on St. Denis, but didn't expect to get involved. Well, one day, it was . . . .Can I consult my notes?"

"Are those notes that were made at the time?" the judge asked.

"Yes, Your Honour."

"You may do so, but please look and speak in the direction of the jury."

"October twenty-first, 1991. At 4:32 in the afternoon I received a phone call from Pauline Vinet. She wanted to meet me about a matter of life and death."

"Did you agree to meet her?"

"Yes, of course. I didn't know what it was about, but I've known Pauline many years, and she sounded desperate. I offered to meet her right away."

"Where did you meet?"

"At Le Carabin Restaurant."

"Before I ask you about the meeting, would you please explain to the court how you happen to know her?"

"Yes. I've been on the police force for twenty-seven years. When I joined the force in 1965, I was first assigned to the station in the Southeast Division, which covers the area east of St. Laurent and south of Sherbrooke. I knew the merchants in my district, and Pauline was one of them."

"Was that your only relationship with her?"

"No, I think you might say our relationship was closer, occasionally intimate. I was young and single, and we—"

"We know, thank you."

This is just like the oldtime movies, Rick thought. Just when the story gets interesting, he interrupts.

"When was the last time you saw or spoke to Pauline before the present incident?"

"Must have been in the early seventies. I didn't see her after I was transferred to Montreal Central in '73."

"So you hadn't seen her in almost twenty years?"

"No. Frankly, I'd forgotten her till the day she called."

"Why did you select Le Carabin as a meeting place?"

"Pauline and I ate there in the past, and it was near her old salon. I knew it was still open, because I had passed by a few days earlier."

"How long after the phone call did you meet her?"

"Oh, we met about a half hour later. Actually, I was at the main headquarters on Gosford when she called, and I went to Le Carabin immediately. Couldn't have taken me more than ten minutes to get there. I arrived first and waited."

"And what happened?"

"I sat at a table near the front and watched the door. A few of the older waiters came around and joked with me. It was late afternoon, just before five o'clock, and they weren't busy. I wondered what Pauline would look like. She arrived ten or fifteen minutes after me. I was surprised at her appearance. Don't think I'd have recognized her if I didn't expect her, except for her way of walking. She always had an unusual way of swinging her butt. When she was young I thought it was, well, sexy. But now she looked much older, and heavier. Frankly I was shocked by her appearance."

"And, what happened?"

"She told me she was living with Maurice . . ." Officer Martin looked down at his notes before continuing, " . . . Pomerleau, and that Serge Tremblay, the accused, muscled in on them. She said he—Tremblay— shot a man on St. Denis Street two weeks before, and was scaring the heck out of the whole family. She was especially worried about her daughter Caroline. I knew immediately what she was talking about, because I'd discussed the St. Denis killing with my colleague, Sgt.-Det. Caron. I told her to return home while I contacted the SWAT team to make the arrest. I promised to have a woman call to tell her when everything was ready for the arrest."

"What happened after that?"

"Pauline left. I went to my car, phoned headquarters, and told officer Caron the news. He ordered the men to stake out the home immediately. As a matter of fact, they were there before she returned, and maintained a continuous watch. It was a difficult arrest, because of the way those old buildings are designed. The courtyard makes it hard to enter without being seen. We decided to make the arrest on the street instead of in the courtyard or the house. We have better control in the street, so long as it's not crowded."

"Were you personally involved in making these arrangements?"

"Yes I was. After the first contact with Pauline, I joined Sgt.-Det. Caron on the case until after the arrest was made. Matter of fact, I worked personally with the SWAT team on the arrangements and was there when they made the arrest."

"What were the arrangements?"

"The squad or team is assigned to make every dangerous arrest. We consider an arrest dangerous when the accused is known to be armed. I met with them twice. We reviewed maps of the area and photographs taken by the surveillance team. We even managed to get a set of plans for the building, so if we had to go in the men would be familiar with the layout and would know exactly where to look.

"When everything was ready we parked a panel truck with five members of the SWAT team on the street near Pauline's flat. We assumed that when Tremblay went out he'd walk towards Ste. Catherine Street because that's where the stores are. If he walked the other way, we had a contingency plan. I was in the street near the place where the interception would probably take place."

"And?"

"Like I said, when I gave the signal Pauline received a call that we were ready. We were worried because we saw Caroline go into the flat a few minutes after the call, but there was nothing we could do. I hoped Pauline would be able to keep her in the house when the suspect went out. The SWAT team could see me, and waited for my signal to make the arrest. They knew when the suspect left the house because the surveillance team was in radio contact all the time.

"We waited about fifteen or twenty minutes, before Tremblay came out. He was walking with both Pomerleau and Caroline. For a moment I thought it'd be too dangerous to make the arrest and we'd have to wait till another time when Caroline wasn't present, but we had a lucky break. When they came near the panel truck, Caroline wandered about twenty feet from them. I knew there was a danger to Pomerleau, but gave the signal to go ahead anyway. The guys went into action and it was a perfect arrest. Didn't take more than five seconds. As Tremblay and Pomerleau walked past the panel truck, our men jumped out and forced Tremblay to the ground. I ran over, grabbed Caroline and gave her to one of the men to take home. Then I told the suspect he was under arrest for the murder of Frank Lepine."

"Did he say anything?"

"Just, 'You guys are crazy. Who the—he used a word I'd rather not repeat in court—do you think you are?'"

"I answered 'police', and read him his rights. I took the pistol Tremblay had in the pouch on his waist, and tagged it with my name and number."

"Did you take Tremblay to the police station?"

"No. Because the arrest was made so close to headquarters, we called Sgt.-Det. Caron. He came over and took control of the suspect. I gave him the pistol, and that was the last contact I had with the case."

"Did you see or speak to Pauline Vinet after the arrest?"

"No. I admit I was tempted, but because of our past I thought it best to not do anything."

Talbot picked up the gun and handed it to the witness. "Have you ever seen this arm before?"

Martin turned it over in his hand, and read the ticket hanging from the trigger. "Yes, this is the pistol I seized from the accused the day of the arrest. It still has my tag on it."

"Thank you. And do you see Serge Tremblay in this courtroom?"

"Yes, over there in the dock for the accused near the police officer."

"No further questions."

"Ladies and gentlemen," Judge Berne announced, "The court will adjourn for lunch. Since it is only five to twelve, and in order to not waste time, we will reconvene at two o'clock instead of the usual 2:15." He noticed that juror number one looked ashen and was trembling slightly, and tried to catch Constable Parent's eye, but he was sleeping soundly. The sound of the shuffling chairs awakened him.

* * *

Inside the jury room, Henri Lanctot sat alone in a corner while the other jurors spoke excitedly about Tremblay's arrest.

"Didn't realize they actually had a SWAT team. I thought that was a TV invention."

"I think Martin still has something going for Pauline. Did you notice that he gave the order to go ahead while Maurice was exposed to danger? Probably didn't give a damn for him."

"He worried about the girl, Caroline."

"Wha'd you expect?"

"Do you think he's the father of Alexandre?"

"Never can tell."

"Wonder where Parent is. He's usually in a rush to take us to the restaurant."

"Still, they did a good job. Nobody was hurt."

"Would you believe it took two days, and Pauline didn't know they were being watched?"

"Look at Lanctot, in the corner!"

Henri Lanctot had slumped in the chair and was slowly slipping towards the floor. Francine Roux and Betty Major, being nearest to him, each grabbed an arm and lifted him back into the chair. Betty moved around to the back and began to knead his shoulders. Francine bent over and slapped his face gently. "Wake up, wake up."

As the other jurors crowded around, Rick Hayes said in a deep voice, "Stand back, stand back. Pasquin, you're the foreman. Go out and get Parent."

Pasquin glared. "Who do you think you're ordering around? I'm the foreman."

"You're an idiot! Get Parent," Rick shouted.

"Yes," called someone.

"Go!" said another.

Roger Lebrun opened the door and Pasquin rushed into the hall. Parent wasn't there. The two other guards immediately asked, "What is it?"

"Henri Lanctot fainted or something."

Wilfred Harvey called to Gisele Boisclair, "Get Parent. He's talking to the judge," then rushed into the jury room.

Betty continued to knead Lanctot's shoulders and Francine held a styrofoam cup of water to his lips.

Constable Parent entered a minute later. "What's wrong, what's wrong? Everyone stand back."

Harvey deferred to his superior and began moving the jurors gently from the corner. Only Francine and Betty remained near Lanctot.

Parent motioned to Boisclair as she entered the room. "Gisele, stay here a moment. I have to speak to the judge." He stepped into the hall where the judge was waiting. "Monsieur le Juge, juror number one, Lanctot, has fainted, but he's reviving and seems a little better now. What should we do?"

"Phone downstairs for the nurse. I want you and Constable Boisclair to take the jurors to the restaurant. Leave Harvey behind to watch number one."

"Don't you think it would be better if I stayed?"

"No, I have a trial to protect. The nurse will take care of Lanctot, and if necessary we'll get a doctor. I'm worried about the others; if the entire jury gets upset it can lead to a mistrial. Now get them moving. I'll stay here till everything is under control."

"Immediately, Monsieur le Juge."

"Call my office as soon as you get to the restaurant."

"Oui, Monsieur le Juge."

Parent led his charges down the hall and through the door.

"The nurse has arrived," Linda announced. "Do you wish to go into the jury room to see juror number one?"

"No, I can't speak to jurors privately. Stay near the jury room and ask the nurse to report to me as soon as she knows anything. I'll be in the office behind the courtroom."

About fifteen minutes passed before the nurse reported on Lanctot's condition. "He'll be fine. Nothing in particular seemed to be wrong with him. He said he felt warm. There's often a problem with the ventilation in the building. I understand he has the chair closest to your desk."

"Yes."

"The side of your desk makes the spot uncomfortable and blocks the air flow. He's also disturbed by the way the witnesses were handling a gun, pointing in the direction of the jury. He has a phobia about guns. Seems that years ago an employee of the insurance company where he works went berserk and shot an executive. He wasn't there when it happened, but he never got over the shock of it."

"How's he doing now?"

"Fine. Constable Harvey will take him for a walk outside and then bring him to the lounge near the first aid room. He can rest there and have a light lunch, if you approve. I'll keep an eye on him till two."

"Is there anything else?"

"No. I don't think there'll be any more problems, but if there are, call and I'll come up immediately."

"Thank you."

Moments later Lanctot left the room walking alongside Constable Harvey. His colour seemed slightly better, and he waved weakly at Judge Berne, who nodded back.

* * *

" . . . and Rick, you didn't have to call him an idiot!" Lucy admonished.

"But he is."

"Of course he is. Everyone in this restaurant knows that, but you didn't have to say it."

"Didn't we promise to tell the truth?"

"No, the witnesses did. We only promised to judge according to the evidence."

"So what do you want me to do now? Apologize to the idiot? I refuse."

"Just stop insulting him. If we start fighting among ourselves, this case will never end."

"If I promise, you gonna spend the night at my place again?"

"Rick, you're a juror. Are you asking me for a bribe?"

"Yup."

"Well, I don't know if it's legal, but I agree. Now stop insulting Pasquin."

"I promise I won't insult the idiot again until the trial is finished."

"Rick!"

"I meant I won't insult him to his face."

"Okay . . . .What do you think happened to Lanctot?"

"I don't know. Hardly noticed him before he fainted."

"Lucy," Albert Rousseau interjected, "can you pass the ketchup?"

"Here." She handed him the bottle.

"Albert," said Rick, "you have notes of every word. Why don't you check and see if anything was said that might have caused Lanctot to faint?"

"I did. It couldn't have been anything they said. Do you think he had a heart attack?"

Francine joined in. "I have some experience in these things. I was close to Lanctot too when he fainted, and I'm certain it wasn't a heart attack: no chest pains, no sweating. He just became faint. It happens."

"Why don't we ask Constable Parent?" suggested Rousseau.

"Good idea," Rick replied. Looking towards the end of the table, he called loudly, "Hey Denis! You heard anything about Lanctot's condition?"

Constable Parent put down the lamb chop and wiped his mouth. "No. As a matter of fact, the judge said I should call his office from here."

"Constable," said Pasquin, "all of us want to hear about Lanctot's condition. We ask that you call immediately."

A number of voices said Yes, Now, Please. Parent rose from the table. He had forgotten that the judge had asked him to phone and was glad they reminded him. He hoped the judge would be out for lunch. Parent picked up the phone at the front counter. His close relationship with the proprietor afforded him the privilege of using the phone meant for taking reservations.

He returned to the table a few minutes later. "I spoke to the judge's secretary, and she told me Lanctot is fine. Court will begin again at two o'clock, as scheduled. The judge went out for lunch. If it were serious he'd have stayed around." He looked wistfully at the cold lamb chops on his plate. He should have called when they entered the restaurant.

The report cheered the jurors and the noise level at the table rose appreciably. They were surprised to realize that the experience of a few days in court had drawn them together.

At twenty to two, they left and followed Parent up the street. Henri Lanctot and Constable Harvey stood outside on the steps of the courthouse. "It was nothing," Lanctot explained. "I just felt warm because of the poor ventilation. It's especially bad where I sit, near the judge's desk."

"The rules don't allow us to move, or I'd change places with you," said Pasquin.

"Thank you. Thank you, everybody."

The group entered the building and walked through the marriage registration office to the rear corridor.

* * *

Parent smiled and raised his right thumb to signal that everyone was ready, and Henri Lanctot, still looking weak, led the jury into the courtroom.

Sgt.-Det. Martin took his place in the witness box, and the clerk announced, "You are testifying under the same oath."

"Yes."

"Officer Martin," asked Marie-Lyse Lortie, "how well do you know Pauline Vinet?"

"I knew her well in the past, but as I said, I didn't see her for many years, before the day I received the phone call."

"Did you know she was a fortune teller?"

"Yes," he replied with a slight smile, "as a matter of fact I did."

"Did she ever tell your fortune?"

"No, not that I remember."

"Isn't it strange that you were a good friend of Pauline Vinet, a fortune teller, and she never told your fortune?"

"No."

"Why didn't she tell your fortune?"

"I never ask her to."

"Did she offer?"

"Yes, she offered once or twice, but I refused."

"Now, why did you do that?"

"I don't believe in fortune tellers."

"Why not?"

"Well, I think they make up or invent a future to satisfy the customers."

"Do you think they also make up the past?"

The smile on his face turned to consternation. "No, no, Pauline doesn't make things up. She may seem a bit strange but she's an honest woman."

"Honest women can make mistakes and be frightened, and fight to protect themselves, can't they?"

"Objection!" called Talbot. "The witness is here to testify to facts that he saw and heard. He's not an expert witness, and is not here to give his opinion and philosophy of women."

"I withdraw the question. What do you know about Maurice Pomerleau?"

"I never saw him before the day of the arrest, and know nothing about him. I don't think we ever spoke."

"You testified that you were not involved in the investigation?"

"That's right."

"So you never met or heard of the accused before the day you met Pauline at Le Carabin?"

"That's right."

"What about the other people involved in this case? Had you ever heard of them before?"

"What do you mean? I told you about my relationship with Pauline."

"Juan Luis Torres?"

"Don't think I ever heard of him, till I read last week's newspaper."

Marie-Lyse began to sit down. "No furth . . . . No, just one more question. Did you know the victim, Frank Lepine?"

"I . . . no . . . I . . . ."

"Officer Martin, did you know the victim, Frank Lepine?" she repeated assertively, rising from the crouch.

"I think I know—knew him."

Sergeant Caron leaned over and whispered to Vince Talbot. Talbot rose. "My lord, something has come up, and I ask permission to address the bench, with the jury absent."

Lortie persisted. "Tell me about Frank Lepine. How did you meet him?"

"My Lord," Talbot pleaded, "I have made a request."

Lortie persisted further. "I have a right to cross-examine the witness without interruption. My question is legal and relevant."

"Answer the question," Judge Berne ordered.

"Frank Lepine was a police officer."

"My Lord, My Lord, I must address the bench on a matter of law and privilege," Talbot interrupted.

Judge Berne looked towards the jury, raising his eyebrows, and opened both hands with palms upward in a sign of resignation. "I ask the jury to withdraw for a few moments. Officer Martin, please step out for a moment as well, and don't discuss this case or your testimony with anyone."

After the jury left, Talbot continued, "Would it be possible to ask the audience to withdraw as well?"

"No, Maître Talbot. I remind the journalists present that it is forbidden to report matters that occur outside the jury's presence, till after the verdict. Now, what's this all about?"

"My Lord," complained Marie-Lyse, "I asked a perfectly legal question and crown counsel interrupted."

"Yes. Maître Talbot, the court would like an explanation. What question of law or privilege do you want to raise?"

"I've just been informed by Officer Caron that the victim, Frank Lepine, was a police officer working undercover."

"My Lord," Lortie protested, "this was never disclosed to the defence. There may be grounds for a mistrial, or even a stay of procedures."

"I'll decide that at the appropriate time. Maître Talbot?"

"May I have five minutes to consult officer Caron and officer Martin?"

"Officer Martin is under order to not discuss this case during this break, and that order stands. You can speak to officer Caron here. Maître Lortie, you will have an opportunity to raise a motion for a mistrial or for a stay, after we all know more about what's going on. I'll be in the office behind the courtroom till you're ready."

Marie-Lyse huddled with Serge Tremblay. "Serge, do you have any idea what I've stumbled into?"

"No, none, I promise you."

"Did you know Lepine was a cop?"

"No."

"Ever see him before the night of the murder?"

"No."

"What do you think he was doing at Le Wiz?"

"Probably chasing someone. I never knew him."

"What about that other witness, Oscar Cimon?"

"Him? I didn't even remember he testified. I never saw him before he came to court."

"Is he somehow involved?"

"I don't know."

When Linda looked into the courtroom, both attorneys signalled that they were ready to resume.

"Maître Talbot," the judge asked, "can you enlighten the court now?"

"My Lord, I have been informed that officer Lepine was engaged in an undercover investigation on St. Denis Street that is totally unrelated to this case. If further questions are asked, there is a possibility that lives will be endangered. I respectfully request the court to limit questioning about him."

"My Lord—" Marie-Lyse began.

Judge Berne gestured with his hand for her to be patient. "Maître Talbot, this case involves lives as well. The future of the accused is at stake. I see no reason to limit questions about the victim, and his activities, that may provide or disprove motive or otherwise be relevant. I am going to recall the jury, and this questioning will continue."

"But—" Talbot began.

"Yes?"

"Nothing, My Lord."

"Ask the witness to return as well." The withholding of information that the victim was a police undercover agent infuriated the judge. He wasn't sure how to deal with the discovery. This new evidence would raise questions and doubts in the minds of the jurors. He would have to resist the urge to investigate and enquire, and maintain a passive role. Lortie would have to carry the ball. The jury re-entered and Marie-Lyse resumed her questions.

"Officer Martin, how did you know Frank Lepine was a police officer? Did you work together?"

"No. We met a few years ago taking shooting practice."

"Did you ever work together?"

"No."

"What branch was Frank Lepine attached to?"

"Objection. Hearsay," called Talbot.

"He should know," responded Lortie.

"Officer Martin, please answer if you know, and remember you are under oath."

"Yes, Your Honour. The Narcotics Squad. At least, that's what I thought he was doing."

"Objection."

"Dismissed."

"You said earlier in your testimony that 'there was a lot of talk about this one', when you described the shooting at Le Wiz. What talk were you referring to? Who were the people talking, and where?"

"Objection, hearsay," interrupted Talbot.

"Dismissed. Answer the question."

"Yes. I heard talk around the police station."

"Which one?"

"Gosford Street, here downtown."

"Who was talking?"

"Other police officers."

"What was being said?"

"Objection."

"Dismissed."

"They said it was too bad a cop was killed, even if it was an accident."

"Did you say *accident?*"

"Well, the word was used. What they meant—"

"I only asked the witness if the word *accident* was used and not what was meant," Lortie protested to the judge.

"Officer Martin, please finish what you were saying," Judge Berne instructed.

"They were saying it was an accident, and they meant that Frank Lepine wasn't investigating the accused, Serge Tremblay, or anything like that. He must have been investigating something else. It's like getting run down by a car while chasing a bank robber. It was an accident because it wasn't part of his investigation. But that doesn't mean that Tremblay, the accused, didn't mean—"

"I see," the judge interjected. "The jury will decide what Mr.

Tremblay did or didn't mean, if necessary. Unless you know or have direct information, I don't think you should comment on that subject."

"Thank you, Your Honour."

"Do you know if Oscar Cimon was a police officer as well?" Lortie continued.

"Yes."

"Yes you know, or yes he was a police officer?"

"Yes he was a police officer."

"Do you know what he did? What department?"

"I think he was part of the Narcotics Squad too."

"Was he on duty on the night of the murder?"

"Objection. Irrelevant."

"I don't know."

"What else do you know about the people in this case that you haven't revealed?"

"Objection. Too general."

"Nothing," the witness answered before the judge could rule.

"No further questions."

"Thank you, officer Martin," Judge Berne said, "you are free to go now." The witness looked apologetically at Sergeant Robert Caron and Vincent Talbot, and left the court.

Lortie spoke. "I have a request to make. I wish to reopen the cross-examination of officer Cimon."

"Maître Talbot?" Judge Berne asked.

"Maître Lortie should call officer Cimon during the defence if she wishes. There is no legal reason to reopen the cross- examination—"

"That would limit my right to ask leading questions and may change the order of the closing arguments," Lortie argued.

"—and," continued Talbot, "I'm not sure he's available."

"We'll adjourn for fifteen minutes, and I have every confidence in your ability to find and produce him immediately," Judge Berne said.

* * *

As the jury left the courtroom, Rick whispered to Lucy and Betty, "How do you like those damn cops? The set-up stinks. A cop gets killed on St. Denis and they pretend it's just an ordinary brawl. Did you see the look on the judge's face? He's damned mad too."

"Rick," Betty responded, "police don't like to see their friends killed. There must've been a good reason to keep it quiet."

"You ever have anything to do with the police?"

"Well, sort of. I've never been arrested or anything like that, but the police chief, he's a customer of the barbershop."

"Him too! Say, who isn't a customer of yours?" Lucy exclaimed.

"I'm not . . . yet," Rick said. "Do you give haircuts to ordinary guys like me, who work in machine shops?"

"'Course we do. But most customers in a downtown barbershop work in offices, hotels, and places like that."

"Rick, what's happening?" Lucy asked.

"A hell of a lot more than we thought. Those cops are working St. Denis Street for drugs. They don't send plain-clothes cops to stop fights in bars. I wonder if Maurice isn't involved in some drug ring. Maybe Pauline is; who the hell knows? Good thing the judge ordered Cimon back."

"You really think Pauline and Maurice are involved in a drug ring?" Francine asked as she joined the conversation. "Maurice probably smokes marijuana now and then, might even sniff cocaine, but what dealer would trust him?"

"Not me," Lucy replied. "And Pauline—she gives me the shudders. No one would want to trust her."

"You heard what the judge said, don't jump to conclusions. Wait till you hear all the evidence," Pasquin quoted.

"You the judge's helper?" Rick asked sarcastically.

"Well, I'm the foreman."

"We made you foreman, and if you don't stop mixing in we'll turf you out as foreman."

"Just who do you think you are? I'm not fooled by you, like Lucy over here," Pasquin said.

"You keep out of my life," Lucy challenged. "What me and Rick do is nobody's business—especially not yours!"

"Yeah." Rick moved ominously in Pasquin's direction. "You want to go out and settle this here and now? One punch will burst the buttons off that fancy suit of yours."

Bernard and Henri lined up behind Phil Pasquin in a show of solidarity. Lucy watched Rick excitedly. Betty and Francine stood between the two men, as the other jurors withdrew to the corners. Betty coaxed Rick backwards in a soothing voice. He wasn't used to women standing between him and an adversary, and seemed unsure how to react.

Pasquin realized a fight would be averted and became brave.

"He's no better than the punks in court. If he wasn't wearing glasses I'd show him a thing or two."

"You and who else?" Rick taunted.

"Stop it, you two," Francine urged.

"Yes, stop it," Betty and Kathy repeated in unison.

There was knock on the jury room door. "Is everything all right in there?" Parent called. "Any problems?"

"No problems," Francine replied through the closed door. Then, looking at both Hayes and Pasquin she continued, "The trial's almost over. Can't you two stop bickering?"

"Well, he started by insulting Lucy," Rick complained.

"Yeah. He's not my boss, and if he was I'd quit," Lucy added.

"Quit what?" Pasquin asked.

"Quit working for you. Now leave us alone."

"I'm the foreman."

"Mr. Pasquin," Betty interrupted, "why don't you just sit down in the chair at the head of the table and relax? I'll get you a cup of coffee."

"Okay. Thanks."

"Lucy, there's something I want to discuss with Rick and you," Francine said at just the right moment. "Come over to the corner."

Bernard Richer sat down next to Pasquin. "Phil, these people don't know what it means to meet a payroll, or negotiate with a bank manager. They haven't really lived. I'm with you all the way."

"Thanks. But after this is all over—"

Betty completed his sentence, handing him a cup of coffee. "You'll go back and open more stores and make more money."

"I wish it was over now. I've got important things to do."

"This is also important, Mr. Pasquin. We need experienced level-headed people like you."

"All right, Betty. I'll continue as foreman for you and the others . . . and I don't want to look like I'm quitting because of him." Pasquin stared at Rick Hayes, unwilling to even pronounce his name.

11

When the jury re-entered the courtroom Oscar Cimon was waiting in the witness box. Marie-Lyse began questioning him immediately.

"You didn't tell us you were a police officer when you were questioned last week."

"No."

"Why not?"

"No one asked me, and I didn't think it was necessary."

"What is your official title?"

"Sergeant-Detective."

"And what division are you attached to?"

"Narcotics, drugs."

"Were you on duty on the night of October seventh, 1991?"

"Yes I was."

"What were you doing?"

"I was engaged in an investigation."

"On St. Denis Street?"

"Yes."

"Were you working with the victim, Frank Lepine?"

"No. In undercover work we usually work alone. It's dangerous to work in teams: doubles the risk. If one policeman is recognized, both lives are in danger. Once in a while we report to the lieutenant what we're doing."

"But you knew the victim, Frank Lepine?"

"Yes."

"Or should I call him Detective Frank Lepine?"

"He was a detective and we were in the same squad. He was a good policeman and a good friend."

"But you weren't working together that night?"

"No."

"What was he doing?"

"Objection," interrupted Talbot. "The question calls for an answer that is hearsay."

"Dismissed. The witness may answer if he knows."

"He was on duty, but I don't know what he was doing because we weren't working on the same case. I told you I was working alone."

"Did you see each other earlier that night, before you entered Le Wiz?"

"No. It was a chance meeting and I was surprised to see him."

"Do you mean you didn't know he would be on St. Denis Street?"

"I didn't quite say that. We often go to crowded places where there's drinking and dealing, so I wasn't surprised to see him on St. Denis, but it was a bit of a shock to be in the same bar. Like I said, it makes it more dangerous. We pretended to not recognize each other."

"Did you speak to him in the bar?"

"No, just looked. I didn't even wink. It wasn't necessary and would have been dangerous. In fact, when I saw Frank I decided to go to another bar, but then the fight started."

"Why did the fight start?"

"Don't know. I saw the accused walk over towards this woman, and the next thing, Frank got involved and there was pushing and shoving."

"Did you know the woman?"

"I think I'd seen her before, but I don't know her. I looked at pictures and thought about her a lot since Frank's death. I described her to the lieutenant, and he asked around but no one seems to know her."

"Did you tell all this to the Homicide Squad, to Sgt.-Det. Caron, so they could join in the search for the woman?"

"No."

"Why not?"

"It wasn't relevant and could've upset some drug investigation."

"Which one?"

"I don't know. I told you I didn't know what Frank was working on."

"Did you get involved in the fight in the bar?"

"No, I began moving in to help Frank, but the bouncer or manager called the regular police and they broke it up."

"Did you leave then?"

"No, I decided to hang around."

"Even though it was dangerous?"

"Yes."

"To help Frank?"

"Maybe, if necessary. I didn't really think about it."

"Do you know the accused?"

"No, I don't think I ever saw him before the night of the shooting."

"Had you ever seen Maurice Pomerleau before?"

"Yes. I saw his picture in the newspapers this week, and I've seen him before."

"Did you ever speak to him?"

"No."

"Did you investigate him in any way?"

"No."

"Did you ever see him with Frank Lepine, the victim?"

"I think so."

"The night of the shooting?"

"I don't remember."

"What do you mean you don't remember? You're an undercover policeman and you don't remember people you saw the night a friend of yours was shot?"

"I wasn't involved in the investigation and I didn't know of any connection between Pomerleau and the accused. There was no reason to remember."

"Was Pomerleau involved in the fight in the bar?"

"No, I don't think so. No."

"But you said you saw him with Lepine."

"Yes, I think so, but I don't remember if it was the night of the murder."

"What were they doing when you saw them?"

"Talking."

"About what?"

"I wasn't close enough to hear."

"Was Maurice Pomerleau an undercover policeman too?"

The tension in the courtroom diffused as several jurors and people in the audience laughed nervously.

"No, he wasn't a policeman."

"Was he an informer who was helping the police?"

"I don't know. He wasn't controlled by me and didn't tell me anything."

"What about Frank Lepine? Was Pomerleau an informer for Lepine? Did he report to him?"

"I don't know."

"Is it possible?"

"Objection."

"Everything is possible."

"Did you see Pomerleau in the street after the bars closed on the night of the murder?"

"I don't remember. I don't think so."

"Why don't you remember?"

"I told you. I didn't connect him with the murder. It just wasn't important so I didn't observe or remember."

"Would you have remembered if you had been questioned a day or so after the shooting?"

"Maybe."

"You testified last week that you didn't see who fired the shot."

"Yes."

"So it could have been almost anyone in the street?"

"Yes."

"How many people were in the street that night?"

"Hundreds, maybe thousands."

"And Frank Lepine could've been investigating or following almost any one of them that night?"

"I suppose so."

"And almost any one of them could've shot him?"

"I guess so."

"Was Frank Lepine investigating Serge Tremblay that night?"

"I don't know."

"Do you know Pauline Vinet?"

"The fortune teller? No, I only know what's in the newspapers."

"Are you following this case in the newspapers?"

"Yes."

"Do you know anything else about Serge Tremblay, Maurice Pomerleau or Pauline Vinet that you aren't telling us?"

"Objection—"

"No."

"Do you know anything else about what Frank Lepine was doing on the night of the killing or about his death that you haven't told us?"

"No, nothing else. He was a good cop and he's dead. If I knew more about how or why it happened, I would've told my lieutenant."

"Have you told your lieutenant anything about this case that you haven't mentioned in your testimony in court?"

"No."

"What's the name of your lieutenant?"

"Lieutenant-Detective Albert Ryan."

"Thank you. No further questions."

Vincent Talbot rose. "No re-examination. No further witnesses. The Crown's case is closed."

Judge Berne looked at Marie-Lyse Lortie. "Does the defence wish to call any witnesses?"

"May I have a brief adjournment to consult with my client?"

"Yes."

Oscar Cimon and Robert Caron followed Vince Talbot towards the back of the courtroom. The two policemen were gesturing excitedly. Neither knew the full relationship between Maurice Pomerleau and Frank Lepine, or whether it was connected with his death. It was too late to investigate. Since earlier that day, their preoccupation had been damage control rather than convicting this accused. Fortunately the trial was winding down, but they wondered where Lortie would stumble next, and what she might find.

The Homicide Department would look bad because they advanced the theory that Lepine was an accidental victim and suppressed the fact that he was a policeman. Now the price of their silence would be paid. The newspapers would call for an investigation of the cover-up of police bumbling. Politicians would make excuses, and everyone would forget that a good policeman had been killed. They were engulfed by a strange helplessness, caught up in the current of uncontrollable events.

*　　*　　*

Marie-Lyse was alone with Serge. The guard had stepped back to respect their privacy. Serge was chained to the floor hook, and unable to move more than three feet in any direction.

"We only have a few minutes to talk now. I'm going to call Pomerleau as our witness. If it takes more time the judge will agree to adjourn. That way I don't have to decide if you should testify till tomorrow. Pomerleau will have to explain his relationship with Lepine. Whatever he says, the jury won't believe him and it'll create one hell of a lot of doubts."

"Don't call Maurice!"

"What do you mean? You heard the cross-examination of Cimon. I'll bet anything Maurice was an informer and you knew—didn't you?"

"No, and don't call Maurice. I don't want him to be a witness."

"You were his cellmate. Was he an informer in prison too?"

"No. I took care of him. I told you that over and over."

"Where did he get drugs in jail?—from the guards?"

"I don't know."

"I'll ask him here in court."

"No. I don't want you to question him again."

"But he's your only chance, Serge. Don't you think the jury is wondering what's going on between you and Maurice? If I don't call him, they'll think that you killed Lepine either alone or with Maurice and find you guilty. Say, . . . were you an informer too?"

"Are you crazy? Do I sound like a guy who works for cops? The less I see them the better. I don't need them to protect me. I can take care of myself; always did."

"But Maurice needed them for protection and worked for them, didn't he?"

"I don't know. He never told me that."

"But you knew anyway. Did Maurice take that shot at Lepine?"

"I don't know."

"Was he at Le Wiz the night of the murder?"

"Nnnno."

"I don't believe you. He was there and fired the shot. Why are you covering for him?"

"I'm not covering. He's not on trial, I am, and I don't want to put him on the witness stand."

"Even if it means you'll be convicted of murder?"

"Yeah."

"You'll spend ten years, maybe more in jail."

"I've been there before. I can take care of myself."

"But Maurice—why shouldn't he go to jail if he did it? Why you? Why not him?"

"Maurice wouldn't last a week. You know what they do to cop killers? You know how they handle stool pigeons? He'd be dead in a few days. Send Maurice to jail and you might as well hang him."

"I have to call him as a witness. You're my client, and I can't let you be convicted."

"Okay. You're fired."

"What?"

"You're fired. If you want to question Maurice I don't want you for my lawyer any more."

"But, what about . . . .I . . . ."

"It's my trial and my ass. Maurice doesn't testify. You don't like it, you can quit."

"I've been—"

"You're doing a great job. But Maurice doesn't testify, understand? Tell the judge you don't want to call Maurice."

"I never told the judge I would. I just have to decide if I want to call anybody. You can't testify because of your record and I can't call Maurice. I guess the defence has no witnesses."

"Tell the judge whatever you want, but no Maurice."

*   *   *

The judge and jury re-entered the courtroom. Turning to Lortie, Sam Berne asked, "Maître Lortie, does the defence wish to present any witnesses?"

"No, My Lord."

The jury was startled at the sudden conclusion of the testimony. The story was incomplete and they expected to hear defence witnesses. Looking at the attorneys, Judge Berne asked, "May I assume that you will be ready to make the final arguments tomorrow?"

"Yes," answered Talbot, "it was my understanding that we would argue immediately after the proof was concluded, and I am ready."

"Thank you. And you, Maître Lortie?"

"I will be ready as well."

"Thank you." Judge Berne turned to the jury. "Ladies and gentlemen, as you have just heard, the Crown and the defence declare they have no further witnesses. This portion of the trial is now complete, and there remain the closing comments by the attorneys, my charge or instructions to you, and of course your deliberations and verdict. Tomorrow morning Maître Talbot will present the Crown's argument. He will be followed by Maître Lortie. In the afternoon I will give you my

212

explanations and comments on the law. After I finish, you will begin your deliberations.

"From that time onward you will not have any contact with the outside world until your verdict has been rendered. If you are unable to reach a unanimous verdict tomorrow, it will be necessary to spend a night, and possibly two, at a hotel. Please bring a small valise or overnight bag containing a change of clothing, and whatever else you may require.

"Once again, thank you. Please do not discuss the case with anyone, and please do not try to decide the outcome until after you have heard my instructions and deliberated with your colleagues. Have a good afternoon, and good night. I shall see you tomorrow morning. Thank you. The court is now adjourned."

* * *

Diane Rousseau lay daydreaming on the back balcony in the cool spring sun. The baby would be born within days. Fortunately the last months of her pregnancy had been in winter, rather than during the oppressive summer heat. Everything was ready, but even so she was anxious and a little worried.

"You startled me!" she exclaimed when Albert arrived home. "It's late and I started to worry about you. Then I must have dozed off. What happened to the trial? Is everything all right?"

"Yes, everything's under control now, but we had some difficult moments. Things worked out, and now it seems the trial's almost over. Everything happened at once . . . and a juror fainted, though he's better now . . . and the guy who was killed—now we find out he was a policeman."

"I've never seen you so excited. Take off your jacket, get a chair, and tell me everything—slowly, please."

He went into the house and returned with his steno pad. "We finished with Maurice Pomerleau this morning. The lawyer for the accused questioned him about guns and he seemed to know a lot. Then she gave him the murder weapon. He was too comfortable handling it.

213

Maybe he killed Lepine and they're trying to frame Tremblay for the murder. I don't know if they'll succeed. His lawyer is doing a good job."

"Do you think Pauline Vinet would do that?"

"I wouldn't have said so the other day, but now I just don't know. Maybe she's fighting to keep Maurice."

"You're not going to believe that and let Tremblay off, are you?"

"At this point, I don't know."

"The policeman, Coco—he testified?"

"Yes."

"What's he like? Romantic, sexy, like on TV?"

"He looks like . . . like a policeman: tall, a little fat, hair getting thin and greying. He walks like a policeman too, as if he owns the building, ready to shove aside anything in his way. He described how the police set up the arrest."

"Was it like on TV?"

"Yes, actually." He looked at his notes before continuing. "There were four policemen in a van parked near Pauline's house . . . . What's wrong? You just looked funny and bit your lip."

"It's nothing. I think the contractions are beginning, but the doctor said to not worry till my water broke or the pains were five minutes apart."

"How far apart are they?"

"That was the first one."

"Should we go to the hospital or call the doctor?"

"No, not yet."

"Let's go into the house. It's getting a little cool."

"I wonder if the baby can hear all this through my stomach." Diane rubbed her large belly with a slow circular motion.

"You never know. Come into the house."

"You said the trial's almost over."

"Uh-huh."

"How can you tell?"

"At first Coco didn't tell us everything. Then it came out, almost by accident at the last moment."

"What?"

"Frank Lepine, the dead man, was an undercover police agent."

"You're kidding!"

"No. And then Oscar Cimon came back and testified he's a police agent too. Suddenly there are policemen all over the place and no one knows what happened. How do they expect us to figure this case out when even the police don't know what happened?"

"Maybe the next witnesses will tell you."

"There won't be any more. Tomorrow we hear from the lawyers and the judge. Then we go to our room and vote on a verdict. The judge said to bring a small suitcase. We might have to spend a night at the hotel."

"What if I go into labour while you're in the jury room or the hotel?"

"Don't worry. They have phones all over the place. Tomorrow I'll ask Parent for all the phone numbers and call you every few hours. I might even send a note to the judge and tell him about you."

"Do you think he cares?"

"Of course, except he'd read the note in court and everyone in the world would know."

"Perhaps you should wait before sending any notes."

*　*　*

Pauline thought that Maurice smelled different after he testified. She was sensitive to odours, and this was the first sign that the court appearance had somehow disturbed him. Always taciturn, he was now a shivering shadow seized by an unusual fear. During the day he appeared to be sleepwalking, and at night he was awake. Before, he had kept away from the trial and even refused to read about it in the newspapers. Now he was obsessed with it.

The evening TV news referred to the crime as the 'Wiz Kill'. The report revealed that the victim had been a policeman, and speculated that the bar was a hangout for drug dealers. Pauline failed to see what difference that could make. Serge had killed Lepine, and must be locked up for good. If Serge was released, who would protect her? Why was Maurice worrying? He was innocent. He was in bed with her on the night of the so-called Wiz Kill.

Maurice still slept with her but it wasn't the same. He just twisted and turned and went to the bathroom, and smelled different. She thought his eyes were darker and sunken. There was no doubt he walked differently, shuffling, taking small short steps. He no longer answered when she spoke to him. When he did, it seemed that he hadn't understood her question.

She reached over in bed to touch his hip, but he drew back, then rose and went to the bathroom again. Pauline closed her eyes and drifted off into a trance. She was back in her salon, staring out the window and smiling at the pedestrians. A few returned her glance and one or two gestured with their hands. She thought she recognized two men, a younger Serge Tremblay and his father, Marcel. They were looking into the salon and pointing at her. Then they turned towards the door and walked and walked but never drew closer. Pauline wanted to open the door and greet them, but her arms and legs were heavy, unable to move, as if paralysed.

She awoke with a start. Serge and Marcel were gone, as was the fortune telling parlour. She was back in bed with Maurice. A noise interrupted the silence. Caroline must have awakened early to prepare for school. Pauline tried to get up, but she was unable to move and imagined she was paralysed. She panicked and reached for Maurice. This time her arm moved, but she withdrew it before touching him. She lay back and lifted the clock on her night table. It was only a quarter to seven. Caroline had plenty of time and there was no rush. Her eyes closed.

A rustling of clothes awakened her. She caught a glimpse of Maurice silently leaving the bedroom. Pauline wanted him back in bed but didn't call out. Perhaps he would sense her need.

They had told Maurice nothing would happen in court that day, but he had to be there. Being a witness had been different than he expected. Lortie's persistent questioning had penetrated his shield of noncommittal grunts and nods. Why had she made him hold that gun again? Everyone knew it was found on Serge. He had expected Serge would be convicted and sent to La Macaza. Now he was unsure. He had lost his ability to manipulate and manoeuver and run from disaster. If Serge got off the police would conduct a new investigation, and he'd be brought down to the station and questioned over and over again.

Serge was still trying to protect him, but how long would that last? He had manipulated Serge through a combination of love, friendship, whimpering or bribery, but that might be over. Pauline would throw him out of the flat. Already she had begun looking at him in a different way, and complained that there would be no one to protect her and Caroline if Serge were freed.

Things might still work out if Serge went to jail, but if he didn't then everyone would be after Maurice. Alexandre would be getting out soon, and who could tell how he'd react to his mother's story? Maybe he'd be mad that Maurice had moved into the flat and blame him for what happened. He raised both hands to cover his ears and temples. A dull pain throbbed in his head.

Caroline had gone to school. Pauline was sleeping when he left. The east end hadn't yet awakened. Like a man in a trance, he shuffled along Ste. Catherine East in the general direction of the courthouse. Two or three times he crossed streets on red lights. Drivers, rather than honking as usual, just gently avoided him. His head grew till he could no longer think. Nobody noticed when he sat down outside the Berri-UQAM Metro station. In times of recession passersby ignore the homeless and the unfortunate seated on park benches.

The headache seemed less intense, but his mouth was dry. He resumed walking, entering buildings from one side and leaving from the other, down stairs, under streets, up stairs, remaining indoors and concealed as much as possible, avoiding streets and fresh air. Forces he could not resist drew him to the courthouse. He entered the gloomy ground floor lobby. After emerging from the crowded elevator, he walked close to the wall and sat on a bench outside the courtroom. When the door opened he would sit in the back near the side, where Serge wouldn't see him.

217

*   *   *

The coffee had been brewing and gurgling in the jury room since the first jurors arrived at 8:30. Kathy Johnson sat at the head of the table, cutting pieces of cake from a large Pyrex dish. She took care to assure that the pieces were the same size before putting them on styrofoam plates. She was proud of her baking and the other jurors seemed to appreciate her efforts. She sent a double-sized piece to the judge. After all, he had said that the judge and jury were a team. Luckily she had received a lift, because the others had arrived earlier than usual.

" . . . and I didn't know if we're going to have a son or a daughter," Rousseau explained. "The doctor offered to check the ultrawave—"

"Ultrasound," Betty gently corrected.

"—ultrasound, and tell us, so Diane and I decided to find out, and now we know it's going to be a boy."

"When is your wife expecting the baby?"

"Any day now. She thought she felt a contraction last night when I got home, but it must have been something else."

"Did you make arrangements for her to call you here?"

"Sort of. Parent gave me the numbers of the judge's office and of the phone outside the jury room, where the guards sit."

"What are you talking about?" Rita Belleville asked as she approached.

"Older women and pregnancy," Betty Major retorted with a broad grin.

"Well, I don't think that fortune teller, Pauline Vinet, could still become pregnant."

"Not her," Albert explained. "My wife, Diane. She's due to have a baby any time. I gave her two phone numbers here, but I hope she won't have to call me."

"When you got the summons for jury duty, why didn't you tell them your wife was pregnant and get exempted?" Rita asked.

"I spoke to the sheriff, but she said it wasn't a good enough reason, and I just didn't try again when the judge was hearing people."

"We won't be here much longer," Betty observed. "We all have to get back to work, and Rita, you must be anxious to write those exams at Concordia."

"My professor didn't mind that I'm on a jury. Still, I'd like it to end soon, so I can get back to school and my friends."

12

Vince Talbot set down his papers and began to speak.

"Ladies and gentlemen, you have been chosen to decide whether or not the accused, Serge Tremblay, is guilty of having murdered Frank Lepine in front of Le Wiz on St. Denis Street on October seventh of last year. It is not an easy assignment, and all of us appreciate your efforts.

"Serge Tremblay is fortunate that he is being tried in a court of law, by an impartial judge, and by twelve hard-working and honourable jurors: citizens who have devoted more than a week to listening to the witnesses, and who will spend further time carefully weighing the evidence, to determine if he is guilty or innocent of the charge laid against him by the attorney general.

"The victim, Frank Lepine, was less fortunate. He was tried, sentenced and executed in a few seconds, without the benefit of a lawyer, judge, or jury to decide his fate. His life was prematurely ended by one person, and it is the submission of the Crown that the accused Serge Tremblay is that person, that the evidence presented is more than sufficient to convince you beyond a reasonable doubt of his guilt.

"At the conclusion of the trial you heard evidence that Frank Lepine was a police officer working undercover when he was killed. Police officers are people like you and me. They have friends and wives and children. They have qualities and faults. They have the same right to life and respect as each of us. Frank Lepine was not engaged in a gunfight at the time of his death. He was standing on the sidewalk on a public street when he was shot down in cold blood. Whoever shot him committed homicide.

"The only question you have to decide today is whether the accused pulled the trigger. Such a decision is not easily made, and to do so you must consider all the evidence.

"I remind you that Juan Luis Torres and Oscar Cimon both testified that they were present at Le Wiz on the night of the incident. Each described in his own way what happened. Both said that they witnessed a scuffle around midnight between the accused and the victim, that things got out of hand and the police were summoned to break up the fight. Serge Tremblay wanted to dance with a girl and Frank Lepine frustrated his efforts publicly. Tremblay was insulted and humiliated. The Crown does not have to establish a motive for a crime, but in this case there is a motive: to avenge a public insult.

"That is not all. After the bar closed there was further shoving between the two men. Once again, Serge Tremblay was insulted in public, and his motive became even stronger. Motive does not prove that a person committed a crime, but is a factor to take into consideration. Remember that there is a motive.

"When Frank Lepine fell to the ground, you can imagine the reaction of the crowd. Many stayed; some called for the police. One man, Serge Tremblay, disappeared. Flight from the scene of a crime does not prove guilt, but may indicate the guilty state of mind of a person . . . ."

* * *

Rita went to bars and clubs often. Although she wasn't a St. Denis Street regular, she could have been at the Wiz that fateful night . . . . Pauline said Tremblay and Pomerleau had a sexual relationship. If Tremblay's orientation was towards other men, what really happened between him and Lepine—and why? Could they possibly have known each other previously? No one said they did. Too bad Tremblay didn't testify and inform us. These details could be important. And then there's the elusive, evasive Pomerleau, always hovering about, but somehow never present. What's his part in all of this?

My God, thought Rita, these people are the same age as I am. Tremblay and Pomerleau are both in their early twenties, and Frank Lepine was only a few years older. Suddenly twenty-two wasn't quite as young and carefree an age as it had been a week earlier. A lifetime seemed to have passed since Rita had been chosen as a juror.

This was a trial about people in their twenties. She and Lucy were the only two jurors who belonged to that generation. She looked along the first row and wondered if Lucy shared her thoughts. She probably understood a lot more than people suspected. After all, she lived in a man's world, driving a canteen truck around construction sites. Rita would talk to Lucy during the break. Maybe she'd have some insight into Pomerleau and Tremblay.

* * *

"In this case there is a lot more than motive and opportunity. There is a statement by the accused, a statement to Pauline Vinet and Maurice Pomerleau on the night of the killing. Do you remember what Pauline Vinet said? She was in bed with Maurice, sleeping, when Tremblay woke them up by pounding on the door. He was white as a ghost, and said a guy was shot on St. Denis and might've been killed. What do you think he was talking about? He was confessing that he shot, and probably killed, Frank Lepine. He was carrying the gun, which he himself said had been used in the shooting, and went on to worry loudly whether the fellow was killed or not. Two weeks later he was arrested with the murder weapon in his possession.

"Perhaps you don't like Pauline Vinet or approve of her lifestyle. But you are not here to judge Ms. Vinet. If you believe her—and I think you must—then her evidence alone is sufficient to convince you of the guilt of the accused. She repeated the statement of Serge Tremblay, and he was an eyewitness to the killing . . . ."

* * *

It had never occurred to Albert Rousseau that the person who fired the gun was an eyewitness. There was no logical reason why not, yet it never entered his mind—almost like a mathematical truth staring you in the face that is glossed over repeatedly. True, he thought, if I believe Pauline it isn't necessary to even think about whether the motive was sufficient, or whether Tremblay should have stayed or run. He was uncomfortable with the suggestion that guilt could be inferred from the fact that Tremblay had left the scene. Many people leave the scene of an accident and crime. So what! Not everyone wants to get involved with reporters and police. Quite frankly, he wasn't sure what he'd have done if he had been at Le Wiz that night.

* * *

"Pauline Vinet's testimony is corroborated or confirmed by the testimony of Maurice Pomerleau, and by all the other facts of this case. Again, you may not like or approve of Maurice Pomerleau and the way he lives. We know he has a criminal record, and doesn't adhere to the work ethic. You may believe that he doesn't always tell the truth. He's like a broken clock whose arms do not move, but remember, the arms of a broken clock tell the correct time twice a day. He told the truth when he described the conversation that took place in their flat in the middle of the night. You know he told the truth, because you know the Maurice Pomerleau clock indicated the same time as the Pauline Vinet clock, and all the other facts confirm this."

"Don't forget the murder weapon, the gun. Tremblay was the subject of a dramatic arrest. Remember how he kept Pauline Vinet a virtual prisoner in her own home. When she was able to contact the police, the SWAT team came to her rescue and made the arrest, a delicate and successful operation. He was arrested with the murder weapon in his possession. Sgt.-Det. Martin, an old friend of Pauline Vinet who responded to her call and organized the arrest, testified that he was present, that he took the pistol from the accused, put a tag on it with his name and number. Remember the early police witnesses. They produced that same pistol, and identified the bullet in the body of the victim as having been fired from the pistol seized in the possession of the accused at the time of the arrest. People don't walk around with another person's pistol in their waistband. Tremblay was the owner of that pistol. He used that pistol to kill Frank Lepine. Serge Tremblay confessed his crime to Pauline Vinet and Maurice Pomerleau. He committed the murder of Frank Lepine. On the evidence offered, you must find Serge Tremblay guilty of murder. Thank you."

Maître Vincent Talbot gathered his papers and returned to his seat. It was twenty to eleven and time to adjourn.

* * *

"Good man, good man, that Talbot," Phil Pasquin commented, leaving the courtroom. "I'd hire him in a moment. The man knows how to close a deal. That's what I like. A man who comes on strong in the stretch and makes the sale."

"Are you sure he made the sale, Mr. Pasquin?" Betty asked.

"Of course I am. Did you see the faces of the other jurors? They were eating out of his hand. This is going to be a sure conviction. Jury will decide in no time at all."

"I don't know. He never did explain what those policemen were doing in Le Wiz, and we haven't heard from the defence or from the judge. I'm going to wait before trying to decide."

"Maybe so, but most of the jurors have already decided. I guess you're just not used to looking people in the face. Ha-ha! In the barbershop customers always have their back to you, but in the clothing business you learn to size up a customer, the moment he walks into the store. I bet most of the members of this jury sized up the situation, and

I tell you they're ready to convict no matter what Marie-Lyse Lortie says. I'll show you." Pasquin signalled for Bernard Richer to come over and join them. "Bernard, what did you think of Talbot's businesslike approach? Pretty good, eh?"

"He speaks well. Much stronger in his argument than in questioning the witnesses."

"He knows how to pace himself and come on for a strong finish. I was just telling Betty—uh, Ms. Major here—that I'd hire that man in my business any day of the week. Bet you would have too."

"Mine was a small business and I'm not sure he'd have agreed to work for a low salary."

"Good point. Makes me wonder why he works here in the courthouse. Crown attorneys aren't well paid. Last year, there were articles in the papers that they were unhappy, and planning a slowdown or something. I'll bet he could earn two or three times as much as a private lawyer."

"Maybe he likes his work," Betty offered. "It's exciting. Some people like to do interesting things and are prepared to earn less."

"Not in the real world. Do you charge some barbershop customers less because you like to cut their hair? I'll bet you don't."

"No, but there's a difference between cutting a man's hair for twenty dollars and deciding what you're going to do with your life. I wouldn't work in the barbershop if my boss didn't treat me well, or if I didn't like most of the customers."

"Don't have that luxury in my business. I take money from all my customers whether I like them or not."

"But you're selling clothes, not a service. Other people sell suits and coats for you and probably don't even get to see most of the customers."

"That's right, but it wasn't always that way for me . . . .Anyway, I'm ready for coffee. How about you, Bernard?"

"Good idea."

"Ms. Major, Betty, do you feel like having coffee with a customer?"

"Not right now, thanks. In a few minutes." Betty wandered off in the direction of Albert Rousseau and Roger Lebrun.

*   *   *

"The judge is back," Parent called. The jurors headed out of the room and lined up in order. Parent formed a circle with the thumb and index finger of his right hand and gestured to indicate everything was perfect.

"Ladies and gentlemen," Marie-Lyse Lortie began, "like my colleague and Mr. Justice Berne, I wish to thank you for your attention. A jury trial is a difficult ordeal for you the jurors, and for an attorney such as me, pleading my first murder trial before a jury. I hope you will overlook any errors I make, and not hold my client accountable for mistakes resulting from my lack of experience.

"It's not easy for an accused person to defend himself against a criminal charge. The Crown has all the advantages: a large efficient police force, detectives, SWAT teams, pathologists, technicians, laboratories, lawyers. They have everything at their disposal.

"The accused, Serge Tremblay, only has a jury of twelve reasonable people who realize his difficult position and won't convict him unless the Crown has convinced them beyond a reasonable doubt of his guilt.

"The judge will explain to you what that means. He will tell you to not convict Serge Tremblay unless each of you is morally certain that he killed Frank Lepine. Not just one or two, but all of you must be convinced of his guilt beyond a reasonable doubt.

"Serge Tremblay has only you to rely upon. I cannot go into the jury room with you to plead for his acquittal. No one, not even the judge, is entitled to enter your room while you discuss this case. That is why I hope that one or more of you will represent me and argue for the acquittal of Serge Tremblay in the jury room after the closing arguments and the judge's charge are finished.

"When this trial began, Serge Tremblay was a name you probably had never heard. Now you know who Serge Tremblay is, the man who has been in this room with you for more than a week and whose freedom depends on the outcome of your deliberations. You must decide his future—not an easy task. You must review the testimony of the witnesses and decide who to believe.

"Do you believe Maurice Pomerleau is capable of telling the truth? You saw how he looked during the questioning. You know the kind of man he is. He has a serious criminal record. He was in prison when he met Alexandre Vinet. As soon as he got out, he contacted and moved in with Pauline Vinet, the mother of his prison friend. Did he support her? Did he contribute anything to the household? Does he have a job? Is he looking for one? You know the answers to these questions as well as I do. Would you live with Maurice Pomerleau? Would you have him as your business partner or employee? Do you believe him? Can anyone believe him? Does he even know the difference between the truth and a lie? Can the accused or anyone else be convicted on the word of this man?

"Maître Talbot compared Maurice Pomerleau to a broken clock that tells the correct time twice a day. There are twenty-four hours in the day and each hour has sixty minutes. If I am not mistaken that means that there are 1440 minutes in the day. The broken clock is correct for only two of those 1440 minutes, once every 720 minutes. One chance in 720 that Maurice Pomerleau is telling the truth: not very good odds! Can you convict Serge Tremblay on that evidence?"

Albert Rousseau wrote "24 x 60 = 1440" in his notebook. The arithmetic was correct and so was her logic. He couldn't stand Pomerleau, and wouldn't believe him once in a thousand times. This was the man who allowed Serge Tremblay to move into Pauline's flat and did nothing about it. He didn't work. He sponged off Pauline, when her welfare cheques probably weren't enough for her and Caroline. He wasn't even loyal to her. Probably carried on with Tremblay all the time he lived with Pauline. The guy is a big zero, and his evidence is worthless. He wrote "Pomerleau = 0" in his notes and sat back to listen.

"Do you believe Pauline Vinet?—Excuse me, Pauline D. Vinet? Madame Vinet has had a difficult life. She had to cope with two children alone. One of them, unfortunately, is in jail for a serious crime. He's a friend of Maurice Pomerleau. Madame Vinet is a retired fortune teller.

Have you ever had your fortune told? No? Why not? Is it because you don't believe fortune tellers? Because you think they invent stories? Don't feel badly if you distrust fortune tellers. Sgt.-Det. Claude Martin—Coco—didn't have his fortune told by Pauline either, because he thought fortune tellers make things up. He didn't ask Pauline to predict his future, and he knew her intimately.

"I'm not being critical of Pauline Vinet. Life has been difficult for her. She had an operation a few years ago, and has to care for Caroline alone. Madame Vinet is a resourceful woman who told you she'd do anything to protect her daughter. What about her lover? How far would she go to protect him? She told you that it's not easy to find a man when you're over fifty, and not well, and have a child in the house. Do you think she'd make something up to protect her man, to protect Maurice if he committed a crime? It's not easy to find a man when you're over fifty . . . ."

It's not easy to find a man when you're under fifty either, thought Kathy Johnson. I'm thirty-six, divorced, and I know how difficult it is. People don't call like before. The men want something for nothing. A one- or two-night stand is fine, but don't really give a damn about me or my needs. I can understand why Pauline would do anything to hold onto Maurice, even if he isn't the perfect man . . . .What am I saying? I wouldn't want to spend ten minutes alone with that creep. But Pauline likes him, and he is a man.

"I don't ask you to judge or condemn Pauline Vinet. She isn't on trial today, and whatever the outcome she is free to return home and spend the rest of her life with Maurice Pomerleau. Did it occur to you that Pauline was concerned her relationship with Maurice was threatened by the presence of Serge Tremblay? That Pauline Vinet testified to protect Maurice Pomerleau? Pauline Vinet really has nothing to lose. Serge Tremblay does. If you have a reasonable doubt about the truth of her testimony, you should not condemn Serge Tremblay.

"Maurice Pomerleau's testimony is worthless. Pauline Vinet's testimony is doubtful. The doubtful and the worthless cannot add up to a moral certainty of guilt . . . ."

* * *

If Francine Roux had been born a few years later, she probably would have attended law school and ended up pleading criminal cases. After graduation from university, she had worked at the museum. Then she married Ron, and devoted her life to helping her husband and family. She was involved in certain cultural activities like the symphony and the museum, and helped Ron in the office, but deep down she regretted not having a professional career.

She prided herself on being a strong, outspoken, decisive person who rarely erred. Now she was confused, torn between Pauline Vinet and Marie-Lyse Lortie. At first she sympathized with Pauline Vinet and believed her testimony, even if she didn't approve of her lifestyle. There was something attractive about this free spirit with special courage. It never occurred to her that Pauline Vinet might not be a simple victim of society and ill health, but rather a shrewd conniving liar ready to commit perjury to protect her younger lover. Francine secretly approved of the idea of a younger lover, but Pauline should have chosen a man with some backbone and character.

She envied and admired Marie-Lyse Lortie, and wanted to help her. The problem was that she couldn't be on the side of Marie-Lyse and Pauline simultaneously. If she believed Pauline's testimony, then Tremblay was guilty, and Marie-Lyse would lose. If she accepted Marie-Lyse's argument and doubted Tremblay's guilt, that meant that Pauline Vinet was lying.

And what if she made a mistake? What if Tremblay was wrongly acquitted? He might go back and kill Pauline, and Caroline—and she, Francine, would have made it possible. Control yourself, Francine. You wanted to be a lawyer and now lack the courage to be a juror. Relax and listen. You know you're every bit as smart as everyone else on the jury. There'll be time to deliberate and decide. Besides, there are twelve of us, and if we all agree we're unlikely to be wrong. We still haven't heard what the judge has to say. Maybe he'll help us to decide.

*   *   *

"Before this trial began," Lortie continued, "You may not have known the difference between a revolver and a pistol, but Pomerleau knew. Did you see how comfortably and easily he handled the pistol? It wasn't the first time he'd held a gun in his hands. He didn't tell you he was frightened living in the flat with Serge Tremblay and a pistol. Pomerleau could have taken the pistol and forced Serge Tremblay out of the flat at any time. He could have called the police. He could have protected Caroline and Pauline. He didn't because he chose not to. When Pauline Vinet testified, did she choose to protect and defend a man unworthy of her love and loyalty?

"The defence does not have to prove who committed the crime. You don't have to discover the criminal; that's the job of the police. If the police didn't do their job, you don't have to do it for them. They didn't do their job in this case. They hid evidence from you. They failed to tell you that Lepine was a police officer. Do you think they forgot? They failed to tell you that Oscar Cimon was a police officer. Do you think they forgot? They failed to investigate Maurice Pomerleau to see how he fits into the drug scene on St. Denis Street. They failed to answer the questions that you and I and everyone in this courtroom are asking.

Is there a reasonable possibility that the crime was committed by Maurice Pomerleau? What was really going on at Le Wiz? Why didn't the police tell you? Why did they hide the fact that Lepine and Cimon were police agents? Why? If you don't know, it's because they didn't tell you, and now you have a reasonable doubt.

"The death of Frank Lepine was a terrible tragedy — a tragedy that will be even greater if you convict an innocent man of causing that death. Thank you."

* * *

"Are they finished?" Jackie asked as Judge Berne entered the office.

"Yes, they both pleaded well. We've adjourned till two this afternoon, when it'll be my turn. I'll be in my office working. Please don't let anyone disturb me."

"Aren't you going to eat?"

"Not right now. I have to sit quietly and think."

"You'll think better if you eat. I'll get you a sandwich, a good one from across the street."

"Thanks."

It was quiet now. Sam gazed out at the east end of the city. From fifteen floors up the distant low buildings resembled well-worn Monopoly hotels and houses, interrupted by church spires and parking lots — a world inhabited by Lilliputians driving toy cars. The smells and sounds, the contradictions and incongruities, were absent, and the morning activities not visible. Imagination and recollection supplied the images his eyes couldn't see: the bars, restaurants, rooming houses, walk-up flats, the St. Denis Theatre, centre of the annual comedy festival, and l'UQAM, a secular university dominated by two architectural church relics. The previous summer when he walked past the concrete campus, a banner suspended from the bell- tower facade proclaimed, 'CABARET', 'PEPSI DIÈTE'.

At the desk he read his notes for the closing act of this drama. Concentrating intensely, he shut the world out of his thoughts. The only reality was the trial. Two hours later he placed the notes for the charge in a red folder on his desk.

During his first year in the Criminal Division, Sam made the mistake of allowing an usher to carry the file into court. Once, the usher dropped the folder, scattering papers on the floor. He had to endure an embarrassing delay while they were gathered up, and then spend five minutes sorting them in full view of the audience. There were butterflies in his stomach.

He lifted the phone and pushed the button to connect with Jackie.

Anticipating his request, she quietly entered and placed a brown paper bag with a sandwich on his desk. "I'll bring you coffee right away."

"Thanks." He ate without speaking, focused on the contents of the red folder.

Linda looked through the open door. "Have you made up your mind whether Tremblay is guilty?"

"No, I can't decide until I hear the judge's instructions. Besides, that's the jury's decision."

"Monsieur le Juge, you're teasing me again."

"Not really. I've prepared my notes, and have a good idea what I'm going to say, but sometimes at the last minute while talking to the jury something pops into my mind that I didn't notice before."

He declined her offer to carry his notes.

*   *   *

The spectators' benches were almost full when Judge Berne entered the courtroom and mounted the platform. After acknowledging the attorneys and the accused, he addressed the jury.

"As a civilized society, we adopt laws to protect the lives, welfare and property of our members. When one of these laws is broken and a crime is committed, the persons suspected of committing the crime must be apprehended and brought before a court of law to determine whether they are innocent or guilty. Failure to enforce these laws can only lead to a state of uncertainty, fear, tragedy, and indeed anarchy. But these laws must be applied in a manner that respects the rights of the individual, so that an innocent person is not falsely convicted."

In the far corner Parent's eyes fluttered and closed.

"This court consists of a judge and jury, who work as a team. Each of us has different responsibilities. I must ensure that the evidence is presented fairly, inform you of the law, and explain how it should be applied. I am your lawyer, but there is an important difference between me and the lawyer you consult in your private lives. As private citizens, you may accept or disregard your attorney's advice, hire a new lawyer, or decide to do without one and follow your own instincts. But as jurors, in matters of law you must accept my statement and interpretation of the law. If I make an error, other judges can read the record and correct me. My role is often summarized with the phrase, 'The judge is master of the law.' That is not completely accurate; the law is my master."

He turned his head and noticed Phil Pasquin staring as though he were sizing a job applicant or a prospective lawyer. Albert Rousseau was scribbling busily. *There's at least one man who's unlikely to skip over any facts. Rocket must be wondering about the jury's consumption of paper, and what that'll do to the government finances. I hope his wife doesn't go into labour during the deliberations. I would probably have to release him. He's a very conscientious juror.*

"Society has chosen you to determine the guilt or innocence of the accused by deciding what facts to believe and applying the law to those facts according to your oath as jurors. You swore to carefully consider all the evidence and render a verdict based on all the facts. Review and weigh the testimony carefully. You may believe all, part, or none of the testimony of a witness. Use your experience and common sense. You have sworn to decide this case solely on the evidence. Set aside anything you may have read or heard about the case outside the courtroom. Abandon all preconceived notions, prejudices, and impressions gathered from the media or from friends and relatives. Concentrate on the evidence only, so you may establish the facts and reach a verdict based solely on these facts. Just as the law is my master, the evidence presented in this courtroom is your master."

Sam liked that turn of phrase, which he had picked up from a colleague and always used in jury charges. *Only there are no masters here. We're all caught up together in this adventure, judge, jurors, the accused, the lawyers—all in this trial together until the end.*

"You have taken an oath to keep your deliberations secret, both during and after the trial. This is intended to encourage free and open discussion among members of the jury. You account to no one but your conscience for your decision.

"There is a great principle of law at the foundation of our system of criminal justice, which applies throughout this trial and your delib-erations. The accused is never obliged to establish his innocence. He is presumed and remains innocent until the Crown has convinced you of his guilt beyond a reasonable doubt. What is a reasonable doubt? It is the doubt that prevents a reasonable person from being *morally certain* of the guilt of the accused. I use the phrase morally certain because mathematical certainty does not exist in the world of law. The question you should ask is this: Am I morally convinced of the guilt of Serge Tremblay? If the answer is yes, it is your duty to convict, but if a reasonable doubt lingers in your mind, it is your duty to find Serge Tremblay not guilty . . . ."

The jury would have two days to deliberate before the weekend. Hopefully it wouldn't be necessary to spend Saturday in the courthouse. When the weekend is approaching, jurors are more motivated to reach a decision. Some are always in a rush to decide and get back to their routine, while others try to prolong the deliberations. Hundreds of years ago in England they didn't feed jurors, allowing nature to compel a rapid verdict.

"Serge Tremblay has been charged with the second degree murder of Frank Lepine, in Montreal, on October seventh, 1991. The Crown must prove the essential elements or ingredients of the offence. You should not have much difficulty deciding that the death of Frank Lepine was the result of an illegal act. The evidence of the police technicians and the pathologist is uncontradicted. The question you must decide is whether Tremblay committed that illegal act. If you are not convinced beyond a reasonable doubt, you must find him not guilty. However, if you are convinced, then you must decide whether he intended to kill Lepine, or only meant to scare or wound him. If you decide that he intended to kill, then you must find him guilty of murder. On the other hand if you are not convinced of the intention to kill, you must find him guilty of manslaughter."

Some jurors just look indecisive. Bernard Richer, number eight, looks that way. He seems to gravitate towards Pasquin. Kathy Johnson, number seven, looks like a follower too—a good baker, but a follower.

"At the end of each day I asked you to not form a conclusion till you heard all the proof. Now is the time for you to examine the testimony of each witness, to see if it harmonizes with the other evidence, to determine if the witnesses told you not just part, but all of the truth. To assess credibility you may consider their general powers of observation, and how they acted. Were they nervous? Some people are nervous because it's their first experience in court and they're intimidated by the surroundings; others have something to hide. Does the witness have something to conceal or gain? Use the criteria you use every day to decide if someone is trustworthy or deceitful, and if they're telling the truth or not. Weigh the evidence of Juan Luis Torres, Oscar Cimon, Pauline Vinet, Maurice Pomerleau, and Claude Martin. Examine the pistol, the shells, and the medical report. They are exhibits and form part of the evidence."

There's good old number twelve, Rick Hayes. He's probably the jury's expert on bars and guns. Pasquin probably sees him as a threat to the entire men's clothing industry, a haberdashery anarchist.

"I may not always express myself clearly and precisely. If you have any questions or require further explanation during your deliberations, send me a note. I will then ask the advice of the attorneys, and invite you back into the courtroom for the answer. Naturally if the problem is a simple administrative one, like a broken coffee machine or a request to go for an early lunch, I will simply take the appropriate action . . . ."

He had been speaking for almost an hour and still retained the jury's attention, even if he had not yet aroused Parent from the depths of his slumber. Just another few minutes to go. Sam paused to sip some water, and glanced at the attorneys to see if they would react. They both were listening, and had few notes in front of them. That was a good sign: little likelihood that he had made an error of sufficient magnitude to invite a motion for a mistrial. Despite the drink his throat was dry, as he turned to the jury once again.

"When you have agreed on a unanimous verdict, send me a note and I will convene everyone back into this courtroom. After you enter, the clerk will ask:

Who is the foreperson who will speak for you?

Are the jurors agreed on a unanimous verdict?
What is your verdict?

When your foreperson replies, the accused, the attorneys, the audience, and I will hear the verdict at the same time. Ladies and gentlemen, good luck in your deliberations and thank you for your patience. You may retire to the jury room."

"All rise," Linda called.

*   *   *

They were happy for the opportunity to stretch their legs. The noise of moving chairs and shuffling feet aroused Parent. He blinked, realized what had happened, and opened the door for the jurors to exit.

After they left, Judge Berne turned back to the lawyers. "The court will adjourn till we have word from the jury. I shall remain in the building, and request the attorneys to keep the clerk advised of your whereabouts. Thank you."

As Judge Berne left the court, Parent rushed up and greeted him. "An excellent charge, Monsieur le Juge, excellent."

"How would you know? You slept like a dead man throughout. Not a sound, not even a snore."

"Pardon, Monsieur le Juge. It's the pills that make me sleep."

"Are you sure it's not my charge that put you to sleep?"

"Non, I fell asleep even before you began to speak."

"Yes, and made it harder for me. Next time you want to sleep, ask one of the other constables to sit in that chair, and go some place where the judge cannot see you."

"Yes, Monsieur le Juge."

"What did you want to ask me earlier, before the court started?"

"Well, as you know there is a severe budgetary crisis in the court-house."

"Yes?"

"They no longer send three jury constables to the hotel unless there is a special order from the judge. We have to stay up all night, and it is very difficult to function without sleeping, so I was wondering if you would issue an order—"

"—for an additional jury constable so you can rest at night?"

"Yes, Monsieur le Juge."

"Non, Constable. You spent the afternoon sleeping in the courtroom, and are undoubtedly fully rested for the night's duties. Non?"

"Oui. You are quite right. I shouldn't have asked."

It was 4:20 when Judge Berne returned to his office. He had spoken to the jury for ove an hour.

"How did you do?" Jackie asked.

"I don't know. I'm afraid it was a big bore. Parent fell asleep as soon as I opened my mouth and didn't awake until the adjournment."

"Don't feel badly. Parent has been around a long time, and wouldn't fall asleep unless he had complete faith in you."

"Thank you. My self-confidence is restored. I guess the real test will come when the jury begins to ask questions."

"Well, were there any motions for a mistrial?"

"No."

"So relax. I'll get you a coffee. Where's Linda?"

"She was having such a good time that I told her she could return to the third floor and wait for news from the jury. However, they could take several days to reach a verdict. I expect she'll have her fill of the third floor before it's over."

13

Maurice sat quietly in the corner of the deserted courtroom, staring at the clerk as she completed and shuffled a seemingly endless pile of documents. He had anticipated a ceremonial opening as on previous mornings, but nothing had happened. The guard just opened the door, and Maurice went in and sat down. The room resembled a bar in the early afternoon, before opening for business. Maurice assumed Serge was in a cell somewhere in the building, but neither he nor his police guards were visible. And the jurors—he hadn't seen them since the previous afternoon.

He heard the sound of muffled footsteps on the carpet. Serge's lawyer entered the room, nonchalantly carrying her court gown over her arm. She draped the gown over the back of the chair at the counsel table and sat down. "Any news?"

"Nothing so far," the clerk answered. "Jury returned at 9:20 this morning, and they've been in their room since."

"Where's Maître Talbot?"

"Up in the crown prosecutor's office. Do you want to speak to him? I have his private number."

"No, just asking."

"He'll be down shortly. Those crown prosecutors are all the same when they're waiting for a verdict. They disappear, pretending there's work in their offices, but they can't stay away from the courtroom. He'll be down before ten. Just wait and see."

"Do you know where Serge Tremblay is?"

"In the basement cells. They'll keep him there till the judge orders him brought up. The government's cutting police budgets, so prisoners are kept in the basement as long as possible. Saves having to assign special guards to watch them."

"Cutbacks, reductions, no money, lower budgets, that's all I ever hear around this building," Marie-Lyse commented. "Glad I don't work here any more."

"Mm-hm. The secretaries had to take two days off without pay. They can't do that to court clerks because we only work when the court's in session."

"The judge?"

"Came by early and waited in the back hall for the jurors to come from the hotel. Spoke to Constable Parent for a minute or two and returned to his office. Like the rest of us, he's just hanging around. I've worked with him before. He'll pop his head into the courtroom every hour or so."

"Breakfast has arrived!" Vince Talbot strode briskly into the room carrying a cardboard tray loaded with styrofoam cups of coffee, a box of donuts, and a bag of munchies. "There's a special promotion over at Dunkin' Donuts. Buy a dozen donuts, and they give you a free bag of munchies. The special starts January first of each year and ends December 31. Been going since 1973." He carefully placed the cups on the table in front of the witness box. "Cream, two percent milk, sugar, saccharin, and twelve donuts — six different varieties. Marie-Lyse, the crown attorneys are at your service. The law obliges us to make full disclosure to the defence, so I opened the box of goodies in order that you can examine its contents."

"Vince, you're great."

"You nervous?"

"Uh-huh."

"We all are. I've been at this more than ten years and I still can't concentrate on anything while the jury is out. And I work for the Crown; it must be even worse for the defence."

"I can't compare."

"Have a donut. It's going to be a long wait."

"How do you know?"

"I don't, but it always seems long. Coffee?"

Marie-Lyse reached for her purse. "Let me give you some money. You must have paid for this yourself."

"No, I'll only accept money from the winner of the pool."

"The pool?"

"Yes, we're going to organize a little pool and try to guess the time of the verdict. Everyone in the room writes a time on a piece of paper and puts two dollars in the pot. Closest guess wins all the money and pays for the coffee. There's Linda. Linda, will you join the pool?"

"Oui." She pulled out two dollars and put it on the table. "I'll get the jury constables. They love to gamble. Constable Parent even applied for a job in the security department at the new casino."

"How do you know?"

"He told me. We've become friends since this trial began. He calls me the *co-pilot*."

"Did he get the job?"

"No, they said he looked too much like a policeman, and it wouldn't be good for the casino's image. Might frighten the customers."

Maurice strained to hear each word. He knew all about the coffee at Dunkin' Donuts, or Chez Dunkin as they called it in their latest advertising campaign. The faces in the room were all familiar, but he was used to seeing them in court gowns, not shirts and sweaters. The casual conversation unnerved him. He had come expecting to see or hear about Serge, and all these people discussed was coffee and betting pools.

During the trial the participants had appeared like actors in a TV serial. Now outside their roles, they were unreal, as if the characters from Cheers interrupted the program to perform a commercial. They all looked so different. Serge's lawyer seemed much younger, dressed in a skirt and sweater, much less frightening. Too bad she hadn't been dressed that way when she questioned him the other day.

Maurice trembled at the recollection of being on the witness stand. He felt warm all over, then cold, then warm again. The headache returned, his throat was dry, and the familiar donut box reminded him that he hadn't eaten that morning. He wondered what the jury was doing.

*   *   *

Up on the fifteenth floor, the phone rang in the outer office, and Jackie called to Judge Berne, "It's Linda. She has news for you."

"Thank you . . . .Yes, Linda? . . . An envelope from the jury . . . .Tell the clerk to advise the lawyers, and arrange for the accused to be returned to the courtroom. Then come up, and please bring me the note."

It would be a bad sign if the first question from the jury showed confusion in the minds of the jurors and required lengthy consultation with the lawyers. That often happened at a later stage when jurors were tired, but hopefully not at the beginning of the deliberations.

Linda entered and handed him a large brown envelope. "By the way," she said, "the verdict was given today in the trial of Billy James: not guilty."

The judge found himself pleased to hear this decision. He opened the envelope in Linda's presence and read:

The jury wishes to hear tapes of the testimony of Pauline D. Vinet and of the second appearance of Oscar Cimon.
Phil Pasquin, Foreman
Juror number six

He wondered what they might be thinking in asking for the testimony of these two witnesses. He put on his gown to go back down to the courtroom.

"Lolita and I are going out for lunch early," Jackie called when he was too far down the hallway to respond. He glanced at the clock: five to eleven. He wondered why she was going out to lunch at that hour. Well, it wasn't really his business. She'd probably seen something on sale and wanted to get to the store before they sold out.

The attorneys had slipped into their court gowns. Serge entered the prisoner's dock, flanked by two policemen. Maurice was the sole spectator, huddled in the far corner of the room.

"I have received a note from the jurors," Judge Berne announced. "I shall read it and then request the clerk to show the note to the attorneys and file it as exhibit J-3." Marie-Lyse sighed audibly when she realized it wasn't a verdict, and the butterflies in her stomach rested their wings. "There are two ways to proceed. Either I bring the jury back into the courtroom, and we all listen together in open court while it is re-broadcast over the loudspeakers, or, if both attorneys agree, I can order a copy of the master tape and allow the jury to listen to the tapes privately. What do you recommend?"

Marie-Lyse rose. "The defence has no objection to proceeding in the second manner; that is, to allow the jurors to hear the tapes privately."

"And the Crown?"

"Agreed."

"Fine," Berne said. "Would you please bring in the jury."

Five minutes later the buzzer sounded and the jury entered. They were dressed more casually, but didn't seem any the worse for having spent a night in the hotel.

"Ladies and gentlemen, I have received your note and consulted the attorneys. The tapes will be prepared and sent to you in the jury room when they are ready. This requires time, so they may not be available till after the lunch break. In the meantime I suggest you continue to discuss the evidence. Please remember it is important that you listen to the entire testimony of each witness. Thank you. You can now return to the jury room."

*   *   *

Betty Major recoiled at the thought of lunch. Usually she had a quick sandwich because many customers liked to have their hair cut during the lunch hour, and she wasn't inclined to idle around alone in a restaurant at 2:30. But in the courthouse long lunches were a daily ritual. The jury spent too much time eating. No one had warned her about the one-and-a-half-hour lunches. Even if she wasn't hungry, she had to sit around the table with the others, and before she knew it she was eating more and more. She'd felt stuffed since the beginning of the trial. No wonder the judge looked like he was putting on weight, and the jury guards were bursting out of their pants.

She thoroughly enjoyed being a juror, except for the long periods of sitting still. As a hair stylist she was on her feet all day. The change was getting to her.

The previous afternoon, after the jurors had begun their deliberations, they discussed whether they'd be going to the hotel. She had hoped that they'd be able to agree and leave quickly, but Henri had made it perfectly clear that he welcomed the holiday from work, and whatever the others felt, he wouldn't agree to any verdict before he slept in the hotel for a night or two at government expense. His stubbornness surprised her, even though she had learnt long ago that even seemingly meek men can be stubborn. If Henri wanted to sleep in a hotel, all twelve of them would have to do likewise.

They were lodged in a separate section. They had been well received, but were surprised to discover that the television sets had been removed from their bedrooms, and the phones only connected with their jury guards. They were totally secluded.

Yes, Betty thought, men aren't always what they seem. Phil Pasquin had seemed to be such an important man, when he came to the salon and sat reading his *Playboy* backwards, talking to no one. She had imagined he must be a top executive, but in the jury room he had shown his true colours as an insecure blowhard, constantly seeking attention and recognition. Some jurors were so unhappy with him that during the night they met secretly in one of the bedrooms to discuss the possibility of choosing a new foreman. Oh well, with Pasquin as foreman they'd have to agree on a verdict quickly, because they couldn't endure him for long.

Imagine the coincidence of meeting Francine Roux here. Betty was pleased that her favourite customer had a nice wife. The next time he came for his haircut, she'd talk with him about their experience.

She expected that they would agree on a verdict before Friday night. She might even go to the shop Saturday morning and surprise Tony.

* * *

Throughout the night Albert Rousseau had been anxious. He had Denis call and assure his wife that he'd return home at the first sign that the labour had begun. Actually Parent said that if anything happened he'd call and ask the judge, but he doubted that the judge would prevent his being with Diane at the hospital. Albert was a juror, not a prisoner, although during the night he felt imprisoned and punished. Jurors weren't supposed to receive calls from the outside but Parent made an exception when Diane phoned in the morning.

* * *

Sam knew it would be a long day. The wait for a verdict is interminable, and he had to remain available while the jurors were deliberating. He decided to go outside for a walk during the jury's noon break.

"Constable, how are your jurors holding up?" he asked Parent.

"They seemed fine, except Albert Rousseau, juror number eleven. His wife's pregnant and ready to pop at any time."

"What happened?"

"Nothing yet, but before we left the courthouse he insisted that I call and tell her exactly where we'll stay, and when we got to the hotel he wanted to call himself."

"And..?"

"We made a deal. I called a couple of times on his behalf. She sounds worried. What should I do if we get a call that she's in labour?"

"I'll decide if and when she calls. Anything else?"

"Oui, Monsieur le Juge."

"What?"

"I allowed him to speak to her. I hope you don't mind."

"No, but I suggest you stand by to make sure he doesn't discuss the case, and limit those calls to one or two a day."

"Good."

"I'll be going out of the building for a while during the lunch recess. Please call my office when the jury is ready to eat. I expect they'll spend the afternoon listening to the tapes."

"Oui. Monsieur le Juge. Bon appetit."

* * *

Maurice watched the jury leave. He had been unable to attract Serge's attention. Nobody cared that he was sitting in the corner of the room, transfixed, like a silent voyeur peering through a window. His temples throbbed, as though a vice were tightening around his head. His stomach was empty but he knew he would be unable to eat. He tried unsuccessfully to moisten his throat and swallow. He turned toward the wall and drifted into an uncomfortable sleep.

"Monsieur, monsieur, the court has adjourned for the lunch break. You must leave now. Monsieur . . . ."

Maurice blinked at the uniformed security guard. "Is there a verdict?"

"No, the jury has gone for lunch, and you must leave the room immediately. They'll be back after two. There will be no verdict before they return."

Maurice shuffled to his feet and stood, swaying.

"Monsieur, are you able to walk? Should I call the nurse?"

"No." He clasped the back of the bench and walked unsteadily to the door.

* * *

Sam returned from a walk in Old Montreal, and went directly towards the jury room. The jurors had taken his instructions seriously, and were about to spend hours listening to the tapes before discussing the facts of the case. Faint muffled sounds penetrated to the corridor where Constables Harvey and Boisclair were playing cards at the table. He looked into the courtroom. Talbot was speaking to Sergeant-Detectives Caron and Coco Martin. The court clerk was at her desk filling out forms, and Parent looked on, leaning against the rail by the empty prisoner's dock. As they began to rise, Judge Berne gestured for them to remain seated.

"I'm just looking in to see how everyone is doing."

"Is there further news from the jury?" Talbot asked.

"No. If anything happens, the clerk will inform you."

"Would you like some coffee? We just bought a fresh container."

"No thanks. Please don't let me disturb you."

"Monsieur le Juge, would you like to participate in the pool?" Linda asked.

"Pool?" he repeated in mock horror.

"Yes, the lawyers and guards have each paid two dollars and guessed the time when the verdict will come. The closest one wins the pot."

"I don't think it would be quite proper for me to join, but here's two dollars towards the coffee. I may wish to have a cup later. Linda, do you think the jury will surprise us with a verdict before seven tonight, and give us the day off tomorrow?"

"Monsieur le Juge, as you know, ushers are only paid for the days they work. Besides, it's past the time I predicted for the verdict. It'd be better if the jury slept at the hotel. Then we can work tomorrow, and I'll have another chance to win the pool."

"I'm going up to my office. Stay here if you wish, but call me if there's any news."

* * *

The office was quiet and Sam dozed off in his chair. Jackie and Linda were both looking down at him when he awakened. Linda placed a folded paper in his hand. "They gave it to the guard without an envelope."

Judge Berne stared at the note:

The jury wants to know why Serge Tremblay didn't testify in his own defence.

> Phil Pasquin, Foreman
> Juror number six

He dreaded the question. The law prohibits any comment on the fact that the accused did not testify. His answer would have to be evasive. Any comment or perceived comment can give rise to a mistrial. He reread the note several times. The issue could not be avoided.

"What does the jury want now? Another tape?" Jackie asked.

"No. It's a real question this time. I'll have to go down and try to answer them."

"Will you be long?"

"Hard to tell. Depends on the attorneys' reaction."

"Well, maybe I should ask now: Can I go out for lunch with Cecile and Lolita at eleven o'clock tomorrow?"

"Eleven?" he asked incredulously. "That'll be two days in a row that you ate lunch at an hour when civilized people are just finishing the morning coffee break. Is there an explanation?"

"Do you mind?"

"No, but I'm curious. What are you hatching?"

"It's the fire drill."

"Fire drill? We had a bomb scare last week."

"That was real so it doesn't count. We haven't had a fire drill for almost a year."

"And now is the time?"

"Alors, now you begin to understand. We don't wish to walk down all the stairs from the fifteenth floor. They always make fire drills around eleven in the morning, because that's the busiest time, so we decided to have an early lunch until the crisis is over."

"But what if they don't have fire drill tomorrow?"

"Then we'll have an early lunch on Monday too."

"Does that mean I can look forward to your making the same request Monday?"

"No, that won't be necessary. I forgot to tell you: The coordinating judge called. She's sorry but you'll have to take another trial next week. They assigned you a narcotics importing case in Saint-Jérôme."

"That's a fifty-kilometre drive from here."

"Yes. How could anyone import narcotics into St. Jerome? It's not a port and only has a small domestic airport."

"You forget that Mirabel International Airport is near there. The airport and the prison have made St. Jerome one of the busiest court-houses in the province."

"Your trial starts Monday, but the jury selection isn't until Tuesday. If necessary, the opening can be postponed a day. So you see, there won't be any problem if I eat lunch early for the next week or two."

"How did you manage to arrange all that?"

"I didn't. Some people are just lucky."

"Maybe I'll be lucky and receive a verdict before the weekend."

"Bon chance."

"Thanks. I'm going back downstairs to answer that question."

*   *   *

There was an air of expectancy when the judge entered the court-room. "I have a question from the jury . . . ."

Marie-Lyse Lortie was convinced that the verdict was imminent. Her expression turned into a scowl as he read the note. "You can't tell them anything, can you?" she blurted out.

"No. The task is to say nothing without appearing evasive or making the jury feel foolish. Maître Talbot, what do you suggest?"

"I don't think you can do any more than read them the law."

"They'll try to draw all kinds of conclusions," Lortie said. "Can't you add something?"

"Well, if you both agree, I'll repeat part of my opening comments about the right of the accused to remain silent, and the burden of proof, and then I'll read them the law. Maître Lortie, would that be satisfactory?"

"Yes."

"Maître Talbot?"

"I don't know. Could we adjourn for a few minutes so I can think about it?"

"Yes. Please let me know when you're ready. I shall remain in the vicinity. The court is adjourned."

Fifteen minutes later Talbot acquiesced, and the jury was invited to enter the court again. Judge Berne spoke cautiously.

"I have received your question and consulted the attorneys for both the Crown and the defence. I wish to repeat some of the comments I made when you were first chosen as jurors.

"The Crown has the burden of proof, the obligation to convince you beyond a reasonable doubt that the accused is guilty of the crime charged. The accused does not have to prove anything, and cannot be compelled to testify. He is presumed, and remains innocent, throughout this trial, until the Crown has made you morally certain of his guilt. Now I shall read you a section of the law respecting evidence:

> The failure of the person charged . . . to testify shall not be made
> the subject of comment by the judge, or by counsel for the
> prosecution.

Under the circumstances, I can make no further comment. Ladies and gentlemen, you may now return to the jury room."

Something funny's going on here, Francine thought to herself. First they concealed that Lepine was a police agent. Now the accused won't speak, the judge won't comment, and the lawyers sit by like dummies. What do they all know that the jury doesn't? I wasn't born yesterday. They're keeping something back. Really, everyone talked about the crime, but we didn't hear much about Tremblay. What's his record? When a patient comes to the office, the first thing we do is get the medical record. The police must do the same thing. Tremblay must have been in jail and they didn't tell us. I wonder if he ever killed anyone before.

Then there's Pauline Vinet to consider. She wouldn't lie. Tremblay would kill her for trying to frame him. Who knows if he didn't try to kill her before she went to the police. Tremblay must be stopped and I'm going to make the jury stop him.

*   *   *

Sam forced himself to spend the next few hours in his office assembling files and reading. There'd be little time to prepare for next week's trial. Occasionally he looked out. It was still light, and he could see cars scurrying down the expressway. By six o'clock there was still no news from Linda or the guards. Obviously the jury had not concluded its deliberations, and had no further questions. He walked slowly to the elevator, making sure he had the office keys. Downstairs, as he crossed the main lobby he noticed Marie-Lyse Lortie pacing anxiously. In French the waiting room is called *la salle des pas perdus,* or the room of lost footsteps. The room of "lost hours" might be more appropriate.

Walking down the rear corridor, he glanced into the courtroom. It looked as though it had been frozen in time. The only change since his last appearance several hours before was that all the donuts had been eaten.

Parent moved out of the alcove. "No word since your last visit, Monsieur le Juge. They stopped listening to the tapes, came out and walked up and down the corridor. Later there was a loud shout. That usually means someone has come over to the majority, but we don't know whether that's a majority for guilty or not guilty."

"Did you make hotel arrangements for tonight?"

"Oui, Monsieur le Juge."

"Anything else?"

"Yes, the plumbers were working in the small office. They apologized to me and said that both faucets now have new washers. Do you know what they were talking about?"

"Yes, but it's too complicated to explain."

"The witness, Maurice—he returned after the lunch adjournment, and he's been in the corner ever since. Like a man in a trance. He just sits and stares, and shivers."

"I noticed."

Constable Harvey came down the hallway. "The jurors just asked if they could go to the hotel now."

"Constable, please call the bus company. Then line up the jury. I want them brought into the courtroom for a few minutes as soon as they're ready. Linda, please tell the attorneys we'll open the court in a few minutes, and ask the guards to bring in the accused."

* * *

The bedraggled jurors showed the effects of their deliberations. The men had undone their collar buttons, their ties were askew and hair dishevelled. The women looked as if they had slept in their clothes. They would welcome the rest at the hotel. Judge Berne's smile was returned by only two or three jurors.

"Ladies and gentlemen, it's been a long day and you are engaged in a most strenuous activity. We all know how difficult it is, and appreciate the seriousness with which you have undertaken this last and most important phase of your work as jurors. The bus will soon arrive to take you to the hotel for the night. There's an old proverb that the night brings counsel. I wish you a pleasant evening and good night, and will see you back here at the courthouse tomorrow morning. You may now return to the jury room to pack your belongings and await the arrival of the bus."

He scanned the room, acknowledging the attorneys. The security guard walked towards Maurice, slumped in his seat and watching through narrowed eyes. It was almost seven o'clock: a long day.

*   *   *

Maurice drifted five blocks to the corner of Ste. Catherine and St. Denis. The warm April evening brings new life to the Latin Quarter. Sidewalk cafes and restaurants teem with students, smoking, eating, drinking, reading, and talking. Many stores remain open, hoping to glean business from students at l'UQAM. At exam time, academic stresses compete for attention with budding trees and renascent nature.

Like most Montrealers, Maurice was puzzled by the large number of students who thronged the area. He didn't realize the buildings are only signposts. The heart of the university is concealed beneath the streets, where an expanding warren of tunnels, classrooms and shops cluster around the Berri-UQAM Metro station.

He wandered past the university's main entrance and continued till he stood in front of Le Wiz, where he sat down on the lower step of an exterior staircase. The sudden noise of an opening door startled him. Le Wiz wouldn't open for an hour or more. He was hungry, thirsty, and cold as he peered into the dark silent bar and tried to remember.

The lawyers and court officials, even Serge, hadn't noticed his presence in the courtroom earlier in the day, and now the rest of the world was oblivious to him. The hundreds of faces—white, brown, yellow, black, bearded, clean-shaven, male, female, animated, deadpan, dirty and clean—were all unknown. His ears failed to distinguish words amidst the cacaphony of street sounds. He wanted to call out, but what could he say, and who would listen? Who cared? Perhaps Pauline, but he couldn't find the energy or desire to return to the flat. Caroline would have the TV on loud, and Pauline would talk endlessly. His head would hurt.

He drifted in and out of consciousness as evening descended. Neon lights illuminated the restaurants and bars, and the sweet smell of marijuana hovered over the area. The pain in his head subsided and he wanted to eat. The crowds continued to flow in both directions. Papers fluttered from the pocket of a moving stranger and landed near the foot of the staircase. He felt a slight tremor, as he leaned forward and retrieved a bus transfer from the sidewalk. It would remain valid for one hour.

He grasped the rail and lifted himself onto unsteady feet. After his head cleared, he began to walk very slowly eastward, staying close to the buildings. Two or three times he stopped to sit on a cement planter and recover strength. Pauline would be glad to see him, and there'd be food in the flat. Serge might be there too . . . .No, Serge didn't live there any more.

The inverted arrow indicating the subway beckoned. The entrance would be warm, and inside there were benches where he could sit. He felt tired and weak again. The lights dimmed and the sounds grew fainter. People rushed past him and disappeared. They seemed to be talking to each other, but he heard nothing.

The passage narrowed and sloped downward like a giant funnel, forcing him to quicken his pace. His legs wouldn't obey the command to slow his steps, and he was propelled through the tunnel on a rubber conveyor. The back of his mouth was dry, but he could taste and smell the sweat on his lips.

The ramp stopped moving and he sat down on the floor. It was dark and gloomy. Now and then legs approached, passed and disappeared. He peered at the moving forest of legs.

His hearing returned, first faintly and then with increasing volume. The hall overflowed with the noise of footsteps, voices, and metal brushing against metal. People were talking, some were shouting, and a distant voice sang. He heard the sounds but couldn't understand the words. The light seemed brighter. He pushed himself back against the brick wall for support, stood up and took a few steps, clinging to the wall for support.

The tunnel ended and he was dazzled by the sudden light. He fumbled as he put the transfer in the turnstile. Then he followed in the wake of the crowd pouring down the stairs to the lower subway platform.

Squinting, he saw a single light beam rush forward. His throbbing headache intensified. He lost control of his legs and sensed they were carrying him toward the approaching beam of light. There was a crescendo of shouting and grinding metal, then a blinding flash.

Afterwards there was only an ominous silence. Minutes later a muffled voice announced throughout the subway system:

AS A RESULT OF A TECHNICAL PROBLEM IN THE BEAUDRY STATION, SERVICE ON LINE NUMBER TWO WILL BE INTERRUPTED FOR FIFTEEN MINUTES.

Maurice Pomerleau was dead.

14

"Monsieur le Juge, Monsieur le Juge," Nantel called as Berne emerged from the elevator, "I've been waiting for you since early this morning."

"Yes, what is it? Is everything all right?"

"Non, Monsieur le Juge. I must speak to you privately on a matter of importance and urgency."

"Come into my office."

Judge Berne reached into his pocket for the key. Nantel deftly moved ahead of him and opened the door to the private area. "Monsieur le Juge, this morning I was reading my morning newspapers to review the reports of the criminal trials—"

"Yes, did they mention my case?"

"No. Yes, but that's not why I'm here. The reporter from *Le Journal* called me."

"How?"

"You know the phone in the back hall for the judges? People can call that number to reach me. My desk and files of news clippings happen to be nearby."

"I see. Do you receive many calls from reporters?"

"Non, non. In fact this was the first time. He obtained my number from the security guard at the front desk."

"Was he seeking information?"

"No, he wanted to tell me something about your case that hasn't been printed in *Le Journal* yet. Perhaps he wanted you to know and was afraid to phone your office."

"This is highly irregular."

"Yes, Monsieur le Juge. Normally I don't talk to a judge about information that is not published, but this is a special situation."

"Yes, Nantel."

"Last night, Maurice Pomerleau was killed in the Beaudry Metro station. The police are investigating and do not know if it was murder or suicide or accident. It happened around ten o'clock, too late for today's *Journal*. This news wasn't on television either; they try not to mention accidents in the Metro, because it might discourage passengers. That's why they call them technical difficulties."

"I know, I know, as do all the Metro riders. Are you sure of this information?"

"I read all the newspapers and magazines, and I assure you there is no more reliable source than *Le Journal*."

"Nantel, thank you. I'll have to check this information with the attorneys and then . . . ."

"Oui, Monsieur le Juge?"

"And then try to figure out what to do. Thank you for your help."

Nantel had been apprehensive about speaking to Judge Berne. Now the agitation within him dissipated, and the frown that had marked his forehead was replaced by a broad smile that transformed his appearance. He pulled a photocopied article out of his pocket and handed it to Berne. "Yesterday's news. Pot's boiling, Monsieur le Juge; pot's boiling."

"So it is. So it is."

The noise in the outer office signalled Jackie's arrival. A moment later she looked through the open doorway and observed, "It'll be another day of waiting and pacing."

"Longer, but more exciting than you think. Monsieur Nantel heard through personal contacts that Maurice Pomerleau was killed last night."

"Non!"

"Oui. By a train in the Beaudry Metro station. After you settle in, please call the crown office and tell Vince Talbot that I want him to confirm the information with the police. And, ask Linda to check to see if the jury has arrived."

"What will you do? Reopen the hearing? Declare a mistrial?"

"Nothing yet. I just want to think, and possibly consult a colleague or two."

"If necessary, I'll cancel my early lunch with Cecile and Lolita."

"Thank you. Please hold all calls not related to this case— and oh, Monsieur Nantel, thank you again."

"It was nothing." As Nantel left, he winked and repeated, "Pot's boiling, Monsieur le Juge."

* * *

The jurors had spent a difficult night at the hotel. They were divided into two equal camps, and strains were showing. Several times Albert Rousseau had picked up the phone to call his wife. He seemed to forget that the telephone service had been disconnected, and was surprised each time to hear Parent's voice at the other end. In the morning Diane called the hotel, and Parent allowed them to speak directly. She was lonely but well, and there had been no further labour pains. Rousseau resolved to hasten the pace of the deliberations. The problem was that four of the jurors simply would not change their minds. For a while they had been evenly split. Then two jurors changed their minds, and it looked like the others would join the majority, but they held fast to their positions. The four remaining jurors simply would not budge. This could go on forever, he thought. He identified the principle points of difference by perusing his notes, and found new arguments to influence their positions. Roger was the key. If he caved in, Rita would follow. Then, Pasquin and Bernard couldn't hold out forever. He was

determined to speak to each of the holdouts privately. He had responsibilities to his wife, and the first was to end the trial quickly so he could
join her.

Phil Pasquin sat alone in the corner of the meeting room the hotel
had assigned to them for breakfast. He was desperate to leave and return
to his business where he was respected. This court system was another
world; the less he had to do with it the better. Who in their right mind
would remove the television sets and disconnect the phones in a hotel?
Last night they had seen a film on the large TV set in the meeting room,
but he hadn't enjoyed it.

He couldn't understand what had happened to him in the last few
days. First the jurors elected him chairman, and now he was part of a
dwindling minority. They refused to follow his direction, and some no
longer spoke to him. It was all the fault of Rick Hayes. Every time he said
something, Hayes disagreed. Lucy Morin did whatever Hayes wanted,
and sooner or later the others also agreed.

If this continued he'd send a note to the judge to stop this trial.
Enough was enough. Why should twelve honest—well, twelve citizens be
locked up as hostages for Serge Tremblay, Pauline and Maurice? Let the
police and the judges find unemployed people to serve on juries, and
allow working people to return to their jobs.

When he returned he'd launch a new collection of men's clothing:
The Judge's Selection, La Selezione de Magistrato. Conservative, double-breasted dark suits with an Italian cut retailing at $399.95 would be
just the right product for the fall season. People in his organization
would be impressed that he'd thought this up during a murder trial.

Only Parent treated him with respect, and there was another side
to him too. During the night, Pasquin was unable to sleep and wandered
into the hall. Parent suggested a friendly game of gin rummy, and before
long Pasquin had lost more than fifty dollars. It wasn't the money so
much as the idea that he was defeated by a jury constable wearing a tight,
poorly-fitting uniform.

* * *

Vince Talbot was dumbfounded when Jackie called. He'd had his fill of surprises during the examination of Oscar Cimon and was waiting patiently for the verdict. Despite pressures from police officers anxious to see one of their own avenged, he would react calmly, no matter what the jury decided. Crown attorneys must take the facts as they find them.

"What's the origin of the judge's information?" he asked.

"A usually reliable source. He wouldn't ask me to call if he didn't have a serious concern."

"Have you contacted Marie-Lyse Lortie?"

"No, he won't do anything till you check the story with the police. I'll wait for your call."

Sgt.-Det. Caron joined Talbot at the crown office minutes after receiving the report. "That judge must have a high- powered infrared telescope in his office, or else he listens to the police network. There's been nothing in the newspapers or on the radio."

"That doesn't matter," Talbot replied. "We have to know some facts. Was it murder, suicide, or an accident?"

"We don't know. It happened around 9:30 last night. That's a busy hour on Thursday nights, students leaving classes, stores closing and bars opening. The subway station's just one stop from l'UQAM and there are plenty of students in the area. It could have been anyone or anything, except Tremblay. He was safely in jail last night. Maurice was dealing small amounts of drugs. Maybe he didn't pay his wholesaler."

"Maybe they found out that he was an informer, and Frank Lepine was his manager."

"Stop that. You and me, crown attorneys and police, are on the same side. I don't know the full story about that."

"Why not?"

"Those guys in the Narcotics Squad still won't talk."

"Okay. Any other ideas about Maurice?"

"It might have been sexually motivated. Maurice swung both ways, and that part of Ste. Catherine East is becoming the gay centre of Montreal. Who the hell knows?"

"So what do I tell the judge?" Talbot asked.

"The truth. Confirm the death and tell him we're investigating.

There must be a hundred people who saw the body after the accident, but we haven't found anyone yet who saw him jump or get pushed. After the disclosures at the trial about Lepine being a police officer, we're going to take plenty of heat over this one.

"Yesterday Pomerleau just hung around looking dazed, but we didn't think anything of it. Maybe the medical report will explain what happened. The doctors at the lab are pretty good."

"Have you checked out Pauline Vinet?"

"Coco went over to see her a few minutes ago. We'll hear from him shortly."

"I'll call the judge. Marie-Lyse too. She has a right to know, and may as well hear it from me."

"What about the jury?"

"That's the big question. I never had this sort of thing happen before, a witness killed while the jury was deliberating. Hate to have the judge call a mistrial. If there's a new trial, Maurice won't be here to testify. Mind you, for all the good he did, our case might be stronger without him to confuse the picture."

"Vince, the guys downtown want a conviction. Tremblay's a bad one and he shot Frank in cold blood."

"The guys downtown could have provided all the information up front."

"Yeah. I'm going out to call the office, and I'll be back soon."

* * *

Marie-Lyse had dismissed Maurice and Pauline from her mind, concentrating entirely on the jury. Now she was jolted by Talbot's phone call. She rushed from her office and caught a taxi. It was urgent that she speak to her client.

Minutes later she was in the courthouse basement, pacing the waiting room adjacent to the cells as she tried to develop a strategy. She could ask the judge to reopen the hearing and allow the jury to hear of this new development. But would he? And where would that lead? The police didn't know yet what had happened, and the simple fact of the death of Maurice could mean everything or nothing. It could be an accident, or remorse, a form of admission or confession. But that was too tenuous to place before a jury.

Were the police getting even with an informer who had failed them or shot one of their buddies? No, that was paranoia. The police don't always play by the rules, but they'd hardly resort to pushing a suspect in front of a subway train. That would be too stupid, too dangerous, and too obvious. Maurice might have been mixed up with pushers and dealers who wanted to get rid of him. That would make more sense, but how does that affect the guilt or innocence of Serge?

She heard the cell doors close and knew that Serge would be available. A uniformed arm beckoned her towards the restricted area.

"Any news from the jury?" Serge asked.

"Not a word. They're probably arriving from the hotel around now. It'll take them a few minutes to settle in."

"How come you're down here in the cells, instead of upstairs?"

"Something happened last night. Maurice is dead."

"What?" Serge caught his breath.

"I said Maurice is dead. He fell or was pushed in front of a train at the Beaudry Metro station."

"Are you sure?"

"Yes."

"How'd you find out?"

"Talbot called a few minutes ago."

"Was anyone with Maurice?"

"They didn't say."

"What does that do to the trial?"

"Probably nothing. The hearing of witnesses is over. Only thing left is the verdict."

"But I want to testify now! There are things I should tell the judge and the jury. Look, I didn't even speak at my own trial."

"That's right. You didn't even tell *me* the whole story, and now it's too late for talking."

"What do you mean?"

"Maurice isn't here to answer any more questions. And you—no one will believe you, no matter what you say. If you try to blame Maurice, they'll say you made it up after his death when he couldn't contradict you."

"No."

"Yes."

"Does the jury know about Maurice?"

"No."

"Is there some way they can be told?"

"No, it's too late to tell them. If you're convicted and we appeal, maybe then the Court of Appeal would hear new evidence. Or, if the jury can't reach a verdict, there'd be another trial with a new jury. Then you could testify, or we could argue that Maurice's death is proof that he killed that cop at Le Wiz."

"When will the jury find out about Maurice?"

"After the verdict, when they read it in the newspapers."

"Can't I do something now?"

"Pray, if you know how."

"Will it be much longer?"

"I don't know."

"So I just have to sit and wait?"

"Uh-huh."

"And you can't help me?"

"No."

"Maurice was my friend."

"He may have set you up for a life sentence."

"He was my friend. Did what he had to, to protect his ass. He didn't want to hurt me, only to protect himself, and now there's nothing to protect. Please go away, Marie-Lyse. I need to be alone now."

"Do you mean that?"

"Yes, go back upstairs." She turned to leave, but he called after her. "Wait, come back . . . .I want to talk."

"I told you it's too late."

"But I want to talk to you. I want you to know what happened."

"I can't do anything."

"You can listen. Just listen to me. Maurice was the only friend I ever had in my life. Can you understand that? I would have done anything for him, killed for him, because nobody else cared a damn for me. I had no mother, and my father hated me. All I ever had was Maurice, and now he's dead. I kept quiet for him. I kept quiet, and now I might go to jail for . . . a dead man."

"Do you want to tell me what happened at Le Wiz?"

"Maurice wasn't there. I had left him with Pauline and he knew where I was going. She hung on to him and he couldn't leave. I was alone at Le Wiz and wanted to talk to this girl. Well, before I said anything, this big guy Lepine came over and started shoving me. I didn't know he was a cop. I shoved him back; a fight started, and we threw some punches— nothing serious. I went out and then came back."

"And?"

"When they closed, I went outside and Maurice was standing there on the sidewalk. He knew where to find me, and came after Pauline fell asleep. Well, I was surprised to see him, but not half as surprised as he was to see Lepine. I turned and, sure enough, Lepine happened to be just behind me and gave me another shove. I didn't want nothing to do with the cops and started to run away. Then there was a shot, and I saw that Maurice was holding the gun."

"What happened next?"

"We both ran. I told him to get the hell back to the flat to Pauline, and I'd get rid of the gun."

"But you didn't?"

"No, I knew the police would be after me and I was afraid to be unarmed. I was going to get rid of it as soon as I could find another one, but I just didn't."

"Why did Lepine shove you the second time, out in the street?"

"He probably wanted Maurice to see how tough he was. At the time I didn't know it, but Maurice told me the next day or the day after, that he gave Lepine information about dealers in the Latin Quarter. He got out of La Macaza a few days before I did and was alone in Montreal. The second day, Lepine caught him dealing and offered to protect him as long as Maurice fed him information. After I got out and Maurice started living with Pauline, he didn't have much to tell Lepine, because he didn't go out much. The night of the murder, Maurice wanted to protect me, . . . or maybe he was protecting himself when he shot Lepine."

Marie-Lyse's dark eyes were moist. "Serge, why didn't you tell me? I could have called the police lieutenant. He must have known about Maurice. I could have questioned Maurice again, and sooner or later he would have broken."

"I couldn't hurt the only friend I ever had. I wanted to protect him, and now he's dead."

* * *

At noon the jury had given no indication yet of wanting to eat. There was a knock from inside the door of the jury room. Parent rushed up. It couldn't be the verdict; they had been too quiet. It was another note to the judge. "Co-pilot," he said to Linda, "here's another note. Do you want to take it up to the judge's office?"

"I'll call first."

Judge Berne had left the office and was on his way down to check developments. As Linda put down the receiver he appeared in the hall. She handed him the envelope and waited while he opened it.

Judge Berne:
We are tired and confused. How much longer must we continue to deliberate? What happens if we can never agree?
 Henri Lanctot, Rita Belleville, Roger Lebrun, Betty Major
 Lucy Morin, Phil Pasquin, Kathy Johnson, Bernard Richer
 Francine Roux, Claire Savard, Albert Rousseau, Rick Hayes

Sam was puzzled that all the jurors had signed. The other notes had been signed by the foreman. This might meaning something, but he had no time to think about it. The deliberations had reached a watershed, and something had to be done immediately to reassure them, and convince them to continue deliberating. Otherwise he would have to declare a mistrial, which he wanted to avoid at all costs. He would exhort them to agree.

The public benches were filled with spectators. Lawyers and court-house personnel on their lunch hours must have sensed the moment of decision approaching. The news had spread about Maurice, because all the chairs for the press were occupied. The reporter for *Le Journal* must have told the others. Even Nantel had dropped in, and sat stoically in the last row near the door. The doors from behind the courtroom opened simultaneously. Judge Berne entered and the jury followed.

"Ladies and gentlemen, I have received your note and consulted the attorneys for both the Crown and the defence. We realize—all of us realize—that you have been working hard to reach agreement. It is not an easy matter. However I must urge you to make an additional effort. You spent a week listening to the evidence, and more than a day and a half discussing the evidence. I know that you are not all in agreement, and expect there is a minority opinion and a majority opinion. I invite those of you in the minority to re-examine the opinion of your col-leagues. See if you can understand their viewpoint, rally to their side and agree on a unanimous verdict.

"However, I must repeat that you are responsible to your con-science and if you cannot join the majority, if you are not convinced, it is your right, your duty to yourself and to the system to stand firm in your views."

He looked along the jury benches making eye contact with the jurors one at a time. Betty and Francine returned his look openly. Phil Pasquin averted his eyes. His tie was askew and there was a coffee stain on his jacket sleeve. The proud executive must have lost some of his confidence in the jury room.

Judge Berne returned Kathy Johnson's tired smile, and then, remembering the cake she had sent him, looked away. Perhaps Jackie was right and she had fallen in love with him. It would be ridiculous. He was too old.

"Ladies and gentlemen, I know you must feel isolated in the jury room. Although we are not allowed to be present during your delibera-tions, each of us here in the courtroom is with you in spirit. All of us rely upon and will accept your judgement. Don't feel that you're alone.

"In a sense this is like the time my first child was born. In those days the father was not permitted in the delivery room, and waited in the visitors' lounge on the other side of the wall. Although I was not allowed to be with my wife in a physical sense, in spirit I was with her.

"I cannot join you in the jury room, but I am with you in spirit, as are the attorneys and indeed everyone in this courtroom. You are our representatives who can and will decide the just outcome of this trial. I ask you to please make this additional effort. You may now return to the jury room."

As they rose and left, Judge Berne heard Kathy Johnson confide to Rita Belleville, "You know, if I'd had a father like him, I would never have left home to get married."

Linda announced the adjournment but the audience lingered, expecting some new development. Marie-Lyse and Serge had a whispered conversation over the rail separating the prisoners' box from the courtroom.

*   *   *

Judge Berne stood concealed in an alcove in the corridor, waiting patiently. He leaned forward, doing push-ups against the wall. There was a knock from inside the jury room.

Parent ambled down the hall. "The jury wants to know if they can have a pizza sent in. They're tired of eating out."

"Good sign. Send out the order. I hope it doesn't take too long at this hour."

Parent gave a broad wink. "We have our friends in this area. After all, we're good customers."

"Linda," Judge Berne said, "I think you're about to win the pool. There's a theory that when the jury is close to a verdict, they like to stay in the jury room and eat pizza. Of course, there is another theory that they like to go out and have a last big meal before they deliver the verdict and separate."

"I prefer the first one."

"Linda, don't say a word to anyone. This may be absolutely nothing, and I don't want gossip going around the building based on what you say."

"Can I go for lunch?"

"Yes, but eat in the cafeteria, and make sure Parent knows where you are, in case the jury reaches a verdict."

"I'll wait here for now."

"Fine. I'll remain in the building too. I'll be in my office or in the judges' dining room."

Sam returned to his office and began to pack books and files into his briefcase. It was nice to do something that didn't require concentration. Ewaschek's book hadn't arrived, and he'd have to take the borrowed copy to St. Jerome next week.

Jackie returned and asked, "Was there a fire drill?"

"No."

"Verdict?"

"No."

"So I missed nothing?"

"No. Was the restaurant crowded?"

"A few people."

"And I'll bet they were all personnel from the upper floors of the courthouse."

"Yes, how did you . . . ?"

"Intuition. Now that you're back, please hold the fort. I'm going down to the judges' dining room. If anything happens, you can reach me by phone or send Linda."

The menu in the judge's dining room was taped to the elevator wall. It changed weekly, yet always seemed the same: spaghetti with meat sauce, ham and cheese sandwich, fried fillet of sole, chicken breast, western omelette, salad bar. Every meal included soup or juice, vegetables, desert and coffee.

Parent was waiting at the door to the dining room.

"What are you doing here, Constable?"

He handed him a sealed envelope. "It's the verdict, Monsieur le Juge."

Judge Berne opened the envelope. "You're right. Please go back to court and tell the clerk to summon the attorneys and have the accused brought back up."

Parent flashed a broad smile and disappeared. Judge Berne picked up the telephone in the corridor and dialled his office.

"Judge Berne's office," Jackie announced.

"It's me. The verdict is ready. I'm going down to the courtroom. Please find Linda and tell her."

"Where are you calling from? The number flashing on my monitor isn't familiar."

"The corridor on the fifth floor. And please call the coordinating judge to advise her. She's a verdict freak, and will want to be there if possible. You're also invited."

Within minutes he was back near the courtroom. After checking that the attorneys and the accused were present, Linda returned, excited.

"Everyone is there, and the courtroom is full. I don't know where they all came from. Jackie, Nantel—even the coordinating judge is present."

"Line up the jury."

He watched them file out into the corridor. Their ashen faces suggested that it had not been easy to agree on a verdict. One of them was missing. Finally Claire Savard, number nine, took her place in the line. He signalled to the jurors and entered the courtroom. The jurors followed through the other door.

After the audience sat down, Judge Berne announced, "Ladies and gentlemen, I have received a note from the jury which reads: 'The jury is ready to render its verdict.'" He turned to the clerk. "Would you please file this note as exhibit J-5. Mr. Tremblay, please stand."

Marie-Lyse stepped back to be as close as possible to her client. She rested a hand on the partition enclosing the prisoners' dock. Serge took hold of her hand.

The clerk rose. "Members of the jury, who will speak on your behalf?"

Phil Pasquin rose slowly, glancing at some of the other jurors for reassurance. He cleared his throat. "I will."

"Are the members of the jury agreed on a unanimous verdict?"

"Yes, we are."

"What is your verdict?"

"We find the accused not guilty."

Serge Tremblay was absolutely still at first, simply staring at Pasquin. He looked at the judge, as if for confirmation. Judge Berne understood and nodded. Serge slowly let out a long deep breath, with eyes closed. The effects of the painful uncertainty and concealed stress would take time to dissolve. He felt a profound gratitude towards the jurors, but was unable to show it. He turned towards Marie-Lyse, who shone with victory. He became almost dizzy with relief at this great turn in his life.

"The court accepts your verdict. Serge Tremblay, a jury of your peers has found you not guilty.

"Ladies and gentlemen of the jury, you have been faithful to your oath and discharged this most important duty according to the very highest standards. On behalf of the entire judicial system I thank you for your efforts. The court is adjourned."

Judge Berne stood and left the courtroom. "Linda, come as soon as you can. I'm going to meet the jurors personally. They'll need some comfort and encouragement, and—congratulations, you won the pool."

Linda's eyes opened wide, and she raised her hand to cover her mouth. "I won!"

* * *

An hour later, Judge Berne was back in his office. "Well, Jackie, what do you think of the verdict?"

"The jury deliberated long enough to weigh all the evidence carefully, so I'd trust their judgement."

"Yes. The tension builds and builds; then all of a sudden it's over . . . . What's that damned noise?"

"ATTENTION, ATTENTION. THIS IS A FIRE DRILL! EVERY-BODY MUST LEAVE THE BUILDING IMMEDIATELY. EVERYBODY MUST LEAVE THE BUILDING IMMEDIATELY."

"The fire drill—they never have a fire drill on a Friday afternoon."

"Except this time. Fifteen flights of stairs, again! It looks like we won't be lingering at the courthouse one extra minute today. Grab your jacket, let's get moving!"